NO TIME FOR TEARS

NO TIME FOR TEARS

Kitty Neale

Severn House Large Print
London & New York

This first large print edition published 2009
in Great Britain and the USA by
SEVERN HOUSE PUBLISHERS LTD of
9-15 High Street, Sutton, Surrey, SM1 1DF.
First world regular print edition published 2006 by
Severn House Publishers Ltd., London and New York.

British Library Cataloguing in Publication Data

Neale, Kitty
  No time for tears. - Large print ed.
  1. Adultery - Fiction 2. Fathers and daughters - Fiction
  3. Battersea (London, England) - Fiction 4. Domestic
  fiction 5. Large type books
  I. Title
  823.9'2[F]

ISBN-13: 978-0-7278-7753-6

Printed and bound in Great Britain by
MPG Books Ltd, Bodmin, Cornwall.

To my wonderful husband, Jim, for
all his support and editorial help.
I love you, darling.
Whither thou goest, I will go.

Acknowledgments

Once again my heartfelt thanks go to Bill and Dorothy Goodbody, Bill for sharing more of his experiences of being an amputee in the 1960s, and Dorothy for answering my many emails on the subject. Dear friends, I love you both.

Author's Note

Many place and street names mentioned in this book are real. However, others, and some of the topography, along with all of the characters, are just figments of my imagination.

One

Arthur Jones tucked his crutches under his arms and, balancing himself, smiled at his five-year-old daughter. 'Come on, Angela, it's time for your bath.'

Sally tensed, but tried to look unconcerned. Her husband was a handsome, huge, bearlike man, with dark hair and grey eyes, but his face showed the ravages of recent pain. 'Are you sure you can manage?' she asked.

'Of course I can. Stop treating me like an invalid.'

'Sorry,' she said, but still watched nervously as they left the room. Their daughter could be a handful, and if the bathroom floor became wet, it would be slippery. Would Arthur be safe on his crutches?

When Angela was born with red hair, a shade lighter than her own, and eyes just like her father's, her name was soon shortened to Angel. Yet by the time she was eighteen months old it became apparent that this was no celestial being. Spoiled by grandparents and her great-grandmother, she became precocious and adept at getting her own way. Sally smiled wryly. She and Arthur were no better, spoiling her too, but despite Angel's behaviour, she *was* adorable.

Sally rose to her feet and, walking over to the window, she looked out on to Maple Terrace. In their tiny front garden a few daffodils bloomed, signalling spring and new beginnings. And that's apt, Sally thought. After many months in hospital this was Arthur's first day home, and she felt a surge of happiness. When he'd had a car accident last November, it had been a traumatic time. At first they'd thought he would soon recover, but the compound fracture of his lower leg had led to complications. First gangrene, and then a bone marrow disease called osteomyelitis. Arthur had been through hell, finally making the brave decision to have his lower leg amputated.

'Angel!'

Sally heard the yell and, heart thumping, flew to the bathroom. 'What is it? Are you all right?'

Arthur was sitting on the side of the bath, his trousers and shirt soaked. 'There's no need to panic. We're both fine – well, apart from this little minx soaking me with water.'

White bubbles formed a small crown atop Angel's red hair and, as she stood up, more coated her body. She held out her arms imperiously. 'Get me out now.'

'I'll do it,' Sally said hurriedly.

'Right, that's it,' Arthur growled as he reached for his crutches. 'As you seem to think I'm incapable, I'll leave Angel to you.'

Clumsily he left the bathroom, whilst Sally grabbed a towel and wrapped it around her

10

daughter. She'd put her foot in it again, over-protecting both Arthur and Angel, and it was obvious he hated it.

'Daddy's cross,' Angel said as they went to her bedroom.

'He's just tired, darling. Now come on, let's get you dry and into your nightclothes.'

'I want to put my nurse's uniform on again. He needs some medicine.'

The tiny play outfit for Angela had been a Christmas present, but she'd refused to wear it until Arthur came out of hospital. It was a hit now, the child acting the role of a nurse to her father since she arrived home from school. Sally smiled, saying softly, 'No more today, darling. It's late and time for bed.'

Angela's face crumpled, 'But Daddy said I can be his nurse.'

'It's past your bedtime, and even nurses have to sleep. Now come on, be a good girl,' and rubbing her daughter dry, she held out her pyjama jacket.

Angel consented to put her nightclothes on, but when Sally picked up a book and suggested a story she shook her head, pouting, 'No, I want Daddy to read it.'

'I told you. He's tired, darling.'

'Want Daddy.'

Sally held back the blankets, saying as her daughter scrambled into bed, 'All right, I'll get him.'

When she walked into the living room it was to find Arthur slumped in a chair. 'Angel wants

11

you to read to her.'

'Are you sure I can manage it?' he asked, voice dripping with sarcasm.

Sally's face saddened. When Arthur had arrived home that morning, he seemed fine, but as the day wore on she could sense a growing tension. 'I'm sorry, love. I know I'm being overprotective, but it's your first day home and I don't want you to overdo things.'

'I don't need fussing over like a mother hen. If I can't cope with something, I'll tell you.'

'All right,' she said, but as Arthur stood up she thought she saw him wince. Was he in pain? With her eyes slightly unfocused, she used her spiritual gift to gaze at his aura, but before she could concentrate sufficiently, Angela burst into the room.

'Daddy, come on.'

'All right, but only *one* story.'

He left the room, but not before Sally noticed how tired he looked, perhaps another reason for his tetchiness. Once Angel was asleep she'd see that he relaxed until bedtime and maybe he'd allow her to give him some spiritual healing.

At last we're alone, Sally thought. Angela was asleep, and Arthur was sprawled out on a fireside chair with his eyes closed. She focused on his aura, seeing only a little darkness around the wound that looked nothing to worry about. Once again she allowed her intuition to flow, but was unable to sense any pain. She grimaced, remembering how awful the gangrene had been and recalling how it had started with the appearance of black blisters on his toes.

He opened his eyes, saw her looking at his stump, and his lips tightened, 'Judging by the look on your face, you must find it repugnant, Sally?'

'Of course I...' her reply was interrupted as the doorbell rang. With a small shake of her head she rose to answer it, forcing a smile of welcome when she saw Arthur's partner, Joe Somerton, on the step.

'Hello, Sally. I would have rung first to see if it was all right to pop round, but I haven't got your new telephone number.'

Sally kicked herself. Arthur's homecoming coincided with moving into this ground floor flat, one that she loved. Tree-lined Maple Terrace was a far cry from dingy Candle Lane where they had lived with her mother and gran. 'I should have thought to give you our new number. Sorry, Joe.'

He smiled, his blue eyes soft. Joe was tall, handsome and rugged, with blond hair over chiselled features, and as Sally stood aside to let him in, he touched her arm, saying softly, 'There's no need to apologize. With Arthur coming home you've had enough to think about. Now are you sure I won't be intruding?'

'Don't be silly, of course you won't.'

As they walked into the living room Arthur grinned at Joe, his welcome warm, 'Wotcher, mate.'

'Wotcher, Skippy?'

As if on cue both men began to sing, 'Skippy, Skippy, Skippy the bush kangaroo.'

Sally had to smile. As usual Joe was making a joke of Arthur's leg, something he'd done when visiting him in hospital. At first she'd been horrified, but Arthur had responded well, and if anything Joe's flippant attitude had snapped him out of depression. The two were great friends as well as partners, and now interrupting the song she called over their voices, 'Can I get you a drink, Joe?'

'A coffee would be great.'

'What about you, Arthur?'

'Yes, the same, please.'

Sally went through to the kitchen, and whilst waiting for the kettle to boil she felt a familiar surge of shame. She loved Arthur, would always love him, and nothing could change that, but when she'd first met Joe Somerton there had been an instant attraction.

She heaved a sigh, thankful that she'd been able to hide her feelings, that neither Arthur nor Joe were aware of how she'd felt. Thankfully the attraction had been short-lived, a silly crush, and nowadays she just welcomed Joe as a friend. He had come into their lives after returning from Australia, and it had been his idea to go into property development, inviting Arthur to join him as a partner. They had sunk all their savings into the venture and it was a huge risk, but knowing how much it meant to Arthur, she had supported his decision. Now, taking cups and saucers out of the cupboard, she concentrated on the task in hand, hearing just the rumble of their voices in the distance as she spooned Camp coffee into the cups.

Arthur felt exhausted, but forced the feeling away, focusing on his friend. 'How are things going on the site?'

'Things are progressing well. The foundations for the first row of terraces are in and so far we're keeping to schedule.'

'That's good, and I can't wait to start work. You've waited long enough and it's time I pulled my weight.'

'There's no hurry, and it's amazing what you managed to achieve from that hospital bed. It was your idea to promote the houses straight away, and Sally came up with the name for the development. "The Meadows" – it has a nice ring to it.'

'Have the brochures turned out all right?'

'Yes, they're great,' Joe said, reaching into his briefcase to pull one out and handing it to Arthur.

He looked at the artist's mock-up of the development and had to agree. The site was in Reading, Berkshire, the houses clustered around a central green. They would sell, he was sure of it. The timing was right, with young couples earning more and looking to get a foot on the housing ladder.

It was a far cry from the removals business, and Arthur wasn't sorry that he'd left his father's firm. He'd been a driver, a humper, his father doing all the office work, and with a wry smile he realized that he'd left at the right time. He wouldn't be able to drive a removals van now, let alone lift furniture, so Joe asking him to go into partnership with him had turned out to be a blessing.

'You're miles away, mate,' Joe said.

Arthur lifted his eyes from the brochure. 'Yes, sorry, I was just thinking about our partnership. I had my accident just before we started the development, and despite what you say, you've had to handle everything on your own. I haven't even seen it yet.'

'We can soon put that right. How about I pick you up tomorrow and run you to the site? Well, that's if Sally doesn't mind.'

'Why should she mind? Anyway, she won't be here. Sally will be going to Candle Lane every day to look after her gran.'

'I'd forgotten about that. How is Sadie?'

'She's recovering from the stroke, but can't be left on her own.'

'It doesn't seem right that Sally has to look after her.'

'I couldn't agree more, but try telling her that. When the old girl had her stroke, Sally dragged me back to live in Candle Lane, and it wasn't much fun I can tell you. Christ, it was all women. Sally, her mother, grandmother, and of course Angel who, though only a child, has the wiles of a female. I'm fond of them, but it drove me mad.'

'Well, mate, you've got your own place again now.'

'Yes, but for a while I didn't think I'd ever coax Sally away from Candle Lane.'

'She must think a lot of her gran.'

'She does, and it isn't surprising. When Sally's mother was left on her own, she had to work to support them. Sadie moved in to help out and virtually brought Sally up.'

The conversation halted as Sally came back into the room, carefully balancing a tray. 'Coffee all round,' she said.

Arthur took one, saying, 'Right, Joe, what time are you picking me up tomorrow?'

Sally was about to hand a cup of coffee to Joe, but now paused. 'Arthur, surely you're not going back to work? You've only just come out of hospital.'

'I'm going to have a look at the site.'

'I thought you said you'd wait until you got your artificial leg.'

'I've changed my mind.'

'Are you sure it'll be safe on the site?'

'Christ, will you stop mollycoddling me! I feel fit enough to work and it's my decision, not yours.'

For a moment they stared at one another, but then Arthur saw her shoulders slump and with a strained smile she said, 'All right, I'm sorry for nagging, but I can't help worrying about you.' She then broke eye contact, turning to talk to Joe. 'Would you like to join us for dinner in the evening? I've invited Patsy Laurington, the girl who lives upstairs.'

Arthur grinned at his friend. 'I met her soon

after I arrived home this morning, and she's a bit of all right.'

'In that case, lead me to her.'

'We'll have dinner at eight. Is that all right, Joe?'

'That's fine.'

Arthur took a sip of his coffee, and then asked Joe a few more questions about the housing development. He tried to take it all in, but with no experience of the construction game he felt out of his depth. There was so much to learn. Was he up to it?

It was after ten when Joe rose to his feet, and Arthur wasn't sorry. He could hardly keep his eyes open and would be glad to get to bed. After so long in hospital it would be strange sleeping next to Sally again, but he looked forward to holding her in his arms.

Sally saw Joe out and, after washing the coffee cups, she laid the table for breakfast.

'I'm going to bed,' Arthur called. 'Are you coming?'

'Yes,' she replied, hurriedly drying her hands and following him into the bedroom. One of his crutches caught the edge of the rug and he stumbled. Sally blanched as she rushed to his side. 'Are you all right?'

'Yes,' he said, regaining his balance. 'But it might be a good idea to take these rugs up for the time being.'

Arthur stood awkwardly by the bed for a moment and, worried that he wouldn't want her to see his fumbling attempts to undress, Sally turned her back, removing her own clothes. She then flung on her dressing gown, still not looking at Arthur as she headed for the bathroom. It was cold and Sally shivered, but to give Arthur time she washed slowly before cleaning her teeth.

Arthur was in bed when she returned, his eyes closed. He had always slept on that side, and had chosen to do so again, but that meant his stump would be next to her. What if she knocked it, causing him pain?

She eased herself carefully into bed, keeping a little distance between them, nerves causing her to lie stiffly by his side. Tentatively she reached out a hand to touch him, but heard a soft snore. Poor Arthur, he must have been exhausted and had already gone to sleep. She wanted to put her arms around him, to snuggle close, but once again fear held her back. Fear not only of hurting his stump, but of the memories that returned to haunt her at the thought of intimacy. She carefully turned over to face the wall, but sleep was elusive as her mind remained active.

It had been so long since they'd slept in the same bed, and even before Arthur's accident, lovemaking had been impossible. When they'd returned to Candle Lane after Gran's stroke, Angel had to share their bedroom. It made intimacy difficult, and it had died altogether when Angel had awoken in the mist of their lovemaking, frightened by what she saw. After that, Arthur refused to make love to her whilst the child shared their room, sex becoming a thing of the past.

With no idea how long it would take for Arthur's stump to completely heal, she didn't know when they'd be able to make love again, but it didn't matter. If anything, it was something she'd rather put off. For now it was enough that he was home and lying beside her. She smiled happily, finally drifting off to sleep.

Two

When Sally awoke in the morning she stretched out her arms, and though it was cold in the room, she was pleased to see that a beam of sunshine lay across the bed.

She sat up and, seeing that Arthur was still asleep, she gazed at his face. In sleep he looked relaxed, the ravages of pain softened, and her heart swelled with love. She wanted to lie down again, to snuggle close, but once again the fear of waking him held her back.

Arthur must have been exhausted to fall asleep so quickly last night, and now Sally's expression changed to one of worry. He was going to the building site today, surely a dangerous place for a man on crutches. Joe had an appointment first so wouldn't be picking him up until after nine. Flicking a glance at the clock Sally saw it was only six thirty. Careful not to disturb him, she climbed out of bed and, hoping it would build up his strength for the day ahead, she decided to let him sleep for as long as possible.

Sally enjoyed the silence of the house as she washed and dressed. All too soon she would have to get Angel up for school and then go to Candle Lane, this the first day of their new routine. A drink made, she sat at the kitchen table, sipping it as her eyes roamed the room. It was lovely to be in their own flat, the worry and unhappiness of the past fading in her joy at having Arthur home again. With a happy sigh she drained her cup and then rose to her feet. It was time to begin the day – time to get her daughter up and ready for school.

'Come on, sweetheart, wake up,' she said, giving the child a gentle shake.

Sleepy eyes gazed up at Sally. 'I was flying, Mummy.'

Sally's eyes widened. She too had dreams of flying, vivid ones of skimming low over roof-tops, the moon casting a translucent glow on the tiles. It felt so real, so joyful, and now Angel was experiencing it too.

She smiled at her daughter, wondering as she always did, if she'd inherited her spiritual gifts. So far Angel had only mentioned the *before time,* something that had started when she was about eighteen months old and just talking. In her toddler lisp she would say that in the before time, washing was done in a tub with a poss-stick, and that irons were placed on the fire to heat them up. It had been very strange, almost as though her daughter had lived before and was remembering a previous life. Gradually though it had died out and nowadays Angel had no memory of it.

Sally now sat down on the side of the bed, pulling her daughter into her arms. 'Did you enjoy dreaming that you were flying?'

'Yes, and I want to go back to sleep so I can do it again.'

'Sorry, darling, you've got to get up.'

Angel pouted a little, but scrambled out of bed and in no time Sally had her in the bathroom, getting her washed and dressed.

Later, just as she was preparing breakfast, Arthur appeared, clumping across the room on his crutches, his hair tousled and, to Sally, looking deliciously sexy.

'Hello, love,' she said. 'You're up then.'

'Daddy!' Angel cried.

'Morning, princess.'

'What do you fancy for breakfast?' Sally asked.

'What are you having, Angel?'

'Porridge.'

'Then I'll have the same,' Arthur said.

She poured him a cup of tea. 'Are you all right, love?'

'I'm fine. Why shouldn't I be?'

'You seemed overtired last night.'

'I said I'm fine so stop worrying.'

Sally hid a frown. Arthur still seemed tetchy,

22

but with Joe calling last night she hadn't had a chance to speak to him about healing. Maybe later, she thought, as she stirred the porridge. If his wound was giving him pain, he was sure to agree.

She poured the breakfast into bowls, placing them on the table whilst her thoughts continued to drift. Since Arthur's accident she hadn't been to the hall to join others in offering spiritual healing, and missed the camaraderie. It had been Arthur's mother, Elsie, who'd recognized her abilities, encouraging her to develop the gift. Elsie was a wonderful woman who had her own spiritual abilities, and Sally was close to her mother-in-law.

The clatter of a spoon falling to the floor broke into Sally's thoughts. She bent to pick it up, noticing at the same time that Angel had finished her breakfast. The time had flown past, and now it was eight fifteen, time to leave. 'Come on, Angel, get your coat on.'

Angel did as she was told, and then ran to kiss her daddy goodbye. Sally did the same, kissing Arthur on his cheek. 'I'll be back as soon as my mother comes home from work.'

'I may not be here. Joe will be picking me up in about an hour and I'm looking forward to seeing the site. I don't know what time I'll be home.'

'It's your first day, and maybe you should make it a short one.'

'Don't start again, Sally. I'm quite capable of doing a day's work.'

23

'Sorry, I don't mean to fuss. We must go. See you later, love.'

He smiled thinly, calling to Angel as they left, 'Bye, sweetheart and be a good girl at school.'

'Bye, Daddy,' she called back.

Holding her daughter's hand, Sally made her way to Candle Lane, arriving to find her mother hovering in the hall. 'Thank God you're here. If I don't get a move on I'll be late for work.'

'Nanny, have you got any sweeties for me?'

'No, sorry, darling, but I'll fetch some home with me. Now come on, give me a kiss before I go.'

Angel ran into Ruth's arms, clinging to her nanny for a moment and obviously bewildered by this new routine. Ruth was finally able to extract herself, saying as an afterthought as she hurried out, 'How's Arthur?'

'He's fine. See you later, Mum.'

As the door closed behind her mother, Sally went into the kitchen, Angel on her heels. 'Hello, Gran.'

'Hello, love, and what are you doing here?'

'You know why I'm here, Gran. I'll be staying with you until Mum comes home from work.'

'What on earth for? You should be with Arthur.'

Sally sighed. Since Gran's stroke she was often forgetful, and had mood swings too which made her difficult at times. 'Arthur's fine, and anyway he's going to the site with Joe today. Would you like a cup of tea before I take Angel to school?'

'No thanks, I've just had one.' She then held out her arms. 'Ain't you gonna give me a kiss, Angel?'

The child ran to her side, grinning widely. 'I'm Daddy's nurse now, Gamma.'

'That's nice, and do you wear your uniform?'

Gamma, Sally thought as she watched the scene, the name Angel had adopted for her great-grandmother when she first started to talk. Somehow it had stuck, and now none of them bothered to correct her.

Angel puffed with importance as she answered Sadie, 'I wear my uniform and I take my daddy's temture.'

'Temperature,' Sadie corrected, 'and my, ain't you a clever girl.'

'Come on, Angel, it's time for school,' Sally urged.

The child reluctantly left Sadie's side, Sally calling, 'I'll be back soon, Gran.'

Sadie closed her eyes as her granddaughter left the room. She hated being a burden and it wasn't right that Sally had to come round here every day to look after her. Why wouldn't they listen to her? She didn't need nursing, and even if she did, it wasn't Sally's place to do it.

Ruth had to work, she knew that, and though she loved her daughter, there was no getting away from the fact that she had a selfish streak. All right, it would be a bit humiliating to apply for National Assistance, but surely that was better than laying the burden of her care on to

25

Sally.

Her elder daughter was as bad, going off on a cruise and then deciding not to return. Mary was in Spain, living the life of Riley, but now Sadie's eyes saddened. In truth, she felt that she'd had a large hand in Mary's decision to leave. Yet what did her daughter expect when she turned up one day to say she was going to marry a black man? The daft cow had wanted her blessing, but there was fat chance of that. Instead, she had done her nut.

Sadie thought back to the scene she'd caused when Mary brought the man into the house, and in no uncertain terms she'd chucked the bugger out, telling Mary that she'd disown her if she married him.

Her daughter had accused her of racial prejudice, and maybe it was true, but she was no different from most of the neigbours, all resenting the West Indians who were moving into the area. There were some who stood up for them, of course, Sally being one of them, but Sadie wasn't going to budge in her opinions. If a stop wasn't put on immigration soon, they'd be overrun.

Mary had been devastated when she broke up with him, but instead of consoling her daughter, all she had felt was relief. Was it any wonder then that Mary had gone off on a cruise to lick her wounds?

Sadie fidgeted in her chair, exhaling loudly; for never in a million years had she expected that Mary wouldn't return. Despite their differences she loved her elder daughter and couldn't believe that she wasn't coming home again.

Mary and Ruth were similar in looks, both pretty with brown hair and blue eyes, but with very different personalities. As children, Ruth had been the needy one, whilst Mary had always been self-sufficient, growing into an uppity and bossy adult. Sadie had no idea where she got that from, but now she squirmed and finally chuckled. If truth be known, Mary was the daughter who was the most like her. She might appear hard, but it was just a veneer that hid a soft and vulnerable centre. She wrote, of course, and if her letters were anything to go by, she was happy, but Sadie longed to see her again.

Once again she shifted in her chair, easing a cushion behind her back. Sally would be back soon, and no doubt she'd get the kettle on to boil, and on that thought Sadie licked her lips in anticipation of a nice cup of tea with a spoonful of condensed milk to make it nice and sweet, her mind, at last, still.

It didn't take long to drop Angel off at school, the child running happily into the playground, and as Sally walked back to Candle Lane she found her thoughts going to Arthur, wondering how he'd cope on the building site. Stop it, she berated herself, stop worrying. Joe was sure to keep an eye on him, and if he thought it was too much for Arthur, he'd drive him home.

Sally smiled softly now, knowing that, as

Arthur had said, she had to stop behaving like a mother hen. Arthur was her husband, not her child, and they had been married for five years. She'd known him since childhood and had been ten years old when he and his family had moved next door to them in Candle Lane.

Their arrival heralded a cascade of changes in her life. Her father, or the man she had *thought* her father, ran off with another woman, and though her mother had taken his desertion badly, it had brought Sally her freedom. He hadn't been able to stand the sight of her and she'd been forced to stay in her bedroom whenever he was home, but his leaving brought release, and she had become fast friends with Arthur's sister, Ann.

For a long time, the only thing that marred her happiness was her fear of men. Sexually abused as a child by her uncle, she was terrified of intimacy. Sally now smiled softly again, remembering how Arthur had changed all that. The boy next door had turned into a handsome man, one she fell in love with, and one who had taken away her fears. Arthur had made love to her so gently, so tenderly and, best of all, Angela had been the result.

Her expression suddenly changed, a small frown appearing. She didn't want to think about it, but once again the memory forced itself to the front of her mind. It was the one thing that marred her happiness, these niggles of worry at the back of her mind that wouldn't go away. It wasn't long ago that she'd been grabbed by two

28

men – violent men who had mistaken her for someone else. They had beaten her, almost raped her, and she'd suffered a miscarriage.

Would the awful experience cause her old sexual fears to return? And though she didn't want to admit it, hadn't she been glad when Arthur went straight to sleep last night? No, no, she mustn't think like that. She couldn't let those awful men ruin the rest of her life. She had to fight these feelings, and when Arthur wanted to make love, she'd respond willingly.

Now, straightening her shoulders, Sally almost marched the rest of the way along Candle Lane, calling as she went inside, 'I'm back, Gran.'

'Yeah, I can see that. I may be old, but I ain't blind.'

Sally sighed. Her gran didn't sound in the best of moods and the day stretched out ahead of her. She'd do a bit of housework for her mother, but then there would be little to occupy her until it was time to pick Angel up from school. She loved her gran and had volunteered to look after her when she'd had a stroke, but sometimes the days seemed endless. 'Gran, after I've tidied up for Mum, do you fancy having a go at a jigsaw puzzle?'

'Yeah, all right,' she agreed, her eyes brightening. 'But make me a drink first, love. I'm spitting feathers now.'

Sally looked along her mother's kitchen: the long narrow room appeared bleak. In the far corner was an old, cracked, china sink with a wooden draining board, and in the other, her mother's old gas cooker. There was a cabinet against the wall and in front of this a battered table and chairs. At this end of the room, and looking squashed in around the hearth, was a sofa and two fireside chairs, ones that had been in the living room until it had been given up to Gran when she came to live with them.

Everything was done in this room, cooking, eating, watching television, but it lacked colour and warmth. Sally's eyes darkened with sadness. Her mother had worked hard to support them, but had little to show for it, this room emphasizing the bleakness of her life.

'What's the matter, Sally? You look a bit down in the mouth.'

'I was just thinking that Mum hasn't had much happiness in her life.'

'What's brought this on?'

'Seeing this place with fresh eyes, I suppose. It's cheerless in here, Gran.'

Sadie's eyes flicked from side to side. 'Yeah, I suppose it is, but that doesn't mean your mum's unhappy. Have you heard her complaining?'

'Well, no, I suppose not.'

'There you are then. She enjoys her job and prefers working to staying at home to look after me.'

'If you say so, but I could have a go at decorating in here.'

'Leave it out, Sally. The room is fine as it is, and anyway, I can't stand the smell of fresh

30

paint.'

Sally shook her head in defeat and then, going to the far end of the room, she filled the kettle before putting it on to one of the gas rings to boil. Whilst waiting she surreptitiously studied her gran's aura. It looked all right, with just a little darkness around her arthritic joints, but the fear of her having another stroke haunted Sally. Her gran might be short and stout, but she was a formidable woman when thwarted and had always stood up for her, even taking her side if she fell out with her mother. Gran was moody at times, but more and more often her old personality shone through. She was a loving, wise woman who had raised her whilst her mother had to work.

When the kettle boiled, Sally filled the teapot, and after it had brewed she carried a cup across to her gran. 'Here, drink that, and then I'll give you a bit of healing. I can see your arthritis is playing you up.'

'So, you've been looking at me aura thing again. When a nipper you used to call it our lights and it gave me the willies, I can tell you. Still, I've got used to it now, and I must admit you can really ease me pain.'

Sally smiled, and when her gran had finished her tea she asked her to sit on a kitchen chair, then stood behind her. With her eyes raised in a silent prayer, she raised her hands, running them parallel to her grandmother's body and feeling the familiar tingle that radiated from her palms. Elsie had been so patient when she'd

31

taught her to heal, explaining that she had to let the energies flow through her, not from her. It had taken a while, but gradually she'd mastered the technique, and though unable to tackle serious illnesses, she could at least ease pain.

After about twenty minutes, she stopped, glad to see that when her gran stood up, her limp was hardly noticeable. 'Thanks, Sally,' she said. 'I feel much better now, but how about another cup of tea?'

'Gran, I think with your love of tea we need to buy an urn.'

'Less of your lip, madam,' Sadie said, but she was smiling widely.

Sally smiled back. Oh, she loved her gran, she really did, and was unable to imagine life without her.

'Well, Arthur, what do you think?' Joe asked.

Arthur struggled out of the car, tucking his crutches under his arm. The earlier sunshine had been replaced by clouds, and now a soft rain fell in a thin veil that obscured his view as he looked at the building site. What looked like a sea of mud ran down the centre, but to one side building materials were stacked high, and the first row of houses were emerging. 'It looks great.'

'Come on,' Joe said, motioning towards a prefabricated hut. 'Such as it is, that's our site office. I'll give our foreman a shout and he can bring us up to speed.'

Arthur saw planks of wood leading to the

door and gingerly swung over them, doing his best to hide his feelings. The site was a quagmire, impossible to manoeuvre on his crutches, and he felt helpless, useless. There was nothing he could do here, and glancing around he saw some of the men looking at him. They quickly lowered their heads, but not before he saw the pity in their eyes.

As they went inside, Arthur's eyes roamed the hut, seeing the plans attached to one wall and charts that meant nothing to him. He sat down on one of several wooden folding chairs, placing his crutches to one side.

'One sugar or two?' Joe asked as he made them a drink.

'Two, please.'

Joe handed him a thick white mug, and then took a seat at the makeshift desk. 'It's good to have you on board, mate.'

'Doing what?' Arthur asked.

'Blimey, what do you think? The site doesn't run itself. To maintain the schedules there are materials to be ordered, and as project managers, it's our job to keep things up and running smoothly. We have to see that each stage is managed properly.'

'What do you mean?'

'The bricklayers will do their job, as will the roofers, but there are all the other tradesmen to sort out; the plasterers, plumbers, carpenters and electricians. They all need access at different times, different stages, and it's up to us to see that they have all the materials they need, and that they don't overlap each other.'

'I thought you said we have a foreman.'

'We do. Billy looks after the men and reports to us if there are any problems.'

Arthur shook his head doubtfully. 'Christ, Joe, I haven't got a clue where to start.'

'Neither did I at first, but you'll learn. We may make a few mistakes, but what we pick up in experience here, we'll take on to our next project. I must admit there have been a few cock-ups, but nothing too serious, and we're on schedule. Well, so far that is.'

'Until I get my prosthesis, I can't even walk the site.'

'Don't worry about that. There's enough for you to do in the office and in marketing the houses.'

The enormity of what they had undertaken hit Arthur for the first time, and he wondered what they had got themselves into. They had no experience, no skills, but had jumped into the project, so sure that they could handle it all. They had sunk all their saving into the venture, and if it all went pear- shaped, they'd be left with nothing but a pile of debts. He took a deep breath. Joe said he'd learn, and he'd do just that, putting everything he could into making this work. Their future depended on it.

Sally glanced at the clock. It wouldn't be much longer before she had to pick Angel up from school and after that a couple of hours before her mother arrived home. 'What are you having for dinner, Gran?'

'I think your mother forgot that she'd only be cooking for two. She did enough potatoes and cabbage to feed a bleedin' army and there's loads left over. I think she's using some of it up on a corned beef hash.'

'Right, once I've collected Angel from school, I might as well get it ready. Mum will only have to warm it up when she comes home.'

'Smashing. It'll be lovely with a fried egg on top.'

Just before three thirty Sally went to collect Angel from school, and now the child was sitting at the kitchen table, absorbed with a colouring book and crayons. Sally busied herself with mashing potatoes, adding the cabbage before forking in the corned beef. She then put a generous amount of lard in the frying pan and, when hot, added the mixture, turning it over when it was crisp and golden on one side. The other side done, she turned off the gas before going to join Angel at the kitchen table. Sadie was dozing in her chair, mouth wide, and she didn't awake until Ruth arrived home, Angel's loud excited voice breaking into her slumbers.

'Did you get me some sweets, Nanny?' the child cried, running across the room.

'Of course I did. They're in my bag,' Ruth said, sinking on to a chair and kicking off her shoes. She then pulled out a packet of Players, lit a cigarette and blew a cloud of smoke into the air.

'I've made your hash, Mum, and it just needs heating up. I'd best be off now though. We've got friends coming for dinner and there's a lot to do.'

'Friends for dinner. That sounds posh, and who are these friends?'

'It's only Joe, and Patsy Laurington, the girl who lives upstairs. Come on, Angel,' she added, 'time to go.'

'But I want to stay with Nanny.'

Sally could see Angel's bewilderment. Until Arthur had come home from hospital they had lived here in Candle Lane. Now though they had moved to Maple Terrace, and Angel wasn't used to the new routine yet. 'But what about your daddy?' she coaxed. 'He'll be looking for his nurse and it must be time for his medicine.'

Angel's head cocked to one side, her eyes narrowed in thought, but obviously her father won the day as she grabbed her sweets before running to Ruth. 'I've got to go, Nanny.'

'I know, pet, but I'll see you in the morning.'

'What about me? Don't I get a hug?' Sadie said, holding out her arms.

After Angel hugged Sadie, they chorused a goodbye, and as they left the house, Sally's mind was on dinner and what to cook for Joe and Patsy. Would her matchmaking work? Would they fall for each other? She hoped so. She liked them both, and if they became an item, they might just end up living upstairs. What fun that could be.

Three

'Hello, come on in,' Sally said, smiling a welcome as she took in Patsy's outfit. Her upstairs neighbour was wearing a navy and white striped minidress, with white knee-length boots. Blonde hair framed her pretty face and her make-up was immaculately and skillfully applied. Patsy was tiny, less than five feet tall, and she reminded Sally of a beautiful porcelain doll. 'I love your dress, Patsy.'

'It's from Biba in Kensington and I couldn't resist buying it.'

Sally looked down at her own outfit, feeling frumpy beside her as they walked into the living room, but she was sure that Joe would fall for Patsy on sight.

'Joe, this is Patsy Laurington,' she said.

He jumped to his feet, eyes widening and hand outstretched. 'Pleased to meet you.'

'It's nice to meet you too,' Patsy said as she took his hand, her neck craning as she looked up at him.

Sally hid a smile, thinking that so far it was going well. She could see the admiration in Joe's eyes and Patsy was flushing prettily. They looked a bit odd together, Joe over six feet tall and Patsy so tiny, but the girl was sure to bring out Joe's protective instincts.

'Are you two going to sit down, or what?' Arthur commented.

Their hands were still clasped, and Patsy giggled, disengaging hers hurriedly and looking flustered as she took a seat.

'Would you like a glass of wine?' Sally asked.

'Er ... yes please. My goodness, wine, it sounds very sophisticated.'

'It's only Chianti,' Sally said as she picked up the raffia bound bottle to pour Patsy a glass. 'What about you, Joe?'

'No thanks. I'll stick to beer,' he said, but Sally saw that his eyes were still on Patsy.

She handed the red wine to Patsy and then excused herself to hurry to the kitchen. It was the first time she'd cooked this meal, one that she thought seemed simple when she looked at the recipe, and hoped it would turn out all right. The water in the pan was boiling and, following the instructions, she fed the spaghetti into the water.

'Can I do anything to help?'

Sally turned to smile at Patsy. 'You can slice the bread if you like.'

'What are we having? It smells lovely.'

'Spaghetti Bolognaise, but it's my first attempt at making it.'

'I'm sure it'll be great,' Patsy said, adding as she sliced the bread, 'Joe seems nice.'

'He's a smashing bloke.'

'And he and your husband are partners?'

38

'They are, and good friends too. They're building low cost houses on the outskirts of Reading and hope to attract first time buyers.'

'It sounds very impressive.'

'It's a new venture for them both, and though they seem sure that young couples will be looking to get on the housing ladder, there are risks involved. I just hope it works out.'

Sally turned to look at Patsy as she spoke, for a moment thinking she saw a calculating look in her eyes, but then wondered if she'd imagined it as Patsy smiled at her without guile. 'Their idea sounds wonderful to me. If you can get a mortgage, why pay rent when you can buy your own home?'

'This is nearly ready so if you'll take the bread through, I'll follow with dinner shortly.'

Patsy piled the bread into a basket and tripped off on her stilettos, whilst Sally tested the spaghetti and found it done. She drained it, added the bolognaise sauce and, hoping it tasted as good as it looked, carried it through to the living room. 'Grub up,' she said, placing the dish on the table.

If nothing else, the meal served to break the ice, and after only five minutes they were howling with laughter. None of them were very good at handling the spaghetti, their attempts at wrapping it around their forks, hopeless.

Joe sucked on a long strand, and as the last of it went into his mouth, he licked his lips. 'It might be a bugger to eat, but it tastes great.'

'Yes, it's lovely,' Patsy said as she delicately

wiped her mouth.

'I'm sorry about your new dress, Patsy.'

She looked at the stain and shrugged. 'Don't worry about it, but maybe the next time I attempt to eat spaghetti, I'll wear a bib.'

'I think that goes for all of us,' Arthur said, looking ruefully at his shirt front. 'What's for pudding?'

'I'm afraid it's only ice-cream. I was a bit strapped for time.'

'Ice cream sounds great,' Joe said. Standing up he began to stack the plates.

Sally did the rest, and as he followed her through to the kitchen she couldn't resist the question. 'Well, what do you think of Patsy?'

'She's lovely,' he said.

'I thought you'd like her.'

For a moment, as they looked at each other, a hint of sadness appeared in Joe's eyes. 'Are you all right now, Sally?'

Sally knew what he was referring to, and would always be thankful for his support following her attack. Joe had been marvellous, encouraging her to overcome her agoraphobia, and now she nodded saying, 'Thanks to you, I'm fine.'

'Good, and as for Patsy, I think I'll ask her for a date.'

'Do that,' Sally encouraged, and after dishing up the ice-cream, Joe helped her to carry it through to the others.

The rest of the evening went well, Joe and Patsy becoming more and more relaxed as the wine and beer flowed.

'Do you work in this area, Patsy?' Joe asked.

'Yes. I'm a mobile hairdresser and most of my clients are in and around Battersea.'

'Do you cut men's hair?'

'Er ... yes, but I don't get many male clients.'

'Did you hear that, Arthur? Patsy here could give you a bit of a trim.'

'What's wrong with my hair?'

'Well, unless you're going for the Beatles look, it's a bit long.'

'Maybe, but no offence, Patsy, I'd rather stick to the barbers,' Arthur said, but then doing his best to hide it behind his hand, he yawned widely.

Joe saw it, saying as he rose to his feet, 'We'd best be on our way, Patsy. I think Arthur needs his beauty sleep.'

Sally looked at Arthur, saw how tired he was and frowned worriedly. Had he returned to work too quickly? She too stood up, and after the goodbyes had been said, Joe called as she showed them to the door, 'See you in the morning, Arthur.'

'Yeah, see you, mate,' he called back.

When Sally returned to the living room it was to find Arthur slumped in the chair, his eyes closed. 'Why don't you go to bed?' she urged.

He opened his eyes, asking tiredly, 'Are you coming?'

'There's a stack of washing-up and I can't face getting up to it in the morning. I'll do it now.'

41

For a moment he frowned, but then struggled to his feet, 'All right. Night, love.'

She gave him a quick kiss on the cheek and then went through to the kitchen, heaving a sigh at the great pile of dishes in the sink.

Joe stood behind Patsy as she opened her front door, surprised when she said, 'Do you fancy coming in for a coffee?'

'I'd like that.'

'Mind you, it's only coffee I'm offering.'

'That's all I expect,' he said, following her upstairs, admiring her shapely legs and slim ankles.

While Patsy made the drinks, Joe looked around her living room. Unlike the restful décor of Sally and Arthur's flat, this one was all garish colours. Bright orange predominated, the psychedelic wallpaper making his eyes swim. He leaned back on the black vinyl sofa, moving a shaggy cushion from behind his back, and then Patsy was back, handing him a Pyrex cup and saucer.

She sat beside him and for a while there was an awkward silence. Joe stirred his coffee, then seeing a photograph of a baby girl displayed on the sideboard he used this to open a conversation. 'Nice kid – is she a relative?'

'Yes,' Patsy said shortly, offering no further explanation.

Silence again, and then Patsy blurted, 'I'm a divorcée.'

'Are you?' Joe said in surprise. She looked so

young, too young to have been married and divorced.

'I was only seventeen when I married and soon found it was a dreadful mistake.'

'What went wrong?'

'I'd rather not talk about it,' she said sharply.

Joe shifted uncomfortably. They'd been fine in Arthur and Sally's company, but now the atmosphere between them was tense. Perhaps Patsy was worried that he'd try it on. Hoping to alleviate her fears he moved along the sofa, putting a little distance between them.

Patsy now looked surprised and leaning forward she placed her cup on the coffee table. She then shuffled close to him again, her expression soft and her eyes inviting as a small smile curled her lips.

Joe's brow rose and, hoping he hadn't misread the signs, he placed his cup next to hers before pulling her into his arms.

Their kiss was passionate, and as it deepened Patsy's tiny teeth nipped his lower lip. Joe groaned, becoming aroused as his hands began to roam her body before resting on a small, but pert breast.

She stiffened instantly, pushing him away, her voice sharp as she said, 'Joe, I think you'd better leave now.'

'I'm sorry,' he said.

'I know I'm divorced, but I'm not that sort of girl.'

'I didn't think you were, but well, you are rather lovely and you can't blame a chap for

43

trying.'

A small dimple appeared on her cheek as she smiled. 'Thanks, but it's late and time you left.'

Joe rose to his feet. 'Can I see you again?'

'Yes, I'd like that.'

'How about tomorrow night? Dinner, or a movie?'

'Dinner would be nice.' She stood on tiptoe, kissing him swiftly on the cheek, and then led the way downstairs. 'Goodnight, Joe,' she whispered as he stepped outside.

'I'll pick you up at eight tomorrow night.'

'That's fine,' she said, adding before closing the door, 'I'll look forward to it.'

Joe climbed into his car, but as he drove home along Maple Terrace there was a worried little frown on his brow. He liked Patsy, and there was no denying that she was a looker, but there was just something he couldn't put his finger on – something not quite right.

He manoeuvred the corner, heading back to his flat in Earls Court, still with Patsy on his mind. He'd asked her out, but now hoped he hadn't made a mistake.

Four

Sally chewed worriedly on her lower lip. Arthur had been home for ten days now, but something was wrong. He was growing distant, remote, and though she had asked if he was in pain, he said he wasn't, refusing any healing. She'd studied his aura, saw only a little darkness, and wondered if phantom pains were the problem. He'd suffered them in hospital, along with itching in a foot that was no longer there.

Every night when they went to bed Arthur immediately fell asleep without so much as a kiss goodnight, and wanting now to feel his arms around her, Sally was at a loss to know what to do. Arthur was tired, moody, and she was sure it was because he had returned to work too quickly.

As usual the early morning routine sped by, and giving herself a mental shake, Sally beckoned her daughter. 'Come on, Angel, it's time to go.'

'Bye, Daddy.'

'Bye, Princess,' he replied.

Sally went to Arthur's side, and leaning over she kissed his cheek. 'See you later, love.'

He didn't look at her, only mumbling, 'Bye.'

Sally took Angel's hand, her eyes awash with sadness as they left the house. Maybe she should talk to Joe, suggest cutting back on Arthur's hours, and as he and Patsy were going to join them that evening, it was as good a time as any.

It didn't take them long to reach Candle Lane, but Ruth only had time to give Angel a quick hug before she rushed off to work.

Sally forced a smile, leaving only minutes later. 'I'm running a bit late, Gran. I'd best get Angel to school.'

'I don't know why you have to come here every day.'

'You know why. I'm here to look after you,' Sally explained patiently again; this was becoming a morning ritual.

'Rubbish. I don't need looking after!'

'We'll talk about it when I get back,' Sally said, grabbing her daughter's hand and hurrying out of the house.

When they reached the school gates, a teacher stood in the playground, vigorously swinging a brass bell. Quickly kissing Angel, Sally urged the child inside. For a moment she watched as her daughter joined a row of children filing into the building, and then she turned to make her way back to Candle Lane.

Sadie greeted her with a smile when she arrived, her ill humour already gone, and Sally heaved a sigh of relief. Once again the day stretched ahead of her, but at ten o'clock there was a knock on the front door.

One of the neighbours, Nelly Cox, stood on the step and Sally stood aside to invite her in. 'Hello, Nelly.'

'Wotcher, Sally. What sort of mood is Sadie in?'

'She's much better nowadays, and her mood swings are not as bad.'

'Right, I'll come in then.'

Sally only half listened to the conversation as the two old ladies chatted, but her ears pricked up when she heard Laura Walters' name. The Walters lived next door, and until Laura had suffered a heart attack, she'd been an alcoholic. Her husband was a drinker too, but he'd left, deserting Laura while she was recovering in hospital. They had a seven-year-old son, Tommy, who had been the bane of Sally's life. She had done her best to keep Angel away from the boy, hating his foul language and habit of nicking things from the local shops. However, her attitude had changed when they discovered his mother's alcoholism and it explained why the boy ran wild on the streets, often hungry and dressed like a ragamuffin. Thankfully all that changed when his mother gave up the booze, and now Sally asked, 'What did you say about Laura?'

'I was just telling Sadie that she might be drinking again.'

'No! I can't believe it.'

'Jessie Stone popped in to see her yesterday, and said that Laura was acting a bit odd.'

'Jessie is nothing but a gossip,' Sally protested. 'Just because Laura wasn't herself, it doesn't mean she's drinking again. She might have been ill.'

'I don't think so. Jessie said that Laura was furtive, trying to get rid of her, and not only that, her voice was slurred.'

'Oh dear. I don't like the sound of that.'

'Me neither, but I ain't surprised. There's still no sign of her husband, and it must be hard on Laura that Denis walked out on her like that.'

'That's no excuse,' Sadie snapped.

'Maybe not, but if you're an alcoholic just one drink puts you back on the slippery slope.'

'Oh, and since when did you become an expert on the subject, Nelly Cox?'

'Now then, Sadie, there's no need to be sarcastic. I'm only repeating what I've heard.'

'I'm not being sarcastic and I'll say what I like in my own home. If you don't like it, then you know what you can do.'

Sally jumped to her feet, surprised by her gran's sudden mood change, and tried to divert the subject. 'Do you fancy a cup of tea, Nelly?'

'No, thanks. I'm off.'

With no other choice, Sally escorted her to the door, and as she stepped into Candle Lane, Nelly said, 'Sorry, love, but I could see that Sadie was on the turn and I didn't fancy being in the line of fire. When she gets in a two and eight she's impossible.'

'It's all right, I understand, but it's rare nowadays.'

'If you say so, and maybe I'll pop along to see

48

her again tomorrow.'

'Do you think Jessie is right about Laura?'

'I dunno, love, but no doubt we'll soon find out,' Nelly said, lifting a hand to wave as she bustled off.

Sally watched her for a moment before going back inside, feeling a wave of sadness. Nelly Cox was a lovely old lady who seemed lost since her husband had passed away. Sally had tried to help, offering spiritual healing, but had been unable to touch the man's terminal illness, and with no children, Nelly was all alone now.

As she made her way home, Nelly saw that Jessie Stone was gossiping on her doorstep as usual, this time with another neighbour, Maureen Downey.

'I see you've been to see Sadie,' Jessie said as Nelly drew alongside them. 'How's she doing?'

'She's fine,' Nelly said without stopping as she hurried past. Jessie was the worst gossip in the lane and she couldn't stand her. The woman spent more time on her doorstep surveying everything that went on in the lane, than she did indoors.

Maureen Downey was as bad, and now Nelly scowled. Not long ago she'd had a Social Worker knocking at her door, sent there by the snotty young woman. Maureen had reported her, saying she had vermin and was incapable of looking after herself. Bloody cheek! All right, she had let the place go since losing her husband, but that didn't mean she was ready for an old folks' home. She'd shown them, of course, and now her place was kept as clean as a new pin again.

As she let herself in Nelly threw off her coat and, walking into her kitchen, she looked around with satisfaction. It looked lovely, the table covered with a lace cloth, and a small plant in the centre.

Moving across the room she sat on a fireside chair and leaning forward to poke the fire to life, she added a few nuggets of coal. She shivered, waiting for the flames to dance into life. It was mid April but still chilly, and she'd need fuel until at least the end of May. Like Ruth, she virtually lived in the kitchen, her front room being kept for best. She had few visitors and it was daft really, but anyway, it would take too much coal to have both rooms heated.

Nelly fidgeted, pushing her wide backside further into the seat. Her thoughts now turned to Sally, and she smiled fondly. Ruth was lucky to have such a lovely daughter, but sometimes she didn't seem to appreciate the girl. It wasn't right that Sally had to look after her gran, and there was no getting away from the fact that the old girl was a trial nowadays. Before her stroke Sadie had been a different woman, and though formidable at times, she had been even tempered and kind. Now, though, she was sometimes like a harridan and Nelly didn't know how Sally put up with it.

Nelly sighed, wishing she had a granddaughter like Sally. Instead, when George died she

50

had been left alone, with no other family. Oh, they had wanted children so much, but it wasn't to be, and now as her husband's face swam into her mind, Nelly chuckled. They may not have had any kids, but trying for them had been fun and she chuckled again remembering their very enjoyable antics.

Her eyes closed. As the clock ticked in the stillness, Nelly found herself drifting, only to sit up sharply minutes later. For a brief moment she thought someone had touched her on the top of her head, and turned swiftly. 'Who's there?'

There was no answer, no one to be seen, and now Nelly's brow creased. She could have sworn there was someone in the room with her. 'Is that you, George?' she whispered.

Silence, just silence, but goose pimples ran along Nelly's spine. 'If that's you, George, then knock it off. You're giving me the willies.'

The humour of the situation hit Nelly then and she laughed. Hark at me, talking to the dead. It's just as well that young Social Worker isn't here or she'd have me committed. Mind you, Sally would understand, and the next time she saw the girl, she'd tell her about it. Maybe it wasn't her imagination, maybe George *was* trying to communicate with her. Nelly frowned. Or was she just losing her marbles?

The rest of the day passed slowly for Sally, but at last her mother arrived home, and she was surprised to see Tommy Walters with her.

51

'I found him sitting on his doorstep. The poor little sod looks half-frozen.'

'Nelly came round today with a bit of gossip,' Sadie told her. 'She said *you know who* might be back on the booze.'

The boy was too astute, and with an adult-like nod of his head, he said, 'Yeah, I fink me Mum's pissed.'

Sally closed her eyes against his language and Angel scrambled from the table to run to Ruth, roughly pushing Tommy out of the way.

'Now then, Angel, there's no need for that,' Ruth admonished.

'You're my nanny, not his.'

Ruth crouched down in front of Angel. 'Now that's enough of that. There's no need for jealousy, and have you forgotten that it was Tommy who stood up for you in school when you were being bullied?'

Angel looked sheepish and, nodding slowly, she whispered, 'Sorry, Nanny.'

'Say sorry to Tommy, not me.'

For a moment Angel looked petulant, but then she murmured in a barely audible voice, 'Sorry, Tommy.'

'That's all right. Mind you, I only let you get away wiv giving me a shove 'cos you're a girl.'

Angel's face darkened so Sally said quickly, 'Come on, it's time to go home.'

'He's gotta go too.'

'That's enough,' Sally said sharply. 'He'll be leaving soon. Now come on.'

Angel scowled, but kissed her nanny and then

52

Sadie, getting a hug from both of them as they said goodbye.

Sally held out her coat and the child slipped her arms into it, whilst throwing a ferocious look at Tommy. Sally grabbed her hand, calling her own goodbyes as she dragged her daughter out.

As they walked along the lane, Sally looked at Angel worriedly, wondering how to deal with this resurfacing jealousy. She'd been friends with Tommy and as her mother pointed out, the boy had stood up for her when she was being bullied. Despite that, Angel reacted badly when her nanny gave him any attention, and Sally was at a loss to know what to do.

Oh, if only Angel had a brother or sister, she thought, for a moment closing her eyes in pain as she remembered her miscarriage. Once again she was determined not to let it beat her and straightened her shoulders. If she could over-come her fears they could try again, and who knows, she might just get pregnant, despite the problems she had in conceiving.

Arthur heard the key in the door and, forcing a smile on his face, he held out his arms as his daughter ran into the room. 'Hello, sweetheart. Did you have a nice day at school?'

'Yes, and I got a star for my painting.'

'Well done.'

'Did you have a good day too, Arthur?' Sally asked.

With Angel around, Arthur hid his feelings,

53

managing to keep his voice pleasant. 'It was all right.'

'Has Joe mentioned how things are going with Patsy?'

'He hardly mentions her, only saying that he's taken her out to dinner a couple of times. I think they've been to the flicks too, but anyway, as they're joining us later, you'll be able to see for yourself.'

'That'll be nice, but now I'd best get our dinner ready.'

When she left the room, Angel began to chatter, and Arthur did his best to answer her. Yet in truth his mind was on Sally. When he came out of hospital he'd expected everything to be wonderful, but instead he could sense her tension, her withdrawal after just one kiss. Their first night and every night since played on his mind. Sally avoided looking at him, keeping her back to him when they undressed. In bed she kept a distance between them, and he could guess why. She found his stump repulsive and didn't want it near her.

He wanted Sally, wanted to make love to his wife, but rather than face her rejection, every night he feigned sleep. She was making him feel less than a man, and he hated it.

Sally washed the dishes, and the next hour passed quickly. Arthur gave Angel her bath and then put her to bed, returning to sit in the living room with a remote expression on his face. Sally was about to ask him what was wrong,

54

when the doorbell rang. 'I'll get it,' she said unnecessarily, rising to her feet.

Joe and Patsy stood on the step, the girl looking lovely as usual, this time in a bright red miniskirt and white roll-neck jumper. 'Hello you two, come on in,' Sally invited.

As they walked into the living room, Arthur perked up. 'Blimey, Patsy, you're a sight for sore eyes,' he said, looking the girl up and down.

'Thank you, kind sir,' she replied and as she sat down her skirt rode up to reveal more of her shapely legs.

Sally saw that Arthur was looking at them with appreciation and was surprised to feel a surge of jealousy. When was the last time he had looked at her like that? She forced a smile, shaking off the feeling as she asked if they'd like a drink.

It was the start of an evening that seemed full of undertones. Arthur focused most of his attention on Patsy, almost, Sally thought, as if he was deliberately trying to make her jealous. But why?

Joe was good company, chatting away to her throughout the evening and acting as a counter-balance. Yet even he seemed tense as he watched Patsy laughing and giggling her way through the evening.

Sally decided to play Arthur at his own game, and flirted a little with Joe, but her heart wasn't in it and it made her feel foolish.

'How's business, Patsy?' she asked, drawing

her attention away from Arthur.

'It isn't too bad, but I could do with a little car and would love to learn to drive. It's a bugger carting my stuff on and off buses.'

'But I thought you said all your clients are local.'

Patsy flushed and Sally wondered why, noticing too that her voice sounded flustered as she replied, 'Yeah, well, they are, but I've just picked up a couple of new clients in Streatham.'

'Oh, did you advertise there?'

'No, they came by way of a recommendation.'

'I wouldn't mind having my hair restyled. How much do you charge?'

'Leave it out, I wouldn't charge you anything. What sort of style are you thinking of?'

'I don't know really, but I've had it short before, and once I got used to it, I rather liked it. What do you think, Arthur? Shall I have my hair short again?'

'Do what you like,' he snapped.

Sally flinched at his tone and the atmosphere in the room became more tense. Obviously sensing it too, Joe looked at his watch before rising to his feet, 'I didn't realize it was so late. Come on, Patsy, we'd best be off.'

They said goodbye to Arthur, his reply short, and as Sally showed them to the door, Joe said quietly, 'Is Arthur all right?'

'I think he's tired, and maybe his leg is playing him up.'

'He seems fine on site, but if you're worried

56

about him I'll suggest cutting down his hours.'

'Thanks, Joe. I was just about to ask you to do that.'

'I'll do my best, Sally, but you know Arthur and he may not agree.'

'I know he can be stubborn at times, but I'm really worried about him.'

'All right, leave it with me,' Joe said. 'But I can't make any promises.'

Sally gave his hand a grateful squeeze and he returned the pressure, softly saying goodnight. Patsy did the same and as Sally closed the door she sighed with relief, feeling reassured. Joe was a good friend, and even if Arthur refused to cut down his hours, Joe would keep an eye on him.

When Sally went into the living room, it was empty, and she guessed Arthur had gone to bed. She picked up the supper things, carried them to the kitchen, and though it only took a few minutes to rinse them out, when she went through to the bedroom it was to find Arthur already asleep.

Quietly Sally undressed and slipped carefully into bed, but as she drifted off to sleep she again longed to feel Arthur's arms around her, longed to know if she could respond to his lovemaking. Maybe she should make the first move? But at that thought, memories of the attempted rape filled her mind and she shuddered.

In Candle Lane, a full moon was casting an eerie glow in the bedroom as Ruth lay awake.

She was thinking about Tommy, worried that he might be neglected again, yet there was a part of her that welcomed it and she felt a surge of shame.

When his mother had stopped drinking, Tommy no longer needed her, and she'd missed the boy, missed having him under her wing. Now, though, he was back, like a chick returning to the nest and she welcomed him. She had no idea why Tommy drew her, but there was something in his cheeky face and smile that made her heart melt.

Ruth snuggled further under the blankets, her mind now turning to her sister, wondering if she was still happy in Spain. It seemed unbelievable that her strait-laced and snobby sister had done something so daring, and who'd have dreamed that she'd find a job in a hotel on the Costa del Sol. Yet she didn't blame her. They'd both had rotten luck with their husbands and poor Mary had never had children. She shuddered now, remembering her sister's husband, glad that he was dead. If he wasn't, she'd have killed him with her bare hands for what he had done to Sally. Christ, who'd have thought that Mary's husband would turn out to be a paedophile?

With a sigh, Ruth plumped up her pillow. Ken, her own husband, had run off with another woman, and though she'd been devastated at first, it had turned out to be a blessing. Her mind strayed further back in time, to when Ken had been away fighting during the war. She hadn't heard from him in ages, thinking him killed in action. Lonely and afraid she'd started an affair, one that left her pregnant with Sally. He'd been a lovely man, a soldier from a Scottish regiment who had briefly stolen her heart, but then Ken had come home. He begged her to stay with him, promising to bring Sally up as his own and, thinking her place was with her husband, she'd agreed.

When Sally had been born with red hair, Ken hated her on sight and she'd been forced to keep the child out of his way. He became cruel, beating her, but after what she'd done it was no more than she deserved, and at least he kept his hands off Sally.

Ken had left when Sally was ten years old, and since then she'd never had a man in her life. He had sapped her confidence, ruled her, but now a surge of loneliness washed over Ruth. How many years had it been since she'd been held, kissed? Yet now, with her mother ill and needing care, what chance did she have of meeting anyone, even if she wanted to?

Ruth closed her eyes, forcing her frustration away and concentrated on Tommy again. If his mother was drinking again, he would need her, would turn to her, and she would see that he was kept safe.

Five

It was two days later, and eight in the evening. Tommy stood scowling at his mother.

'Tommy, run down to the off-license and get me another bottle of cider.'

'Mum, you've had enough. You're already pissed.'

'What did you say?'

Tommy saw the glimmer of fire in his mother's eyes as she rose unsteadily to her feet, and backed away. Why? Why had she turned to booze again? He'd been good when she came home from hospital, had kept out of mischief, and with his Dad gone he'd tried to look after her. She'd been fine for a while, and he'd loved all the cuddles and affection showered on him, affection he hadn't had since his little sister died. Now, though, she was boozing again, the cupboards empty of food and the house stinking.

She was almost on top of him now, her hand raised to strike him, and fumbling behind his back for the door handle, Tommy shot out on to the street.

'Come back, you little bugger!'

He ignored her shout, his feet pounding along

Candle Lane as though he could outrun his problems.

Tommy finally stopped three streets away, his thin little chest heaving as he leaned against a wall. With his mum in that sort of mood, he'd have to keep out of her way. When his breathing eased, he began to wander aimlessly. Gawd, he was hungry, but with the shops closed there was no chance of nicking something to eat.

He passed Maple Terrace and, knowing she lived there now, he thought about Angela Jones. It was all right for her. She had the life of Riley. Her mum and dad loved her, and she had Ruth and Sadie too. Mind you, he didn't envy her Sadie. The old girl frightened the life out of him. But he liked Ruth, she was great, and he wished she was his nanny too.

His stomach rumbled and Tommy bit hard on his lower lip. He was a boy and mustn't cry. Big boys don't cry, his dad always said. He wondered where his father was, and why he had buggered off. Had he caused that too – just as he'd caused his mum to turn to booze again?

Tommy continued to walk aimlessly, sometimes pausing to sit on a wall but, though he'd never admit it, he was nervous in these ill-lit streets. At last, turning yet another corner, he found he had walked full circle and was back in Candle Lane.

The lights were still on in his house. If he went in now he was sure to get a belting. He'd have to wait until his mum was asleep and then get into his bedroom by climbing the drainpipe

61

at the back of the house.

He shivered, still fighting tears, and, remembering how Ruth had always taken him in before, he decided to knock on her door. She was pretty, with soft brown hair, a nice smile, and she always smelled lovely too, clean, like flowery soap. With his fingers crossed, and his tummy rumbling loudly, Tommy rattled the letter box.

'Goodness, love, it's gone ten o'clock. What are you doing out at this time of night?' Ruth cried.

'I can't go home. My mum's got the hump and I'll get a belting if I show me face.'

'Is she drunk, Tommy?'

He nodded, reluctantly murmuring, 'Yes.'

Ruth shook her head, sighing heavily, but her voice was kind, 'Come in, lad,' she said, leading him into her kitchen.

As they walked in Sadie looked annoyed and Tommy quickly lowered his head, his feet shuffling nervously.

'Sit down, Tommy. Are you hungry?' Ruth asked.

He nodded again as he perched gingerly on the edge of the sofa, but then Ruth stuck a doorstep of bread and jam into his hand. He bit into it with relish, barely chewing a great chunk before swallowing it.

Ruth smiled softly at him and Tommy relaxed as his eyes flicked around the room, seeing this wonderfully warm kitchen as a refuge. Wood crackled in the fire and, as Tommy's gaze settled on the glowing embers his eyelids began to droop. It was only a moment later when Sadie spoke, her words making his ears prick up, but his eyes remained closed.

'He's nearly asleep, Ruth. It's time he went home.'

'Laura's drunk, and from what Tommy said it sounds as though she's on the warpath. I think I'll let him kip down here for the night.'

'You can't, love. Laura may be drunk now, but if she wakes up in the morning to find he's not there, it'll worry the life out of her.'

'Huh, I doubt that, and if she does, it's no more than she deserves.'

'I still don't think you should let him stay. You've fallen out with Laura before and you know she resents you taking the boy in. Take him home, love.'

Ruth exhaled loudly. 'All right, but I'll have a few choice words to say to her, and if she lays a hand on him, she'll have me to deal with.'

Tommy's eyes snapped open and he shot up. Christ, if Ruth had a go at his mum, she'd take it out on him. 'It's all right. You don't have to take me home, I'll be fine.'

'Now listen, Tommy. I know you've done it before, but I don't want you climbing drain-pipes to get in again. It's too dangerous. Come on, we'll go and knock on your door.'

Tommy felt like making a bolt for it, hopping on his feet with anxiety as he cried, 'Please don't say anything to my mum. She'll go potty. I'll be fine getting in. Honest, it's a piece of cake.'

'All right, calm down,' Ruth said, placing a placatory arm around his shoulders. 'If you insist on climbing up to your window, I'll come with you to make sure you're all right.'

Tommy slumped with relief but, as they went out the back way, he saw that the lights were still on in his house. He'd have to be quiet, very quiet, but with any luck his mum would have passed out by now. Tommy opened the back gate, Ruth behind him as he snuck into the yard. He'd done this many times before, and with practiced ease began to scale the pipe, Ruth hissing, 'Be careful, Tommy,' from behind.

He didn't answer, all his concentration on the task in hand, but when he reached his bedroom window and climbed inside, he leant out, saying in a loud whisper, 'I'm fine, and ... and thanks.'

Ruth lifted a hand to wave, her face appearing white and ghostly in the moonlight as she looked up at him. He gave a small wave back and then closed his window, relieved to be indoors safely. It was cold in his room and he didn't bother to get undressed, instead diving under the few threadbare blankets fully clothed.

Curling into a ball he closed his eyes, thinking about Ruth. She was nice, he liked her, and once again wished she was his gran.

Finally sheer exhaustion overwhelmed Tommy and he succumbed to sleep.

In Maple Terrace the following morning, Sally

was in despair. She had prepared breakfast, but Arthur barely spoke unless it was to answer Angel's continuous chatter. She knew he was annoyed that his appointment for the Limb Fitting Centre had been cancelled, but it had been rescheduled, and surely that wasn't enough to cause his continuing foul mood. Something else was wrong, very wrong and, despite his denials, she was determined to have it out with him.

In a way she was glad to leave the flat but, as they walked along Maple Terrace, Angel looked up at her worriedly.

'You all right, Mummy?'

'Yes, darling, I'm fine.'

'You're sad.'

'No, I'm not,' and swiftly pulling out a handkerchief she added, 'I've just got a bit of dirt in my eye, that's all.'

Angel didn't look convinced as Sally forced a smile. The child said no more for a while as they walked along, but then abruptly she said, 'I don't like Patsy.'

Where had that come from, Sally wondered. What had made Angel say that? 'Why don't you like her?'

'Dunno, just don't,' Angel said and, letting go of her hand as they turned into Candle Lane, she ran ahead to number five.

Sally frowned, wondering why her daughter didn't like Patsy. She was always sweet and kind to the child, and she was still frowning when she walked into her mother's kitchen.

'Hello, love,' Ruth said. 'What's up?'

'It's nothing.'

'That's good because I've got to go or I'll be late for work. Bye, Angel, see you later, pet.'

Angel gave her nanny a hug, and then Ruth was on her way, the door slamming behind her.

'Blimey, where's the fire?' Sadie complained.

'What fire, Gamma?'

'Oh, it's just a silly saying for someone in a rush,' she said. 'Now come and give me a cuddle before you go to school.'

Sally glanced at the clock and saw that she too was running a little late. 'Come on, Angel, time to go,' she urged.

As they stepped on to Candle Lane, Tommy Walters was leaving his house, and with a frown Sally took in his scruffy appearance. His hands and face were dirty, his shorts torn, and his elbows hung out of the holes in his thread-bare jumper. He wasn't wearing a coat, and grey socks bagged around his ankles, but he just yelled a greeting before running on ahead.

'Tommy doesn't like me now, Mummy.'

'Of course he does, but he's older than you and prefers to play with his little gang.'

Angel didn't reply, the child unusually quiet, and in no time they were at the school gates. 'Bye, darling,' Sally called, pleased to see her daughter running into the playground to join a group of little girls.

'Well, are you going to tell me what's wrong?' Sadie asked as soon as Sally returned.

Sally floundered for a moment, wondering if she should confide in her gran, but then felt a need to unburden. With a sigh she sat down, saying sadly, 'Since Arthur came home from hospital, he's been acting strangely. He seems distant, remote, and hardly talks.'

'That's to be expected.'

'Is it? But why?'

'He was in hospital for over four months, and in that time the ward became his insular little world. He was cut off from outside worries, with everything done for him, but now he has to adapt to ordinary life again, and in a new environment too. He's bound to find it a bit strange, love.'

'You could be right,' Sally said eagerly. 'Arthur did say that he felt a bit disorientated when he came home. Do you really think that's all it is?'

'Yes, I do, and maybe you're being a bit oversensitive. When Arthur was in hospital, the pair of you had no privacy, and when you lived here it wasn't much better. Your mum and me were always around, and Angel shared your bedroom. Now all of a sudden, you're in a new flat, Arthur's doing a new job, and I expect it's all a bit much for him at the moment.'

Sally's spirits lifted, 'Oh Gran, I feel so much better now and I'm glad I confided in you.'

'Good. Now how about putting the kettle on?'

'It wouldn't suit me, Gran.'

'Yeah, very funny, but I don't suppose it would look any worse on you than the daft fashions youngsters are wearing nowadays. It's all minidresses, long boots, straight-cut hair and black-rimmed eyes that make them look like pandas.'

'I keep meaning to get myself some new clothes and I rather fancy a miniskirt, but I just never seem to have the time.'

'Leave it out, Sally. You look fine as you are and I can't see Arthur letting you wear a short skirt.'

'Oh, you'd be surprised, Gran. My upstairs neighbour wears them all the time, and Arthur ogles her legs with great appreciation whenever he sees her.'

'Yeah, well, that's typical of men. They like to see women in sexy clothes, as long as it isn't their wife who's wearing them.'

Sally chuckled, 'Yes, you may be right.'

As she waited for the kettle to boil a smile remained on Sally's face. She felt so much better since talking to her gran about Arthur, and should have realized how he was feeling. His homecoming, coinciding with moving into Maple Terrace, was strange for all of them, and on top of that Arthur was trying to adapt to a new job, one that was far removed from the removals business. Once they were settled, things were sure to get better and, in the mean time, she'd try to be more understanding.

She was just pouring water into the old brown teapot when the doorbell rang. Quickly completing the task, she went to answer it. 'Hello, Nelly, come on in.'

'Watcher, Sally, I'm a bit early but I've got a bit of news about Laura Walters,' the old woman said as she bustled into the kitchen. She took a seat opposite Sadie, preening with importance. 'Jessie Stone was right. Laura is definitely back on the booze again.'

'I don't think there's any doubt about it,' Sally said, remembering the state Tommy was in when she'd seen him that morning.

'Sally's right, and not only that, the kid was in here last night,' Sadie said, her lips setting into a scowl. 'Don't get me wrong, I feel sorry for him, but it's like we're back to square one. He turned up after ten saying he couldn't go home because his mother was drunk and of course Ruth took him in. She fed him and was going to let him stay the night until I put my foot down.'

'It's disgusting that Laura's boozing again,' Nelly said. 'Jessie Stone is up in arms about it. She collared me first thing this morning, doing her nut, and said that from now on Laura can stew in her own juice.'

'Very Christian of her,' Sadie commented.

'You can't blame Jessie for being upset. She did a lot for Laura and they were becoming quite friendly.'

'Ruth did a lot to help her out too. As you know, Nelly, my daughter's a hoarder, and she gave Laura loads of stuff, including china, and bedding. No doubt it'll all end up in the pawnshop now to provide the woman with money for booze.'

'It's Tommy I'm concerned about,' Sally said as she passed both women a cup of tea. 'He looked like a ragamuffin when I saw him this

69

morning, and I expect he'll be running wild on the streets again.'

'Not if your mother has anything to say about it,' Sadie said. 'She should keep her nose out, but where that boy's concerned, I can't see it happening.'

Sally knew that Gran was right. Her mother *would* interfere, and she could sense trouble brewing. There was no doubt that she would take Tommy under her wing again and, as before, Laura wouldn't stand for it. Sober, Laura was a nice young woman and a good mother but, drunk, she became a shrew.

'Sally, I know I'm changing the subject, but can I ask you something?' Nelly said.

'Of course you can.'

'Well, you see, the other day I sort of thought my George was around me.'

'Did you? What happened?'

'It felt as though he touched my hair, and I actually spoke to him. Not that he answered, of course. Do you think I imagined it, Sally? Do you think I'm losing my marbles?'

Nelly looked so worried that Sally felt compelled to tell her of her own experiences. 'No, Nelly, I don't think you're losing your mind and I'll tell you why. You see, when I was a child I had what my mother called an imaginary friend, yet I knew she was real. She used to come to me when I was hurt, frightened or upset, and I still see her now, but rarely. She comes in a wonderful translucent light, and she too strokes my hair. To me, she's like an angel.

So, Nelly, if you're losing your marbles, then I must have lost mine years ago.'

'What does it matter anyway,' Sadie commented. 'If you thought it was George, and it comforted you, I can't see any harm in that.'

Nelly was quiet for a moment, her eyes darting from Sally to Sadie and then back again. 'Do you believe in life after death, Sally?'

'Yes, I do, but how it manifests itself, I've no idea, and it isn't anything I've delved into. I know there are people in the spiritualist church who say they can communicate with the dead, but I can't do it and don't want to try. I can do a little spiritual healing, and sometimes I get feelings of intuition, but that's all.'

'All!' Sadie said. 'The fact that you can heal is wonderful, and you've done so much to ease my arthritis.'

'Yes, maybe, but I can't touch serious illness. I wonder if all I do is to somehow release some sort of energy inside of people, an energy that gives them the ability to heal themselves.'

'Blimey, Sally, this is all getting a bit too deep for me,' Sadie protested. 'Whatever it is you do, it does me no end of good, and that's all that matters.'

'Yeah, your gran's right,' Nelly said. 'And now you've told me that you've felt someone touching your hair too, I feel heaps better. I was beginning to think I'd have to go into the funny farm.'

'Well, as I said, if that's the case I'd have to join you. Stop worrying, and if you feel George around you again, as my gran said, there's no harm in chatting to him.'

Nelly grinned widely and chuckled as she said, 'Yeah, I'll do that, and anyway, my old man never did like to be ignored.'

When Sally went to collect Angel from school, she kept an eye out for Tommy, but there was no sign of the boy. Now Angel was happily sitting at the kitchen table, painting as usual, and Sally kept busy until her mother arrived home.

'What's up, Mum?' Sally asked when she saw her expression. 'You look a bit down in the mouth.'

'I'm worried about losing my job. Sid's son has been to see him again, and is trying to talk him into retirement.'

Sally frowned. It sounded a bit odd. Sidney Jacob's son hardly had time for his father, his visits rare, so why had he started to turn up now? Before her marriage, she had worked in Sid's haberdashery shop, and had come to love the job and the old man. Last year, her mother had gone to work for him, she too loving the job and her boss. 'What did Sidney have to say about it?'

'Not much, but I think he's considering the idea. Gawd, Sally, I'll be gutted if he closes the business.'

'I don't think he will, Mum. Sid loves his little shop, the customers, and the local gossip. He'd be lost without it.'

'That might have been the case when you worked for him, but nowadays he spends most of his time upstairs. He hardly comes into the shop for more than a couple of hours a day.'

'I still don't think he'll sell up,' Sally said, hoping she was right. 'Anyway, I'd best be off. Arthur will be home and wanting his dinner.'

'All right, love. See you tomorrow,' Ruth said, giving Angel a hug.

The child ran to Sadie, hugging her too as usual, and then they were on their way home.

Sally was looking forward to seeing Arthur and her step was light. Since confiding in her gran she was happier and understood the problem now. It was just that Arthur was unsettled, they both were, but it would get easier with time.

That evening, Bert and Elsie arrived at seven, and as soon as Angel saw her grandmother, she flew across the room.

'Grandma!' she cried.

'Hello, darling,' Elsie said, pulling Angel into her arms before turning to Arthur and saying, 'How are you, son?'

'Not so bad, Mum.'

'How are things on the site?' Bert asked.

Sally and Elsie smiled at each other and, whilst the men discussed business, they went into the kitchen, Angel in their wake.

'Arthur looks tired, Sally.'

'I think he went back to work too soon. Originally he intended to wait until he got his artificial leg, but then changed his mind.'

'Daddy said his leg won't grow again. Why won't it, Grandma?'

'New legs don't grow, sweetheart.'

'But when my teeth fall out, I'll get new ones, and Mummy said the tooth fairy will give me sixpence for the old ones.'

Elsie chuckled. 'I think teeth are a bit different, darling. Anyway, don't you worry about your daddy. He's going to have a special leg made for him and he'll be fine.'

Angel smiled, obviously placated as she stood close to Elsie.

'How's Ann?' Sally asked.

'She's fine, but I wish she hadn't moved to Milton Keynes. With three kids, and two of them twins, she's too far away from me.'

Sally sighed. Ann wasn't just her sister-in-law, she was her best friend, and she missed her too. Soon after getting married, she and her husband had moved to a new town out of London. The children had come quickly, twin boys, followed by a baby girl, but it wasn't often that Sally got to see them.

'I'm going to see Pops,' Angel called, running from the room.

Elsie grinned. 'She still calls her granddad Pops and I can't see it changing now. Anyway, how are you coping Sally? It can't be easy having to go to Candle Lane every day to look after Sadie.'

'It's fine. We've settled into a routine now, and Arthur doesn't mind.'

'I still think it's your mother's place to look after Sadie, but I understand how difficult it is. I know she has to work, but maybe she could apply for National Assistance.'

'Oh, she won't do that. My Aunt Mary suggested it once and Mum flipped. She said that she hadn't gone round with a begging bowl when Ken left, and she wasn't going to start now.'

'It seems strange to hear you calling your father Ken.'

'He isn't my father.'

'No, of course not, but you didn't know that as a child.'

'You're right, I didn't, but it was such a relief when I found out the truth. I could never understand why I had to keep out of his way – why he hated me, so finding out that he wasn't my father was like a huge weight lifting from my shoulders.'

'I remember, and you came into your own after he left. It's a shame that you don't know your real father.'

'Yes, and I'd love to find him, but with so little information, it's impossible. Mum could not tell me much and I know it embarrassed her. All she said is that he's Scottish and that his first name is Andrew. With only that to go on it would be like looking for a needle in a haystack.'

'Yes, I suppose you're right,' Elsie agreed and then changed the subject to one that Sally didn't like. 'What those men did to you was horrendous but you never talk about it. Are you sure you're all right?'

'It's in the past and I just want to forget about it.'

'All right, Sally, and in that case I'm sorry for bringing it up.' And changing the subject again she asked, 'Have you given Arthur any healing?'

'No, he insists he's fine and doesn't want any.' Sally frowned. 'Sometimes though I can sense he's in pain.'

'It's still early days, love, and what about Angel? Has she mentioned the *before time* lately?'

'No, and she hasn't for some time now. It's as if she could remember it for a while, but now it's faded from her memory.'

'It was strange, but nevertheless but I've heard of it before. There are eastern religions that believe in reincarnation.'

'Reincarnation! Do you think that's what it was?'

'How else can you explain it? How could she have known about such things, starting at only eighteen months old?'

'I suppose you have a point, but I'm still not sure about reincarnation. It sounds a bit far-fetched to think we've been here before.'

'Does it sound any more far-fetched than heaven and hell, angels and demons?'

'Well, no, I suppose not.'

'Who's to know which teachings are right, Sally, and if you ask me religion seems to be a matter of geography and nationality.'

Sally frowned, 'What do you mean?'

'If I had been born, say, in Tibet, I would have been brought up a Buddhist. In India, maybe a Hindu, but because I was born here and my parents were Christians, that's the doctrine I was taught. If you ask me, as long as the religion you practice makes you a better person, and gives you something to cling to in time of trouble, that's all that matters.'

Sally nodded. 'Yes, I agree, and it's a shame that there's so much intolerance.'

'Oh, Sally, I do miss our chats. Bert thinks it's all a load of tosh and I've given up talking to him about spiritual subjects. I used to love it when you popped up to Wimbledon to see me, but since you've had to look after Sadie, we never get any time alone.'

'Yes, I miss my visits too, but I have to look after my gran, Elsie. She can't be left on her own.'

'I know, love, but I still think your mother should do it.'

'Grandma,' Angel cried, running into the room again and scrambling on to Elsie's lap, 'Pops said he wants a cup of tea.'

'I'll make him one, and what about you, Elsie?' Sally asked.

'I thought you'd never ask,' she grinned.

The rest of the evening was pleasant, and it was Elsie who put Angel to bed. Then, at ten o'clock, Arthur began to yawn.

Elsie frowned as she gazed at him. 'I don't

think you should have rushed back to work. You look worn out.'

'I'm fine. I'm not doing anything physical, but there's a lot to learn about being a project manager and if I cock things up, the building could be held up for weeks. I'm tired mentally, not physically.'

'All right, son, if you say so, but it's time we went home. Come on, Bert,' she said, rising to her feet.

'Yes, your ladyship,' Bert said, as he too stood up.

'Huh! Very funny, ladyship indeed. Anyway we're off,' Elsie said, looking reassured as she bent to kiss Arthur's cheek. 'We'll be down to see you again in a few days. Bye, Sally, and give my love to your mum and Sadie. Tell them I'll pop in to see them soon.'

'Yes, I'll do that. Bye, Elsie. Bye, Bert,' she said as she showed them out.

Not long after Sally returned to the living room, Arthur rose to his feet, saying he was going to bed. Sally joined him, but as soon his head hit the pillow, he fell asleep.

Unable to believe it, Sally whispered, 'Arthur,' but there was no reply. The bed then shifted slightly, and with a soft snore, he turned away from her.

Six

Nearly two weeks later, and after another day on site, Joe dropped Arthur outside his house. He was about to climb back into his car when he saw Patsy hurrying up the road towards him and his heart sank. He hadn't asked her out lately, and in fact had been avoiding her.

'Hello, Joe,' she said, touching his arm and smiling intimately. 'Are you coming up for a coffee?'

Christ, Joe thought. This was awkward. There was something about Patsy that he didn't like. Something false. When he'd first met her she had seemed so sweet and innocent, but it hadn't taken him long to decide that it was all an act, a veneer covering a hard centre. She was too pushy, too eager to take the relationship further, and much too interested in his finances.

'Come on,' she urged, her grip tightening on his arm.

After a moment's hesitation, Joe decided that honesty would be the best policy. He didn't want to get involved in a serious relationship and instead of avoiding her, he would tell her face to face. 'All right, I'll come up for a coffee.'

Patsy made the drinks and then sat beside him on the sofa, tucking her feet up and showing an expanse of shapely legs. It was one of the things that Joe didn't like, her innocent act combined with brazenness. She was Sally's friend, and that made it a bit difficult, but he hadn't liked the way she openly flirted with Arthur, a ploy obviously designed to make him jealous.

'I haven't seen you for a while, Joe, and was beginning to think that you've been avoiding me.'

'I've been busy, and to be honest, I don't want to get into anything serious at the moment.'

Her eyes hardened. 'So why ask me out?'

'That's just it, Patsy. I asked you out, but it was all going too fast. We'd only been out a few times and you were getting proprietary. I'm not ready for that.'

'Huh, and do you think I don't know why? I'm not stupid you know and I've seen the way you look at Sally.'

Joe's face paled. Patsy had seen it, something he thought he hid well. He was in love with Sally, a feeling he fought each and every day. Arthur was his friend, his business partner, and he didn't want anything to jeopardize their relationship. Not only that, Sally was in love with Arthur, her feelings plain, and there was no way on earth he'd do anything to come between them. 'I don't know what you mean,' he blustered.

'Don't give me that. You fancy Sally, but I wonder how Arthur would feel about it if he found out?'

Joe reared up, his face taut. 'Sally and Arthur are my friends, good friends, so I hope you're not implying that you intend to stir things up with this load of claptrap.'

'Me – stir things up! No, of course not. Now come on, when are you going to take me out again?'

There was something in Patsy's tone, something that smacked of blackmail, but he wasn't standing for that. If she tried to make mischief, he'd handle it, sure that Arthur wouldn't believe anything she had to say. 'I've told you, I'm not looking for a relationship, but there's no reason why we can't be friends.'

She uncurled her legs and stood up abruptly. 'All right, friends it is and that suits me. Now if you don't mind, I'd like you to leave.'

Joe was pleased to go and hurried downstairs yet, as he drove off, he was frowning. He didn't trust Patsy and hoped she didn't try to make mischief.

As Sally prepared dinner that evening, she was doing her best to keep cheerful. Gran had said that Arthur's attitude was to be expected, yet things weren't getting any better between them, and if anything they were becoming worse. She and Arthur hardly communicated, but she was still trying to be patient and understanding. Even so, the atmosphere was strained, and though they tried to act normally when Angel was around, as soon as the child went to bed they would sit watching television all evening, with hardly a word spoken.

She dreaded going to bed now – dreaded lying beside this man who was beginning to feel like a stranger. She wanted to be held in his arms – wanted them to regain their old intimacy, and until they did she was unable to allay her fears. When he had first come home she hadn't expected to be made love to until his stump had completely healed, and at first had been glad of that, but now she had begun to feel resentful. Surely he could show *some* affection?

At eight o'clock, after Sally got Angel off to sleep, she returned to the living room, deciding that this situation couldn't go on any longer. She and Arthur needed to talk, to find out what the problem was, but just as she was about to speak, there was a knock on the door.

Sally went to answer it, forcing a smile when she saw Patsy, and stood aside to invite her in. The girl looked unhappy and, as she stepped into the living room, it was Arthur who asked what was wrong.

Patsy flopped on to a chair, saying with a choke in her voice, 'I saw Joe earlier, and he said he doesn't want to see me any more.'

'Oh, I'm so sorry, Patsy,' Sally said, moving forward to lay a conciliatory hand on Patsy's shoulder.

'I think he's got his eye on someone else.'

Arthur frowned. 'No, I don't think so. We work together all day and he hasn't mentioned anything to me.'

'Perhaps he doesn't want you to know about it.'

'I don't see why. Joe and I have been mates for years and he's like an open book to me. If he had his eye on another girl, I'd know about it.

'Maybe not this one,' Patsy murmured.

There was a strange undertone in Patsy's voice, something Sally couldn't put her finger on and Arthur looked puzzled too, but the girl looked so miserable that Sally's heart went out to her. 'Would you like something to drink?'

'Yes, please, a coffee would be nice,' she said, dabbing at her eyes with a handkerchief.

Sally went to the kitchen, wondering as she made the drink why Joe didn't want to see Patsy anymore. She thought the two of them were hitting it off, but obviously she'd been wrong. Despite what Patsy said, she doubted there was another girl and maybe Joe had hinted at that for an excuse.

When she returned to the living room, her eyes widened in surprise. In the short time she'd been absent Patsy had recovered, no longer looking sad as she sat obviously relaxed and laughing at something Arthur had said.

'Oh, you are funny,' Patsy sputtered. 'It's good that you can joke about your leg. And when do you get your artificial one fitted?'

'I'm going to Roehampton in the morning. I was a bit fed up that my appointment was cancelled and I've had to wait this long. My stump has completely healed and I can't wait to get it fitted.'

'One of my clients has a prosthesis, but you can hardly tell. He barely limps at all, but he's quite elderly and uses a stick.'

'Somehow I can't imagine you cutting an old man's hair.'

Patsy flushed. 'I do his wife's hair and one day he asked me to cut his.'

Arthur nodded and then said, 'I'm determined to walk without a stick. Douglas Bader flew a plane with two false legs, so how can I complain?'

'Good for you,' Patsy said, unravelling her own legs and reaching out to pick up her coffee.

At ten o'clock, Patsy still hadn't left. She laughed and giggled with Arthur until Sally felt like screaming. Over and over again she heard Arthur's words in her mind. He'd told Patsy that his stump had completely healed, yet he hadn't mentioned it to her and still kept a distance between them in bed.

Arthur's eyes continually strayed to Patsy's legs, and in such a short skirt, there was a lot on show. Sally hated herself, but couldn't help feeling jealous, relieved when at last the girl rose to leave.

'I'm sorry about you and Joe,' she said as she showed her to the door.

'Really? Are you sure?'

As Sally caught that strange undertone again, her brow creased. 'Of course I'm sure. I was hoping you two would hit it off.'

'Yes, well, as I said, I think he's got his eye on someone else.'

'I'm sure you're wrong.'

'I don't think so, and you never know, she may become available. Anyway, goodnight, Sally. I'll see you again soon.'

Sally was still puzzling over Patsy's words when she closed the door and returned to the living room but, seeing Arthur struggling to his feet, their own problems became paramount. 'Arthur, don't go to bed yet. We need to talk.'

'Not now,' he said curtly. 'I'm tired and there's the hospital in the morning.'

Sally exhaled loudly. Picking up the coffee cups she carried them through to the kitchen. They hadn't managed to sort things out, but this situation couldn't go on and they'd have to have it out soon.

When Sally awoke the next morning, she found the bed empty beside her. Surprised that Arthur was up first she threw on her dressing gown and went to the kitchen. Arthur was sitting at the kitchen table, deep in thought and seemed unaware of her presence. Maybe they could talk before Angel got up and, grabbing at the opportunity she asked, 'Arthur, what's wrong?'

His face was taut. 'Nothing.'

'I can see you're upset about something.'

'If you must know, I was just thinking that, unlike you, Patsy doesn't see me as less of a man.'

'What's that supposed to mean?'

His face suddenly red with anger, he yelled, 'If you don't bloody know, then I'm not about to tell you.'

'Daddy, why are you shouting?' Angel cried, neither of them noticing that she had come into the room.

Arthur took in a great gulp of air, and then held out his arms. 'Take no notice of me, princess. I must have got out of bed on the wrong side this morning. Come on, give me a hug and that will make me feel better.'

She scrambled on to his lap, saying, 'Are you cross with Mummy?'

'No, of course not. Now, shall we have an egg on toast this morning?'

Angel nodded and Sally began to prepare breakfast, her mind on Arthur's comment. He'd said that Patsy didn't find him less than a man, but what did he mean? Was he referring to his leg? And if so – why? She had wanted to talk to Arthur, not have an argument, but he hadn't given her the chance.

It was a tense morning, the atmosphere strained, but in just under an hour Sally was ready to leave. Arthur was waiting for his father to pick him up for his appointment at the Roehampton Limb Fitting Centre and, as Sally took Angel's hand, she took a deep breath, saying in a conciliatory tone, 'We've got to go, but I hope it all goes well today. I'll see you later, love.'

'Yeah, see you,' he said shortly, but his face softened as he gave Angel a kiss. 'Bye, princess.'

Angel waved, but clung tightly to Sally's hand as they walked to Candle Lane. Sally's mind

86

was churning, going over and over Arthur's words so she didn't notice that Angel was unusually quiet until they turned the corner and her daughter pulled on her hand.

'Mummy.'

She looked down, saw that Angel was looking up at her, face wan and eyes dark with confusion. 'What's the matter, love?'

'Why is Daddy cross with you?'

Sally's face stretched in surprise. 'He isn't cross with me, darling.'

'Yes he is. Doesn't he like you anymore?'

'Of course he likes me.'

'But he doesn't kiss you now, and he isn't nice to you.'

Oh God, Sally thought, what do I tell the child? This couldn't go on, it just couldn't and somehow she and Arthur had to sort things out once and for all. Her own childhood memories were of rows, violence, and though she knew Arthur would never hit her, she didn't want her daughter affected by their arguments.

Arthur watched the door close behind his wife and daughter, his face dark. Nothing had changed. As she had on his first night home, Sally still kept a distance between them. He thought back to their first evening together, remembering how he had opened his eyes to see Sally looking at his leg with revulsion, something that until that moment, he'd had no idea she felt.

She rarely kissed him, and when she did it

was usually a quick one on his cheek, and he couldn't remember the last time he'd held her in his arms. His frustration was mounting. He wanted to make love to his wife, but the thought of seeing disgust on her face again if he tried, held him back. He couldn't face her rejection, he just couldn't.

He was looking out of the window when he saw their upstairs neighbour leaving her flat, and eyed her appreciatively. Patsy didn't seem repulsed by his leg, and he had lightly flirted with her, hoping to make Sally jealous. He shouldn't have done it of course and had been surprised when the girl flirted back. He was also surprised that Joe had broken up with her, and wondered why he hadn't mentioned it. He frowned, determined to ask Joe about it the next time he saw him.

Patsy disappeared from view just as he saw his father's car drawing up outside, and Arthur hurried to let him in. 'Hello, Dad.'

'Hello, son, are you ready for the off?'

'Yes, I'll just get my coat.'

'Stay there, I'll get it for you.'

Arthur wanted to protest, to tell his father that he was perfectly capable of getting it himself. Like Sally, his parents mollycoddled him and he hated it, but for the sake of peace he kept his mouth shut.

As they travelled to Roehampton, conversation was mainly on the removals business, but more than once Arthur saw his father glance around, until finally he said what was on his mind. 'Are you worried about adapting to an artificial leg, son?'

'No, I can't wait to get it, but they're only taking a plaster cast today to make sure they get the right shape for a skeletal fitting.'

'And after that, when will it be ready?'

'I don't know, but I hope it won't take long. I'm sick of hopping about on crutches.'

'Don't expect miracles, son. It'll take you a while to adapt to a false leg.'

We'll see, Arthur thought, thankful that at last they'd arrived. After parking, they made their way to the limb fitting centre, reporting to the desk before taking seats. Arthur's eyes scanned the other patients, seeing amongst them a man missing his leg from the thigh who smiled at him in camaraderie.

When called into the clinic, Arthur watched as the crepe bandage was removed from his stump. The wound looked completely healed, and there was no sign of any swelling around the stump.

A plaster mould was made, and then the doctor said, 'Right, Mr Jones. We'll see you back here in a week for a rudimentary fitting, and in a further three weeks your leg should be ready.'

'Three weeks!'

'Yes, and then you'll be sent to our gym.'

'Why the gym?'

'You'll need to use our apparatus to learn how to walk with the leg, but with a below the knee amputation it shouldn't take long.'

Another appointment was made for the

following week and, fighting his disappointment, Arthur went to find his father.

Bert was outside. He smiled wanly when he saw Arthur, his dislike of hospitals all too obvious. 'All done, son?'

'Yes, until next week, but listen, Dad, I'll ask Joe to bring me next time.'

'There's no need for that. When exactly is your next appointment?'

Arthur told him but as they began their journey home, he was still feeling disappointed. A month before he got his prosthesis, a whole bloody month.

Would it make a difference? With an artificial limb, would Sally find him less repugnant?

Seven

Sally opened the door, greeting him with a smile. 'Hello, Joe.'

'Is Patsy with you?'

'No, I heard her going out a while ago.'

'Right, I'll come in then. I've stopped taking her out and it's making things a bit awkward.'

'Yes, she told us.'

God, she's lovely, Joe thought as he followed her through to the sitting room, but then berated himself. She was Arthur's wife, and they could only ever be friends.

'Hello, mate,' Arthur said.

'I've just called in to see how you got on at the hospital today and to see for myself if you're up to work in the morning.'

'Of course I'm coming to work. I only had a fitting and it'll be a while yet before I get my prosthesis. Until I do, and can drive again, you'll still have to pick me up. Sorry to be a pest.'

'Don't be daft, I don't mind.'

'Can I get you something to drink?' Sally asked.

'Yeah, tea would be great.'

'What about you, Arthur?'

With surprise, Joe saw that Arthur scowled at Sally, his voice curt as he said, 'No, nothing.'

He waited until she left the room, and then said, 'Have I called at a bad time?'

'What makes you think that?'

'You were a bit sharp with Sally. Are you sure I haven't interrupted a row?'

'No, you haven't. And if I was sharp, it's no more than she deserves.'

'Deserves! What's that supposed to mean?'

'She's repulsed by my stump, and makes it pretty obvious.'

'Don't be daft, Arthur. You're imagining things.'

'No I'm not, and if you don't mind, can we change the subject?'

'Yes, if you insist, but I still think you're wrong.'

'Patsy came down to see us last night. She

91

said the two of you have broken up and I'm surprised you didn't mention it to me. A bit of advance warning would've been handy.'

'Sorry mate, I didn't think.'

'What went wrong?'

Joe rubbed a hand around his chin, wondering how to answer, but then Sally came back into the room. She handed him a cup and then sat down, saying, 'I'm sorry things didn't work out between you and Patsy. She said something about you having your eye on someone else.'

Joe stiffened. Christ, it sounded like Patsy was already trying to stir things up. 'No, she's wrong. There isn't anyone else.'

'Yeah, that's what I thought,' Arthur said. 'Mind you, I'm surprised that you've stopped seeing her. She's a bit of all right and I wouldn't mind giving her one.'

Sally jumped to her feet, hurrying from the room, the door slamming behind her.

'Blimey, mate,' Joe said, 'you shouldn't have said that in front of Sally. She looked really upset.'

'So what?'

'Don't you think you should apologize?'

'Look, Joe, I don't want to fall out with you, but this is none of your business.'

Joe lowered his eyes. Arthur was in a rotten mood, and maybe he was in pain or something. It was obvious that he'd called at a bad time, and now rose to leave. These two needed to be left alone to sort out their differences. They loved each other, and he was sure that this was just a flash in the pan, a row soon made up.

'I'm off, mate. I'll pick you up for work in the morning.'

Arthur didn't argue at his swift departure, only rising to his feet and shoving his crutches under his arm. 'All right, I'll come with you to the door, and I'll see you in the morning.'

Sally didn't appear and, after saying goodbye to Arthur, Joe drove home, finding that she remained on his mind. He couldn't imagine why Arthur had the idea that she was repulsed by his stump. It was bloody ridiculous, so ridiculous that he was sure they'd soon sort it out.

A week passed. Patsy looked at her face in the mirror, her lips tight with anger. Joe was still avoiding her and she knew now that there was no chance of getting him back, despite her veiled threats. Oh, she wasn't stupid, and in fact was very observant. It was obvious that he fancied Sally, and it would come in useful with her new plan, one she was sure would work.

Patsy picked up her lipstick, applied a fresh coat, and then made her way downstairs. She'd failed to snare Joe, but now had another fish to fry. She'd use Arthur's weaknesses, ones she had already sussed out.

'Hello, Patsy,' Sally said, her welcome muted as she invited her in.

Patsy ignored it and, walking straight to the living room, chirped, 'Hello, Arthur, how are you doing?'

'I'm fine, and you?'

'I'm all right. You're due to go to the hospital again tomorrow, aren't you?'

'Yes, that's right.'

'Is Joe taking you?'

'No, my father will be running me there again. Joe's away on business tomorrow and in fact I've got the whole day off.'

'Patsy, were you hoping to see Joe?' Sally asked.

'Well, yes, I was, but to be honest I think it would be a waste of time. He told me that he doesn't want a relationship, and I suppose I'll just have to accept that.'

'There are plenty of fish in the sea,' Arthur said. 'With your looks you'll have no trouble netting one.'

'Well, thank you, kind sir,' Patsy said.

'Sit down,' Arthur invited, and she did just that, making sure that she was opposite him and displaying her legs prettily.

Sally offered to make her a drink and, asking for a coffee, Patsy focused her attention on Arthur. He was a good-looking bloke, tall, bear-like in build, and his missing lower leg didn't bother her. She was more interested in the money he was going to make from the building development that he and Joe were involved in.

Sally was a daft cow, a wet blanket, one who was so sure that she had the perfect marriage. Well, she'd soon show her, and by the time Sally worked it out it would be too late.

Patsy smiled secretly. When her scheme

worked, it would change her life, and she now began to put it in action. She leaned forward, her look seductive as she gazed at Arthur, giving him no doubt that she found him attractive.

Would she never go, Sally thought as the clock ticked round to ten thirty. It was awful to see the way Arthur flirted with Patsy, and not only that, Patsy was flirting back. She had thought Patsy nice, but now found herself having doubts about the girl. She had seemed so sweet at first, but was now showing a different side of her personality.

Sally yawned yet again. Finally it must have got through to Patsy.

'Time for my beauty sleep,' she said, rising to her feet. 'Good luck at the hospital tomorrow, Arthur.'

'You don't need beauty sleep,' Arthur quipped, grinning widely and adding, 'See you, love.'

Sally showed her to the door, her back rigid, unable to hid her feelings as she said curtly, 'Bye, Patsy.'

'Your husband's a bit of all right, Sally, but he looked a bit down in the mouth when I first arrived.'

'Yes, I know.'

'I thought he might be worried about his leg or something, and there's nothing like a bit of flirtation to cheer a man up. I think he's feeling better now.'

'Oh, right,' Sally said, wondering now as she

said goodnight and closed the door if she had misjudged the girl.

Arthur was already on his feet when she returned to the living room and, walking across to touch his arm, she said, 'Please, love, can we talk?'

'Not now, Sally. I'm tired. Maybe tomorrow.' And with this he swung his crutches, heading for their bedroom.

Sally's eyes began to fill with tears, but then she shivered as an awful premonition washed over her. Her spine tingled, something she had not felt for a long time, and it frightened her. The last time she had felt like this, Arthur had been involved in the dreadful car accident that resulted in the loss of his leg. Now, once again, she was sure something awful was going to happen, but to whom? She closed her eyes, praying for all those she loved.

In Candle Lane, Ruth was opening the door to Tommy again. She saw the state the child was in and pulled him into her arms, the boy stiffening as though in pain. 'Oh, Tommy, what has she done to you?'

'Nuffing, me muvver didn't do nuffing, but I need to keep out of her way for a while.'

'Come inside,' Ruth urged.

Once again she fed the boy and, with Sadie in bed, there were no protests. Tommy looked unwashed, filthy, his clothes full of holes and, though Ruth was appalled, she was pleased that he'd come to her again.

Wanting to see if the boy was badly bruised, Ruth said, 'How about a nice wash? It'll make you feel better and then you can stay here tonight.'

'No, I can't. She'll go mad if I ain't there in the morning.'

'Tommy, this climbing drainpipes has got to stop. You can sleep on the sofa, and then in the morning I'll have a word with your mother.'

'No, missus, don't do that. She'll go bleedin' mad. I'll be all right, honest.'

Ruth shook her head doubtfully. 'One of these days you'll fall.'

'Course I won't. I've done it loads of times and it's a piece of cake.'

Yes, he made it look easy, Ruth thought, remembering how she'd watched before when Tommy climbed the drainpipe like a little monkey. 'I still think you should sleep here tonight.'

'No, I've gotta go home,' he said stubbornly. 'Anyway, me muvver will need me when she wakes up in the morning.'

He rose to his feet, heading for the door, but as Ruth took his arm to hold him back, he winced. 'What's the matter with your arm, Tommy?'

'Nuffing, I'm fine.'

'Listen, it's my half day off tomorrow and I want you to come round here after school.'

'What for?'

'To have a bit of dinner,' Ruth lied.

'Cor, thanks, missus.'

'Now, are you sure you don't want to sleep on

97

the sofa?'

'Yes, I'm sure.'

Ruth sighed heavily. He wasn't going to give in and, as she had done before, she walked with him to the back of his house. With bated breath she watched as he climbed, but with practiced ease he was soon pushing open his bedroom window. He clambered in, gave her a small wave, which she returned, and then he disappeared from view.

With a heavy heart Ruth went home. Tommy had asked her to say nothing to his mother, but she was sure the child was being beaten again. She wasn't going to stand for that, and no matter what the boy said, she was determined to sort his mother out.

Eight

Sally's premonition was still with her when she awoke the following morning, her feelings of foreboding making her shiver. If Gran were ill, her mother would have rung, but she was anxious as she got ready to go to Candle Lane. 'What time is your father picking you up for your hospital appointment?' she asked Arthur.

'At nine thirty, and then he's dropping me back here afterwards.'

Sally thought about the drive to Roehampton,

her intuition heightened, but Bert was a good driver and she felt nothing to worry about. It was something else, something she couldn't put her finger on. She was running a little late, and had to go, so now said, 'Give my love to your dad, and I'll see you later.'

'Yeah, right,' he said, speaking pleasantly with Angel around.

Sally hurried to Candle Lane, relieved when she arrived to find that everything was all right. Her gran looked fine, in fact more alert than usual as she greeted them.

Her relief was short-lived as a shiver ran down her spine. Was her gran going to have another stroke? She looked at her aura, saw nothing to worry about, but nevertheless she intended to keep a close eye on her all day.

By the time her mother had left for work, the bad feelings had eased, but even so Sally rushed back to Candle Lane after dropping Angel at school, finding as she walked in that her gran was reading a letter.

'Hello, love,' she said. 'It's from Mary.'

'I had one from her last week. She seems happy in Spain.'

'Yes, maybe, but I think I drove her away.' Sadie said sadly.

'Of course you didn't.'

'When she brought that black bloke round here and told me she was going to marry him, you know I went mad, Sally. I thought about the neighbours, what they'd say, and I was ashamed of her. Colours don't mix, and them blacks

99

should stick to their own kind. It ain't right when they chase after white women, and if you ask me they only do it to use them as status symbols. And as for the women that go out with them, well, you've seen how they're scorned and it serves them right.'

'Gran, I don't want to talk about it again. You keep on and on about it, but you know I don't like racial prejudice.'

'I know you don't, but as I've said before, if them blacks keep coming over here in droves, it'll lead to trouble.'

'Yes, if everyone thinks like you, no doubt it will. Why can't we just live and let live?'

''Cos they're different from us.'

'Gran, it's just their skin colour, that's all. They have the same feelings as us, the same dreams and aspirations. They've come here to try to make a better life for themselves, and I don't see anything wrong with that.'

'All right, you've made your point, now get off your soapbox. Anyway, I wish I hadn't made such a fuss about Mary's boyfriend. As I said, I drove her away.'

'You didn't. Mary chose to break up with Leroy and I think she went away to get over him. She'll come home again one day.'

'I hope you're right, Sally, and let's hope it's before I'm six foot under.'

'Gran, don't say things like that!'

'Why not? What's wrong with talking about death? I'll tell you something, my girl, it's the one thing that's certain in this life. We're born and when our number's up, we die.'

'Yes, I know, but I still don't want to think about it,' Sally said, beginning to flick a duster along the mantelpiece, then saying, 'I think I'll give Mum a ring at the shop.'

'What for?'

'Just to make sure that she arrived safely.'

'Why wouldn't she?'

'I don't know, Gran, but I had a funny feeling earlier and it's back again.'

'Gawd, Sally, you still give me the willies at times.'

Sally rang the shop, her mother answering and saying she was fine but, as Sally replaced the receiver, she was frowning. She couldn't ignore the feeling, and now began to worry about Bert and Arthur. Surely they were all right? Surely there hadn't been an accident? She'd wait a while and then ring home, and in the meantime she tackled a bit more house-work.

At eleven thirty Sally saw that her gran was dozing and, unable to stop worrying about Arthur, she decided to ring him.

Arthur answered, saying shortly, 'Hello.'

Sally's legs wobbled beneath her with relief. 'Hello, love, I was just ringing to see if you're all right.'

'Dad just dropped me off and I'm fine,' he said curtly.

'Good, that's all right then. I'll see you later.'

'Yeah, see you,' he said, replacing the receiver.

Sally felt tears welling in her eyes. Arthur had been so short with her. If only he'd talk to her, tell her what was wrong, but he refused to discuss it. Oh God, they couldn't go on like this – they just couldn't.

Sally was still tense when her mother walked in at one thirty and her eyes widened in surprise. It was Wednesday and half day closing at the shop, but even so her mother was rarely home before five. She would stay behind, making lunch for Sid, and then discussing the stock and takings with him. Sid had been the same when she had worked for him, always finding a way to keep her there, and she knew it was because he was lonely.

'You're early for a change,' Sadie said. 'What brought this on?'

'I want to be here when Tommy comes home from school. He seemed to be in pain last night, but denied it. I told him to come round as soon as school turns out and maybe this time I'll be able to have a look at him. Not only that, the child needs feeding up.'

Sadie pursed her lips. 'You're asking for trouble again. Laura Walters ain't gonna stand for it.'

'That's just too bad, Mum. I'm sure Tommy's had another beating, despite his denial, and if he has, I'll have a few words to say to his mother.'

'Why don't you report her?' Sally asked.

''Cos I don't want the kid put in care. Anyway, I'm going to give her a bloody good talking to and maybe I can get her to stop drinking again.'

'Don't be daft,' Sadie said. 'The woman's an alcoholic and talking to her will be a waste of time.'

'I've got to do something.'

'I think you ain't got a hope in hell of getting her off the booze.'

Sally felt sorry for Tommy, but felt sure her mother would sort things out. Her own problems now had to come first, and with a couple of hours to spare until Angel finished school, this was a chance to talk to Arthur out of her hearing, and without fear of any other interruptions. 'Mum,' she said, 'I'm off home. I'll see you tomorrow. Bye, Gran.'

Both women called goodbye, though they looked taken aback at her swift departure. Sally hurried down Candle Lane. She and Arthur needed to talk calmly. Arguing wouldn't solve anything, and in her mind she rehearsed what she intended to say.

It was early May and Sally was perspiring by the time she turned into Maple Terrace, but she was intent on seeing Arthur and didn't slow her pace.

When she reached number seventeen her mind was still churning as she let herself in, but determined to talk without rowing she fixed a smile on her face, making straight for the sitting room.

Sally opened the door – and froze at the tableau before her. *No, it can't be – it can't*, she agonized, her mind refusing to accept what she was seeing.

With eyes like saucers Sally baulked, but was finally forced to take in the scene. Bile rose in her throat and her hand rose to her mouth in horror. Arthur was sitting on the sofa with Patsy straddled across his lap, naked from the waist down. The two were heaving and panting, Arthur's hands gripping Patsy's hips as he pumped her up and down.

His eyes were closed in ecstasy, but hearing her horrified gasp they suddenly flew open. 'Sally!'

Patsy turned, a look of triumph on her face, and that was all Sally saw as she turned and fled the room.

She didn't hear Arthur's frantic call – she couldn't hear anything for the blood pounding in her ears. Then running, the street door left wide open behind her, she headed for Candle Lane.

'Get off me, Patsy!'

'That wasn't what you were saying a few minutes ago.'

Arthur groaned as he pushed her away and, recalling the look on Sally's face, he felt sick. Christ, what had he done?

He'd been surprised when Patsy knocked on the door, saying she'd seen him arriving home and asking how he'd got on at the hospital. He'd invited her in and they'd sat on the sofa chatting for a while, but when Patsy moved a little closer, the atmosphere became charged.

The next thing he knew, her hand was seductively running up the inside of his leg. He'd responded immediately, and Patsy had seen that, her smile knowing as she raised an eyebrow at his obvious erection. He should have stopped her, but felt powerless with lust as she had peeled off her short skirt. Skimpy little knickers followed, and then she was astride him, her tiny hands unzipping his flies.

It had been *all* her. She had guided him in, aroused him to fever pitch, but just as he was reaching a frantic climax – Sally had walked in.

'Get dressed, Patsy,' he growled.

'Don't you want to finish what we started?'

'No!' he shouted. 'My wife just caught us, and you saw the look on her face. Haven't you got any shame?'

'Sally doesn't want you, and in fact I think she has her eyes on Joe.'

'Joe! Never!' Arthur protested, but then his eyes narrowed thoughtfully. 'What makes you think that?'

'I've seen the way she flirts with him, and you must have seen it too.'

'No, I haven't, but anyway, even if it's true she's wasting her time with Joe. He's not only my partner, he's my friend, and I trust him.'

'He's a great looking bloke.'

Yes, Arthur thought, Joe was good looking. Unlike him, he was whole, and was it any wonder that Sally was attracted to him, Patsy too. 'Still fancy him, do you?'

'No, not really. We didn't click, but I fancy *you* something rotten. Are you sure you want me to get dressed?'

'Yes,' he said, unable to help watching as Patsy slowly began to pull her knickers over her hips. He licked his lips, despite everything, tempted, but then heard a sound in the hall. 'For God's sake, Sally's back! Quick, get your skirt on!'

Patsy had just stepped into it when the sitting room door opened, and Arthur's breath left his body when he saw who was standing on the threshold. 'Mum,' he gasped. 'What are *you* doing here?'

He saw his mother's eyes narrow, saw the way her lips tightened, and then she advanced across the room, her face livid as she marched up to Patsy. 'You, miss, finish putting your skirt on and then get out! And you, Arthur, I suggest you zip up your flies!'

Arthur looked down in horror and quickly fastened his zip.

'Get out!' he heard his mother say again and, hastily pulling up her skirt, Patsy walked out.

'God, son, how *could* you? And with that tart?' Elsie said as soon as the door closed.

'She isn't a tart, Mum. Patsy lives upstairs and is a mobile hairdresser.'

'Oh, and that's supposed to make a difference, is it? She knows you're a married man, and as far as I'm concerned that makes her a tart. Christ, son, I just can't believe it. How could you do this to Sally?'

106

'Sally doesn't want me and she's made that plain.'

'Don't give me that as an excuse. I've known Sally since she was ten years old and she's like a daughter to me. She loves you, and doesn't deserve this. Christ, if she found out it could well be the end of your marriage.'

'She already knows.'

'What! Sally knows? But...'

'She caught us and ran out. I can't believe you didn't bump into her.'

'Well, I didn't, but must admit I was surprised to find your street door wide open.'

'You still haven't told me what you're doing here, Mum.'

'Your dad told me that you'd be home this afternoon and I thought I'd take the opportunity to talk to you out of his hearing.'

'What about?'

'It's just that I'm a bit worried about his health. His back's playing him up but he won't see anyone about it.' Elsie then shook her head impatiently. 'That hardly seems important now, not after what I've just seen. My God, Arthur, what on earth possessed you?'

'Patsy doesn't find me repulsive and ... well ... she offered.'

'She offered!' Elsie spluttered.

'Yes, Mum, and she made all the moves. Unlike Sally, she doesn't see me as a cripple.'

Elsie's eyes narrowed again and Arthur could have kicked himself. He wouldn't put it past his mother to have a go at Patsy, and quickly said,

'I've been home for over five weeks now, but Sally has hardly been near me. In bed she keeps a wide distance between us, and she can't bear to look at my leg.'

'If Sally is keeping a distance between you, there must be a reason, and I can't believe it's because she finds you repulsive. Are you sure you aren't imagining it?'

'Yes, I'm sure. Sally makes me feel less than a man and I can't stand it.'

'All right, maybe she is having trouble adjusting, but that's still no excuse for what you've done. Look, I'll go round to Candle Lane and talk to her.'

'No, Mum, keep out of it, and anyway, what makes you think she'll be at Candle Lane?'

'Where else would she go? It's best I talk to her, Arthur, because I doubt she'll want to see you.'

'I said no.'

'Why not? Don't you want her back?'

Arthur pondered his mother's words. Yes, of course he wanted Sally back, but if she couldn't stand the sight of him, what was the point? Maybe when he got his artificial leg she would look at him differently, but he couldn't keep it on for twenty-four hours a day. His thoughts turned to his daughter, and he groaned. If he and Sally didn't patch things up, when would he see Angel? God, he couldn't think straight.

'Mum, I don't know what I want at the moment, and to be honest, if Sally can't accept me the way I am now, there's no future for us.'

'I can't believe you, son. Sally caught you with Patsy, and she must be heartbroken, but all you're thinking about is yourself.'

'Huh, I doubt she's heartbroken,' Arthur retorted, pushing away the memory of the horror on Sally's face when she had seen him with Patsy. 'She's got her eye on someone else.'

'Rubbish! You're just saying that to salve your conscience.'

'No I'm not. Patsy told me she's been making eyes at Joe, flirting with him.'

'I don't believe you.'

'She has, but I trust Joe and she's wasting her time.'

Elsie's eyes narrowed again, and then she stood up abruptly. 'I still think this is just your way to salve your conscience and, despite what you say, I'm going round to see Sally.'

'No, Mum,' Arthur called, but he was wasting his breath.

Elsie stormed from the room like a ship in full sail, calling, 'I'll be back after I've spoken to Sally.'

Nine

By the time Sally had reached the lane, she had slowed to a crawl, her earlier horror now replaced by anger. *How could he? And with her!* Bile rose again as she recalled the scene, and imprinted on her mind was the ecstasy on Arthur's face.

She knew things hadn't been right with their marriage since Arthur came home from hospital, but to do *that*!

When Sally reached number five she paused to draw breath, once more feeling tears flooding her eyes and wanting only the comfort of arms around her. 'Oh, Mum,' she cried as she ran into the kitchen.

'What on earth's the matter?'

'Arthur ... Arthur. Oh, Mum,' and sobbing, she ran forward.

For a moment her mother's arms enfolded her, but then abruptly pushed her away. Ruth stepped back. 'What is it? Has something happened to Arthur?'

Sally's throat was constricted with emotion and she could hardly speak, 'No, but ... he ... he...'

'Pull yourself together and tell us what's happened!'

Hearing the stern tone of her mother's voice, Sally felt as if she'd been doused with a bucket of cold water. Rigid now she said, 'I caught him with another woman.'

Her mother's eyes widened, and for a moment there was silence, but then Sally heard her gran's voice.

'Sally, start at the beginning.'

She sank on to a chair, fumbling with her words at first, then gradually able to recount the scene. Nausea rose again, and hand over her mouth she rushed to the toilet where bending over the bowl she was violently sick. When there was nothing left in her stomach, she perched on the rim of the bath, brow beaded with perspiration and her throat burning.

Her mother appeared in the doorway. 'Sally, are you all right?'

'I don't think I'll ever be all right again.'

'Of course you will. Now come downstairs and let's talk about this.'

'What's there to talk about?'

'Come on, come downstairs,' she repeated. 'I'll make you a cup of tea.'

Tea, Sally thought, her mother's answer to every crisis, as though the brew had some sort of magical qualities to cure all ills. But not this time, she thought as she followed her mother into the kitchen.

Whilst her mother bustled over to the kettle, setting it on to boil again, Sally sat down, her gran asking, 'What are you gonna do now, love?'

'I don't know, but as far as I'm concerned my marriage is over.'

'Listen, love, I know you're hurt, and I don't blame you, but don't make hasty decisions. Men are different to us. They're ruled by what's in their trousers and can sleep with a woman without emotions being involved. Why else do you think there are prostitutes?'

'That's no excuse, Gran. And anyway, Arthur wasn't with a prostitute. He was with our upstairs neighbour.'

'You're not listening to me, girl. Arthur may have slept with another woman, but I'm sure it's you he loves.'

'But he betrayed me, Gran. Betrayed my trust and our marriage. I ... I can't forgive him.'

'You're in a state, and perhaps it's too soon to talk about it.'

Sally glanced at the clock, surprised to see that it was only just after three. She felt that her life had fallen apart, that nothing would ever be the same again, and it had all happened in less than two hours. Closing her eyes she felt a rush of weariness. She knew why, knew that she didn't want to think about it any more, that her mind wanted to shut down. Her mother spoke, but her voice seemed to come from a great distance.

'Why don't you go and have a lie down? I'll pick Angel up from school.'

Sleep, Sally thought. Yes, she wanted to sleep, but even so doubted it would be possible. Yet she didn't want to talk any more, she just wanted to be alone, to crawl into a shell and never come out again. 'All right, Mum,' she said, rising to her feet.

'Wait, Sally. What if Arthur comes round?'

'He won't do that. He's too busy with Patsy.'

'Don't be silly, he's bound to want to talk to you.'

'Well, *I* don't want to talk to him! If he comes round here, as far as I'm concerned you can shut the door in his face.' And on that note she left the room, climbing upstairs like a weary old woman.

Only five minutes later there was a knock on the door. Ruth was surprised to see Elsie on the step. 'Blimey, that was quick! Did Arthur ring you?'

'He didn't need to. I turned up just after Sally ran off and he was still with that tart. Is Sally here?'

'Yes, but she's upstairs having a lie down. This has knocked her for six, Elsie.'

'Do you mind if I go up to talk to her?'

'Of course not, but at the moment I don't think it'll do any good.'

'Maybe not, but I'd still like to see her.'

'Go on up then. I've got to collect Angel up from school, but I'll see you when I get back.'

Elsie climbed the stairs, and knocking softly on the bedroom door she opened it to see Sally sprawled on the bed, one arm flung over her face. 'Can I come in, love?'

'Elsie, what are you doing here?' Sally asked, her eyes bruised with pain as she raised herself into a sitting position.

'I know what Arthur has done and had to talk to you.'

'There's nothing to say. If you know, then you must realize that I'll never forgive him.'

'Listen, Sally, you're hurt, and I don't blame you, but I've spoken to Arthur and he said some funny things.'

'Like what?'

'Are you repulsed by him now that he's lost part of his leg?'

'No, of course not. Did he say that?'

Elsie nodded. 'He also said that since he came home you hardly go near him, and keep a distance between you in bed.'

'What! How dare he!'

'So it isn't true?'

'Of course it isn't. When we go to bed, Arthur falls asleep as soon as his head touches the pillow. He's been awful to live with, distant and cold, but Gran said I should be patient as he needed time to adjust.' Her eyes rounded, 'My God, it sounds like he's blaming me for sleeping with another woman!'

'He also said that you've got your eye on his friend Joe.'

'What!'

Elsie saw Sally's cheeks flood with colour and her suspicions were aroused. 'Is it true?'

Sally looked down, quiet for a moment, and then said, 'Look, I'll be totally honest with you. When I first met Joe, I admit I was attracted to him, but that was all. It would never have gone any further. I love Arthur and thought he loved me.'

'Then why does Arthur think you've been flirting with the man?'

'When Patsy was seeing Joe, they spent a few evenings with us. Arthur gave Patsy a lot of attention, and almost completely ignored me. I think Joe noticed and tried to act as a balance, chatting to me whilst Arthur was focused on Patsy. It got me down, Elsie, and I admit I was jealous, but I only flirted with Joe once because I wanted to get my own back on Arthur. All right, it was silly and childish, but that doesn't excuse what Arthur has done.'

'I see,' Elsie mused, her thoughts racing. She knew Sally well, and sensed she was telling the truth, but still none of this made sense. Arthur seemed to think that Sally was repulsed by his leg, but she denied it. What on earth had gone wrong since her son had come out of hospital? She thought about Patsy, and now said, 'If you ask me, Arthur was led on by that girl. He said that she made all the moves, and I reckon she's nothing but a slut. Please, Sally, don't let this break up your marriage. I know you love Arthur, and he loves you. Can't you find it in your heart to forgive him?'

'I don't think I can, and if anything his excuses have made things worse. I can't believe he's blaming me, and I also can't believe he said that I'm repulsed by his leg. That's utter rubbish, and he knows it. And as for Patsy leading Arthur on – well, he's got a tongue and could have said no.'

It's too early, Elsie thought, Sally's wound deep. 'Give it a few days, love, and maybe then you'll see things differently.'

'I doubt it, Elsie. Oh, I doubt it. Please, can I ask you a favour?'

'Of course you can.'

'I left without bringing anything with me and both Angel and I will need clothes. When you next go to Maple Terrace, can you pack a few things for us?'

'Yes, all right,' Elsie said and, after stroking Sally's hair for a moment, she left the room, her thoughts on Arthur as she made her way downstairs. Oh, son. What have you done?

Ruth had been to fetch Angel and was just coming in the street door as Elsie came downstairs. With an expectant expression she said, 'Did Sally talk to you?'

'Yes, but if anything I think I've made things worse. Where's Angel?'

'I let her play outside for a while.'

They both walked into the kitchen, Ruth then asking, 'What did you say to Sally?'

Elsie recounted her conversation, ending with, 'So you see, she now thinks that Arthur is blaming her for what happened.'

'It sounds like he is to me,' Sadie snapped.

'None of this makes sense. Arthur says that Sally doesn't go near him and makes him feel less than a man. But Sally says he's been distant and cold with her since he came home from hospital. If you ask me, it seems that the two of

116

them have got their wires crossed.'

Ruth frowned. 'That still doesn't excuse what he's done, Elsie.'

'I know, believe me I know, and I'm at a loss to know what to do. Anyway, I'd best be off. I told Sally I'd pick a few things up for her and I want another word with my son.'

'Tell him not to come round here, at least for the time being,' Ruth said hurriedly. 'Sally is adamant that she doesn't want to see him, and not only that, I'm so mad at him that I wouldn't trust myself not to give him a piece of my mind. All right, he lost his leg and that's awful, but when my Sally was attacked by those men, she pulled herself together for his sake. She stood by him and was there for him every step of the way. Now he's done this to her!'

Elsie's eyes clouded with distress. 'Oh, Ruth, I'm so sorry.'

Ruth laid a hand on her friend's arm. 'You don't have to apologize for Arthur. It isn't your fault.'

'But he's my own flesh and blood and I'm so ashamed of him. Not only that, what on earth is Bert going to say? He'll probably disown the lad.'

'I doubt that,' Ruth consoled.

Elsie left with a heavy heart. She saw Angel playing, and stopped to give the child a kiss and a hug, but her thoughts were elsewhere as she made her way to Maple Terrace.

Please God, she prayed, *don't let this be the end of Sally and Arthur's marriage.*

117

Ten

It was seven thirty in the evening when Arthur heard a knock on the door. If it was his mother again she could clear off. He'd had just about enough of her lecturing.

Sally had told his mother a pack of lies, and he was fuming. She'd accused *him* of being distant and cold, when in truth it was the other way round. She also denied being repulsed by his leg and it seemed his mother believed her. Before leaving she had packed a suitcase of clothes for Sally and Angel, saying that he should stay away from Candle Lane for the time being. Bloody cheek! He wasn't a child to be given orders. He'd go to Candle Lane if he wanted to, if only to give his wife a piece of his mind.

There was another rap on the door and, fumbling with his crutches, Arthur went to answer it, finding Joe on the step. 'Come in,' he said shortly.

Joe's brows rose at his tone and as they walked into the living room, he said, 'What's up, mate?'

'Sally's gone back to her mother's. We've split up.'

'Split up – but why?'

'If you must know, she caught me having it off with Patsy.'

'You and Patsy? No ... I can't believe it. Bloody hell, Arthur.'

'Don't look at me like that. Patsy made it obvious that she was available, making all the moves, and – well, it just happened.'

'And Sally caught you. Christ, she must be in a right state.'

'I doubt it,' Arthur said, choosing to forget the look he'd seen on his wife's face. 'If you must know, things have been bloody awful since I came out of hospital. Sally can't stand the sight of my leg, and has made it plain that sex is a no no.'

'I don't know about the sex bit, but I got to know Sally pretty well while you were in hospital, and one thing I'm sure of is that she isn't repulsed by your leg.'

'And just *how* well did you get to know her, Joe?'

'What's that supposed to mean?'

'She's been flirting with you, and you've been giving her plenty of attention too.'

'That's rubbish and I think you know me better than that. If Sally flirted with me it was only because she was upset by all the attention you gave to Patsy.'

'You didn't have to flirt back.'

Joe's face darkened with annoyance. 'I didn't, but I see that Patsy's been stirring it and you're mad to listen to her. She's nothing but trouble.'

'You took her out a few times.'

'Yes, but unlike you, I'm single.'

Arthur scowled, 'All right, so I shouldn't have slept with Patsy, but I've told you, she made all the moves and—' There was a knock on the door and somehow Arthur knew who it was. Did he want to see her again? For a moment he floundered, but then remembering Sally's lies, his anger reasserted itself. 'Joe, would you mind going to see who that is?'

Joe stood up, his face still dark with anger as he left the room. How could Arthur do this to Sally, and with Patsy of all people?

He opened the door, his eyes narrowing. 'What do you want, Patsy?'

'To see Arthur.'

'Don't you think you've done enough damage?'

'You can get that sanctimonious look off your face. It takes two, you know.' And pushing her way in, she marched into the living room. 'Hello, Arthur. We need to talk.'

'Yes, I know we do. Sit down, Patsy.'

Joe wanted to stay, to stand between the two of them, but the look Arthur was giving him was plain. 'All right, I'm going,' he said.

'Thanks, mate. I'll see you tomorrow.'

Joe slammed the door behind him, making his feelings plain, and his thoughts raged as he climbed into his car. He should be happy that Arthur and Sally had broken up, but knew he'd never stand a chance with her. He thought he'd felt a spark between them once, but soon realized it was in his imagination. There was only one man for Sally, and that was her husband. And now, after what Arthur had done, she must be heartbroken.

Should he call round to see her? Yet if he did, and Arthur found out, it would be playing into Patsy's hands. She had planted the seed in Arthur's mind that there was something between them, and the last thing it needed was watering. The best thing would be to stay away from Sally, and now his hands gripped the steering wheel. Christ, that Patsy was a cow and he'd like to wring her bloody neck. Surely she wouldn't succeed in breaking up Arthur and Sally's marriage? No, of course not. Arthur would come to his senses soon, would see Patsy for what she was, but what about Sally? Would she ever forgive him?

Arthur was hardly aware of Joe leaving, his eyes on Patsy and the seductive way she was looking at him. 'No,' he protested as she gyrated slowly forward.

She perched on the arm of the sofa, her expression changing to one of regret. 'I'm sorry that Sally caught us, Arthur.'

'Yes, so am I, and you saw the way Joe reacted. Did you sleep with him too?'

'No, of course I didn't. I'm not that sort of girl.'

'Oh, really?' he said, his voice dripping with sarcasm.

'Yes, really. If you must know, I'm ashamed

121

of the way I threw myself at you. I was brazen and it's not like me at all. It's just that I fancy you so much and I just couldn't help myself.'

'You fancy me?'

'Yes, I really do. You're such a handsome man, and the fact that you're missing a little bit of leg doesn't worry me.'

'It doesn't repulse you?'

'No, of course not, but I know that Sally finds it revolting.'

'How do you know? Has she told you?'

'Oh, Arthur, now you're asking me to break a confidence and I can't do that. Anyway, I didn't need to be told. I've seen the way she avoids looking at it.'

So, Patsy had seen it too, and from what she said it was obvious that Sally had confided in her. Arthur felt vindicated and wished his mother could hear this. She'd know then that Sally had been lying through her teeth. She *was* repulsed by his leg, and now the pain of her rejection twisted his guts.

Patsy slid on to his lap. She leaned forward to kiss him, and he didn't resist.

Patsy got to work, smiling secretly. She had hoped that Joe would be the way out of her present life, but he'd rejected her. She knew why, of course – he had his eye on Sally. Well, she'd made Sally pay for getting in her way, and more was to come. Now was the time to take her plan a stage further and, unlike Joe, she suspected that Arthur was a much softer touch, a man she could easily manipulate.

She mounted him now, her thoughts distant from the act, and set only on the future as he pumped her up and down.

Patsy felt nothing, but had learned to be a good actress, finding that a few groans here and there sufficed. Sex to her was just a means of making money, but suddenly, and unbelievably, as Arthur drove into her, she found herself responding. Feelings she thought dead rose to the surface and she gasped with pleasure. Her hands reached up, dragging off her jumper, and with no bra on she leaned forward to bury her breasts in Arthur's face. Her mind now became oblivious to anything but the sensations that ripped through her body. How long had it been? How long since she had felt like this?

She eased up, taunting him, moving slowly with his tip now barely inside her. 'Wait, darling,' she urged, 'take it slowly.' But then she pushed down, feeling the whole length of his shaft deep within her. 'Oh God ... Ohhh,' she gasped, close now to a climax, and as Arthur exploded inside her, his cries matched her own.

They were silent for a while, each drawing breath, but then Arthur abruptly pushed her off. 'Christ, I can't believe I've allowed it to happen again.'

'I'm sorry, but I just couldn't resist you,' Patsy said, finding to her astonishment that she already wanted Arthur again. Bloody hell, it had been years since she felt like this.

She thought about her clients, the old and sometimes crippled men that she serviced, and grimaced. Mind you, they paid well, and were pathetically grateful. None of them lasted for more than a few minutes, she made sure of that. Made sure that with a few tricks the act was soon over. But in truth she hated it, and though it enabled her to have a nice flat, nice clothes, and a decent standard of living, she wanted out.

She'd been married once and had a baby girl, but soon after she'd fallen head over heels in love with another man. He refused to take on the baby, and unable to face losing him she'd abandoned her daughter. All she had was a photograph of the child, thrown into her bag at the last minute, but it was enough. Maybe she was unnatural, she didn't know, but she'd never felt any great maternal feelings.

Her own mother used to say that what goes around, comes around, and she proved to be right. Payback came when he in turn deserted her. She'd been heartbroken, stranded, penniless, but the experience and need to survive on her own made her hard. Never again would a man hurt her. Instead she'd use them, the decision leading her to the life she lived now.

Mobile hairdressing, Patsy thought, amazed at how many people fell for her cover story. As if mobile hairdressing would be lucrative enough to pay the rent on her flat and provide her with the lifestyle she had now. Christ, she doubted if the income from hairdressing would provide enough for a bed-sit. Still, it was a good cover story, but one she hoped she would never have to use again. If she snared Arthur, she'd have the life of Riley and would never have to work again.

She smiled at him now, disappointed to see worry lines on his face. Would he try to get his wife back? Yes, probably, but she'd put a spoke in the wheels and it wouldn't happen if she had anything to do with it. She now replaced her smile with a sad expression. 'Look, love, don't blame yourself. It was my fault that it happened again, and I'm sorry. You're so handsome and I can't believe that Sally doesn't fancy you any more. She must be mad.' Patsy leaned across Arthur again, making sure that her breasts were in his face as she stroked his hair. 'Is it a long time since you've had sex with your wife?'

'Bloody ages.'

'Goodness, no wonder this happened. Doesn't Sally know that a man has his needs?'

'I was in hospital for a long time and before that we didn't have any privacy.'

'But there's nothing to stop you now.'

Arthur scowled. 'Look, Patsy, I thought you said that Sally had confided in you. If that's the case, you must know that our sex life is a thing of the past.'

Christ, she had nearly put her foot in it, Patsy thought, recovering quickly. 'Sally didn't mention your sex life, Arthur. All she talked about was your leg, but don't worry, I'm sure she'll get used to it. Just give her some time.'

'Huh,' he murmured, his lips now brushing her nipples. 'Why should I? My leg doesn't bother you, and if Sally doesn't like it now, she

125

never will. Anyway, after the frustration she's put me through, I'm not sure that I want her back.'

Patsy smiled with relief and then triumphantly straddled him. Her kiss was passionate and he was soon aroused. He was ready, as ready as she was, huge and throbbing beneath her. 'Oh, yes!' she cried as he entered her.

Eleven

To Sally the following days passed in moments of agonizing pain at Arthur's betrayal, interspersed with moments of deep anger. She knew that Angel was confused. The child was constantly asking to see her father, but so far she had fobbed her off with excuses.

It was Sunday, and the day had started bleak, the sky dark and heavy to match her mood. Then, by three in the afternoon, the sun broke though and Angel begged to be allowed outside to play.

'No,' Sally said, her eyes fixed on the sparse fire burning in the grate.

'Pleeease, Mummy!'

'Sally,' Ruth urged, 'she's been cooped up in here all day and it won't hurt to let her go out for a while.'

She sighed heavily, too caught up in her own

misery to care. 'All right then.'

Angel squealed with delight, but Sally hardly heard her. Some of the things her gran had said kept going round in her mind, but they failed to comfort her. Huh, so men could sleep with women without becoming emotionally involved, but to her that was no excuse.

Their sex life had been non-existent for such a long time, and though she had been nervous at first, as the weeks passed she found herself wanting Arthur, wanting their old intimacy. When nothing happened between them she thought it was because Arthur wasn't fully recovered, and too tired to make love. Huh, until last Wednesday when she had walked in on that dreadful scene. She felt sick at his betrayal, sick that he had turned to Patsy instead of her. Why, Arthur? Why?

Oh, if only she could stop thinking about it ... but it went round and around in her mind. When she fell in love with Arthur, she'd found real love, deep love, and had thought he felt the same. But no, she thought, obviously not. Time ticked slowly by and though Sally could hear her mother and gran talking in the background, the subject Laura Walters, her eyes were still on the small flames flickering in the fire.

'It was a waste of time trying to talk to Laura again,' Ruth said.

'Yeah, well, I could have told you that,' Sadie replied.

'I just hope I ain't made things worse. She was livid when I knocked on her door, and I hope she doesn't take it out on Tommy.'

'The lad seems to have a knack of keeping out of her way, and half the bloody time he's in here.'

'Oh, Mum, the poor kid needs us and he ain't got anyone else.'

Sadie sighed heavily. 'Yeah, I suppose you're right.'

Their voices were a buzz to Sally, and it was over half an hour later when something aroused her, what, she didn't know. Worried she ran to the street door, her eyes scanning the lane. There was no sign of Angel. Frowning she hurried back to the kitchen. 'Mum, where's Angel? She isn't outside.'

'Isn't she? Well, I don't expect she's gone far.'

'Did you see her with anyone?'

'I've been washing up and ain't got eyes in the back of me head. I could have done with a hand too and it's about time you bucked yourself up.'

Sally grabbed her coat, her feet still in slippers as she ran outside. 'Angel! Angel!' she called, hurrying to the end of the lane, her eyes frantically searching in each direction.

Tommy Walters was approaching, his small gang ambling along by his side. 'Have you seen Angel?' she asked him.

'Yeah, I saw her going that way.' He pointed.

Angel had been whining for days that she was missing her dad, and now the penny dropped. Maple Terrace! She should have guessed. Running now, Sally hoped to catch up with her daughter, but there was no sign of her as she turned the corner.

Lips tight, and without keys, she had to knock on the door of number seventeen, her eyes registering shock when Patsy opened it.

'Hello, Sally. Have you come round for your daughter? We were a bit surprised when she turned up on her own.'

'Yes, I've come for Angel,' Sally said, fighting the urge to dig her fingernails into Patsy's face. Holding her head high and hardening her voice, she added, 'Tell her that I'm here.'

'Don't you want to come in?'

'No, I don't! Now please tell my daughter that I'm waiting.'

'But she wants to see her daddy and there's no harm in her staying for a little while.'

Sally's back was rigid. She wouldn't give Patsy the satisfaction of seeing how upset she was. Instead she spat an order, 'I said tell her that I'm here. And now!'

'There's no need to be nasty. We've just had our dinner, and I was about to start rearranging the furniture when the kid turned up. Arthur was dead chuffed to see her.'

Sally felt the blood drain from her face. So, Patsy was already making herself at home and it was now obvious that she'd moved in. She was shifting the furniture, changing the room that she had so carefully arranged for Arthur's homecoming, and what was more, it seemed he was allowing it. How could he? God, how could he? 'Get my daughter. I'm taking her home.'

'I think you'll find that Arthur has a right to see Angel.'

'Right! He's got a right? No, I don't think so. He lost any claim on her when he had it off with you!' Sally knew she sounded coarse, but didn't care; in fact, if she had to look at Patsy's smug face for much longer she'd go for her, she really would.

'Oh dear, if that's your attitude it looks like your divorce could be nasty. I think you'll find that Arthur's solicitor will insist that he has access to Angel.'

'Divorce!' Sally gasped. So, it had come to this. Her teeth clenched, 'A divorce suits me,' she spat. 'Now, as I said, tell my daughter I'm waiting!'

'All right, keep your hair on,' Patsy said as she turned to go back inside.

Only moments later Angel appeared. Seeing her mother she held back. 'I don't want to come home yet.'

'Come here!' Sally demanded and, grabbing her hand, she pulled her along Maple Terrace.

Angel was dragging her feet, still protesting, but Sally hardly heard her. Divorce! How was it possible that their marriage had fallen apart when he'd only been home from hospital since the end of March? God, Arthur wanted a divorce and, at the finality of the thought, Sally's shoulders slumped.

Patsy smiled happily as she closed the door

on Sally. Christ, what a bit of luck. She had popped down to see Arthur, only to find that he was still talking about getting Sally back, and inwardly she had fumed.

Hiding her feelings she told him that the time wasn't right. It was too soon and his wife would still be upset. Sally needed a bit of space, she'd advised, and right now it would be pointless going round to Candle Lane. Despite this, he still wanted to go, but thankfully Angel had forestalled this by knocking on the door.

By calling round to collect her daughter, Sally had played right into her hands. It hadn't taken much to hint that she was living with Arthur and the silly cow had taken the bait. Now, with a few choice words to Arthur, she could pull the pair of them even further apart.

Her lips curled with satisfaction. Yes, with luck, she'd be able to snare Arthur soon. They were already having sex constantly, the man insatiable, but he'd baulked at her sharing his bed. Well, that was about to change, Patsy decided.

She composed her face, looking sad as she walked into the living room. 'Oh, I'm so sorry, Arthur. I did try, but your wife wouldn't let Angel stay.'

'I wanted to see my daughter for more than ten minutes. I miss her something rotten. Surely Sally will talk to me now?'

'I don't think so. In fact she was really annoyed that Angel came round here on her own and said that she's going to see a solicitor first thing in the morning.'

'A solicitor! What for?'

'She going to put in for a divorce, and not only that, she intends to make sure that you never see your daughter again.'

Arthur's face flushed with anger. 'I'm not standing for that! I'm going round to see her, and right now!'

'You'd be wasting your time. She won't talk to you and made that plain. I did try to persuade her to come in, but in no uncertain terms she refused. If you want to make sure you get access to your daughter, you'll need to see a solicitor too, and as soon as possible.'

'Are you sure she's filing for a divorce?'

'Yes. She said that the next time you hear from her, it would be through a solicitor.'

'She *can't* keep me away from Angel!'

'I know, but you've got to face it. Sally won't take you back and you must take steps to see that you don't lose your little girl too.'

Arthur slumped back on the sofa, his eyes dark with anger. 'The bitch! I didn't think it would come to this. So, it's over. Well – that's fine with me.'

Patsy sat beside him, hiding her triumph. Arthur was a proud man, and there was no way he would crawl to Sally begging for forgiveness. He growled with anger and she was instantly aroused, memories of last night's lovemaking coming to mind as she gently rubbed his inner thigh. 'Never mind, darling. If Sally is too blind to see what she's throwing away – I'm not.'

He grabbed her then, fury still evident in his eyes and, as his teeth sank into her neck, she groaned with pleasure. He was taking his anger out in sex, but she didn't mind. In fact it seemed to heighten his passion. Thanks, Sally, she thought, smiling wickedly.

Later, they lay back, both spent, Patsy nestling close to Arthur. Maybe tonight she thought – maybe tonight he'd let her stay. She pictured the special underwear she had upstairs, imagined his face when he saw her in it, and smiled.

'Won't you give Arthur another chance?' Elsie asked as she and Bert sat in the kitchen.

'He has Patsy living with him now,' Sally told them, the events of earlier still vivid in her mind. She loved her in-laws, yet when they had called round less than ten minutes ago, she was in no mood to talk.

Angel was still upset, wanting to go back to see her daddy, but had brightened up when Elsie and Bert arrived, especially when they'd given her a present. She had looked at the new paintbox and colouring book with delight, almost immediately beginning to fill in one of the pictures.

'Sally, I'm not defending what my son has done,' Bert said, 'but you've only just broken up and I can't believe that he's moved that girl in already.'

'He has. I saw it with my own eyes.'

'You must be mistaken,' Elsie protested. 'I'm

sure it was only a one-off thing with Patsy. I went round to see him last night, and I know he wants you back.'

'Don't like Patsy,' Angel said, her brush poised as she abandoned the painting to listen to the conversation.

Sally frowned, recalling that Angel had said that before. Was her daughter displaying spiritual gifts? Had she foreseen this happening? So far there had been no signs – no imaginary friends, only the *before time*. She looked at her daughter, saw her ears were pricked and, not wanting her to hear any more of this conversation, said quietly, 'Elsie, we can't talk in front of you know who.'

Bert frowned, and then crossed the room to Angel. 'How about coming for a ride in Granddad's car?'

'Can we go to see my daddy?'

Sally tensed, relieved when Bert said, 'Maybe another time, but right now I thought we might go to the park and you can have a ride on the swings.'

Angel scrambled to her feet. 'Will you push me really high?'

'Of course I will. Now run and get your coat.'

'Thanks, love, it's good of you,' Elsie told him, smiling warmly at her husband.

'Sally's right, we shouldn't talk in front of the child. I'll be back in an hour and then I want to have a word with my son.'

Angel ran back into the room, her coat clutched to her chest. 'I'm ready, Granddad.'

Bert leaned down, his huge form towering over his granddaughter as he helped her on with the coat and buttoned it up. 'Right, see you later,' he said, taking Angel's hand as they left the room.

'I dread to think what Bert will have to say,' said Elsie. 'He was furious when I told him and wanted to see Arthur straight away. I managed to talk him out of it, telling him that I was sure you'd be back together again soon and we shouldn't interfere. Now, though, I doubt there's much chance of keeping them apart.'

'Yes, Sally, what's this about Arthur moving that girl in?' Ruth asked. 'I know you were upset when you came back with Angel, but you never said anything. I thought you were just annoyed that she'd gone round there.'

'I didn't want to talk about it, Mum, and I still don't.'

Elsie shook her head. 'Patsy wasn't there when I called round last night. I still think you're mistaken, love.'

'I expect Arthur kept her out of your way. When I saw her earlier, she told me that Arthur wants a divorce.'

'She's lying. I don't know what she's up to, but it seems she's determined to make mischief.'

'Living with him or not, there's no getting away from the fact that they're a couple now. I'm finished with him, Elsie.'

'Oh, Sally, please don't say that. What about Angel? She loves her daddy.'

'Arthur forfeited his daughter when he had it off with that tart.'

'Sally, this doesn't sound like you. I know you're angry that Angel went round to see him today, but you can't keep them apart.'

'Oh, can't I? Well, you just watch me.'

Sadie leaned forward in her chair, speaking for the first time. 'Sally, listen to me. No matter what Arthur has done, you can't keep Angel away from him. Little girls cling to their fathers, and if you stop her from seeing him it'll rebound on you. She'll blame you and surely you realize that.'

Sally reared to her feet. 'I don't care! Just leave me alone, all of you, just leave me alone,' she cried, fleeing the room.

'She's in a terrible state,' Elsie said, distressed, as the door slammed behind Sally. 'But I think she's got the wrong end of the stick. I'm sure that Arthur hadn't moved that girl in with him.'

'She said she saw it with her own eyes,' Ruth said, 'and if that's the case there's no way they'll get back together again.'

'Oh, don't say that, Ruth.'

'It'll be no more than Arthur deserves.'

Elsie's eyes filled with tears and dashing at them she turned to Sadie. 'Won't you talk to her? She'll listen to you.'

Sadie exhaled loudly before speaking. 'Listen Elsie, Arthur has been out of hospital since the end of March, and already he's slept with another woman. For the sake of Angel and the marriage, I was prepared to talk Sally round, but not now, not when he's moved that girl in. I'll try to talk her into letting Angel see her father, but that's as far as I'm prepared to go.'

'But, Sadie, I still think that Sally is mistaken. If you ask me that Patsy is up to something and I intend to find out what. In fact, I think I'll walk round there now. When Bert comes back, will you tell him where I am?'

'I think I'll come with you,' Ruth said.

'It would be better if I spoke to Arthur on my own.'

'Maybe, but I want to see for myself if that girl has moved in. If she has, then as far as I'm concerned, Sally has made the right decision.'

'All right, come on then. You'll see it's a load of rubbish.'

'Sally!' Ruth called. 'Me and Elsie are popping out for a while. You'd better come down and sit with your gran.'

Both women now marched along Candle Lane, hardly speaking during the walk to Maple Terrace.

It was Elsie who banged on the door and when Arthur opened it she barged in, saying before he had time to speak, 'What's this about you and Sally getting a divorce?'

Arthur's half smile was more like a sneer, his voice sardonic. 'Hello, Mum, nice to see you too.'

'Don't be funny with me,' Elsie spat, and indicating that Ruth should follow her they made for the living room.

Arthur followed behind and as he took a seat Elsie spoke again, 'Now, son, I asked you a question. Are you getting a divorce?'

'Yes, I am, and I don't appreciate you barging in here as if you own the place.'

'Got something to hide, have you?' Ruth scowled. 'Are you frightened we'll catch you with your fancy woman?'

Arthur's chin rose. 'Your daughter left me. What I do now is none of your business.'

'She had good reason to leave you.'

'Maybe, but if she'd been a proper wife when I came home from hospital, I wouldn't have slept with Patsy. I'll tell you something else – she has no right to keep my daughter away from me.'

'She's got every right. When Sally came round to fetch Angel, she found Patsy in here again. It seems you've already moved the girl in.'

'Is that what she told you? And I suppose the lying bitch said she'd caught us at it again.'

'Don't you dare call my daughter a bitch!'

'If the cap fits,' he drawled.

'That's enough, Arthur,' Elsie said sharply. 'Are you trying to tell us that you haven't slept with that tart again?'

Both women saw Arthur flush, his guilt obvious, but it was Elsie who now spoke, her voice high with shock. 'My God, son, you should be ashamed of yourself.'

'Well, I'm not! Unlike my wife, Patsy wants me and has made that plain. Now if you don't mind, I'd like you both to leave, and Mum, when you come to see me in future, make sure you telephone first.'

Ruth saw the distress on her friend's face and through teeth clenched in anger she ground out, 'You ... you rotten sod!'

'Come on, Ruth, let's go,' Elsie said, throwing a look of disgust at her son as they left.

For a while Elsie was quiet as they walked along Maple Terrace, but then she turned to Ruth, her eyes moist with tears. 'God, I can't believe this! How could my son talk to me like that? He's become like a stranger to me.'

'I don't know what's come over him, but Sally's right. He does want a divorce.'

'I know, and I dread to think what Bert is going to say.'

Elsie found out when her husband returned with Angel. None of them wanted to talk in front of the child, so she waited until they left the house and climbed into the car, then saying, 'Bert, while you were at the park with Angel, Ruth and I went to see Arthur.'

'Did you? Why didn't you wait for me?'

'I wanted to find out if it was true that he had that slut living with him.'

'And?'

'He didn't deny it, and not only that, he's going to divorce Sally.'

'What? We'll see about that. We're going round there now and I'll have a few words to say to my son.'

'No, Bert, leave it. It'll be best to wait until things have calmed down a bit, and anyway, Arthur said we have to ring him first before going to see him.'

'He what?' Bert exploded.

'He said that Ruth and I had no right to barge into his place, and – oh, Bert, I hardly recognized him. He seemed so hard, so cruel...' and unable to hold them back any longer, tears ran down Elsie's cheeks.

Bert saw them, his face reddening with anger. 'First he sleeps with another woman, then he moves her in, and now he says that we have to make an appointment to see him, upsetting you in the process. Right, that's it, Elsie. From now on he's no son of mine.'

'Oh, Bert, don't say that.'

He didn't answer, only starting the car up and putting his foot down on the accelerator as he roared along Candle Lane, whilst Elsie sat beside him, tears still rolling down her cheeks.

Arthur sat back on the sofa, his anger still burning. What right had his mother to barge in here like that, Ruth with her. It was Sally who wanted a divorce, not him, yet *he* had borne the brunt of their anger. Yes, he had slept with Patsy again, but it wouldn't have happened if Sally hadn't left him. And to top it all, the bitch had told them that Patsy had moved in.

Well, that was it, the last straw. His anger continued to mount, festering inside. Sally had turned everyone against him. Slamming his fist on the arm of the sofa he vowed to see a solicitor the next day.

He was still fuming when he picked up one of his crutches and stood up, banging the other one on the ceiling. Patsy wanted him, in fact she wanted him all the time, and though he didn't love her he had to admit the sex was terrific. Yes, there *was* a woman who found him irresistible, and from now on he'd show Sally that he didn't give a damn.

Patsy walked into the room now, smiling as she said, 'You rang, sir? Or should I say, you knocked?'

'Yes, I did. Come here – you little minx.'

Twelve

Laura Walters stared blearily at the grainy black and white photo. It was all she had left of her bonny daughter. An image. A moment frozen in time.

She had tried to stay off the booze, she really had, but since her little girl died it had been a way to blot it out, to drown the pain. If Denis hadn't left her, maybe she could have kept it up, stayed sober, but she was lost without him.

Laura returned the photograph to the tin and picked up another, this one of her wedding. Denis was smiling into the camera, and even in profile, she looked equally happy as she gazed up at him. Scathingly she flung it aside, reaching for a glass of cheap cider. It had all been an illusion, her happiness fleeting and, now that Denis had left her, their marriage a farce.

For a moment she looked at the amber coloured liquid, wishing it was gin, but there was no money for spirits. Laura thought she heard a knock on the door, but ignored it. It would be that interfering cow from next door again, or even worse, Jessie Stone, and she had no intention of letting either of them in. They had been round a few times now, both nagging at her to stop drinking, but what she did was none of their business and she'd told them to bugger off. Anyone would think they were her parents, the way they carried on.

Thinking of parents, Laura's thoughts shifted. She had been a late and unexpected baby, born when her mother was menopausal and her father fifty-three. They had been more like grandparents and she'd hated the restricted life they forced her to lead. No running, no playing, and even as a young child she had cringed when her mother met her from school. Unlike all the other young mums, *hers* looked like a grandmother.

She had an elder brother, but Andrew was already a man when she'd been born and with such a huge age gap there was little connection between them.

On becoming a teenager she'd run away from home and it was many years later before she contacted her parents. When she had rung them, they refused to speak to her, only saying they would never forgive her for the worry she had caused them. She'd wanted to tell them that they had grandchildren, but hadn't been given the chance. It was the last time she tried to contact them.

Andrew, though, had travelled to London to see her, but the meeting had been strained. He had stared with horror at Bessie and Tommy. Just like her parents he was a worryguts, nagging her about her problem, and asking if she was getting treatment. She had flared up, telling him to stop acting like her father. They had parted on bad terms and, other than a letter which she didn't answer, she hadn't heard from Andrew again.

There was another knock on the door. 'Laura! Laura! Let me in!'

Denis – it sounded like Denis! Laura rose unsteadily to her feet, finding that the room swam before her eyes. It took her a moment to gain her equilibrium then she stumbled to open the door, blinking blearily as she said, 'So, you've come crawling back have you. Where's your key?'

'I don't know,' Denis said, stepping inside.

'Who said you can come in?'

'Come on, Laura,' he wheedled. 'I came back, didn't I, and I've got a few bob.'

Laura found she had difficulty focusing, but wasn't drunk enough to miss the fact that he'd returned with money. 'Why did you go off without a word?'

'I couldn't face it.'

'Face what?'

'Losing you.'

Laura continued to stare at her husband, her mind refusing to function. 'But I got over the heart attack and you'd gone when I discharged myself from hospital.'

'Think, woman! Are you forgetting your problem?'

Laura dragged out a chair, shaking her head to clear her thoughts. Yes, she had a problem, a heart defect, but despite the doctors telling her she should never have children, she had borne two bairns. Bloody quacks, she thought, reaching out for the cider again.

Denis grabbed her hand, forcing it away from the bottle. 'You got over your heart attack this time, but if you keep drinking, for how long?'

'Leave it out. You sound like my parents. They tried to wrap me in cotton wool and it drove me mad. Why nag me about drinking now? You drink too, and you haven't exactly been a caring husband. In fact, you hardly came to see me when I was in hospital.'

'I know, but that's because I didn't think you'd survive and couldn't face it.'

'Huh, what sort of excuse is that? I felt fine, and refused another load of bloody tests. They let me out after five days but you'd already buggered off. So tell me, why have you come back?'

'Because I realized that running away doesn't

solve anything. Drunk or sober, I haven't been able to stop thinking about you. Our marriage was fine before our little girl died, but then we both lost our way and started on the booze.' Denis stood up and began to pace the room. 'Things can be different, Laura. I've turned over a new leaf and I haven't had a drink for a fortnight. You can stop drinking too.'

Laura laughed derisively as she picked up the bottle of cider. 'I did stop for a while, but didn't enjoy the experience. Do you want a glass of this?'

'Christ, woman, haven't you heard a word I've said? You've got to stop drinking or it'll kill you! Surely you realize that!'

Laura stared at her husband, but the need to have a drink was too strong. She poured another glass of cider and gulped it down.

For a moment Denis just looked at her, but then his expression hardened. 'That'll be the last drink you have. I'll see to that.'

Next door in number five, Sally clutched the solicitor's letter confirming that the proceedings were in progress. She hadn't wanted to seek legal advice, but after a letter from Arthur's solicitor stating that her husband was filing for a divorce and seeking access to Angel, she'd had no choice.

Nearly four weeks had passed since their break up and she was still sick at the thought of him with Patsy. Not only that, the rift between Arthur and his parents showed no sign of mending and her heart went out to her in-laws. Bert continued to disown Arthur and, though she appreciated their support, she knew Elsie was taking it badly.

Apathy still gripped her, and though she went through the motions of living, inside she was dead. Her mind went back to a time not long ago when she'd felt like this before, a time when after her miscarriage she had felt empty and lost. Arthur had been in hospital, facing his amputation, and she had managed to snap out of it for his sake. A small sob escaped her lips. Now, though, he'd betrayed her.

She thought about Laura Walters, knew the woman had refused to listen to anyone and had sunk back into alcoholism. Now, feeling the pain in her heart, Sally wished she could join her.

Tommy, when not at school, was always in the house, and instead of objecting she was just relieved that he played with Angel, keeping her daughter occupied until bedtime. Angel's demands to see her father drove her mad at times, but she was determined not to give in. The child was confused enough without seeing her father with another woman, and anyway, Arthur didn't deserve access to his daughter.

There was a rap on the letter box, and when Sally opened the door her face stretched in amazement. 'Aunt Mary,' she cried, 'you've come home. Oh, it's wonderful to see you.'

'It's wonderful to see you too,' and as she stepped inside, Sadie came out of her room,

Mary saying softly, 'Hello, Mother.'

'Mary, I can't believe it. You're back.'

'Yes, I was missing you all. How are you?'

'I'm fine,' she said, but then her arms stretched out and as Mary walked into them, Sadie's voice cracked with emotion. 'I can't believe you've come home. Oh, it's wonderful.'

For a moment the two women remained entwined, whilst Sally stared at her aunt, thinking she looked incredible. Mary was tanned and trim, her eyes sparking with health. Her stiff, formal hairstyle and attire had been discarded in favour of soft waves and garments. She looked the younger sister instead of the elder, and Sally wondered what her mother would make of Mary's appearance.

Sadie finally let Mary go, sniffing and wiping her eyes as she said, 'Come on, let's go into the kitchen. I want to hear all about your travels.'

Sally made them a drink, listening to her aunt's adventures, amazed by all she had seen and done. For a while it distracted her, but then seeing the solicitor's letter on the table where she had left it, her face saddened.

'Sally, I've been so full of telling you about Spain that I haven't really looked at you, but now I can see that something is wrong. You've lost so much weight. What is it? Are you ill?'

Sally felt a lump forming in her throat and, barely able to speak, she croaked, 'Gran, will you tell her what's happened?'

'Yeah, all right, love.'

With her head down, Sally listened to her

gran's words, each one like a fresh blow to her heart. 'And to top it all,' Sadie said, 'Arthur's got his fancy piece living with him.'

'No!' Mary gasped. 'I can't believe it. None of you mentioned it in your letters.'

'I asked them not to tell you,' Sally said. 'You were happy in Spain and I didn't want you to feel you had to come back over this.'

'Oh, Sally, I'd have jumped on the first plane. I can't believe this of Arthur and I could kill him, I really could. I'm so sorry, my dear. You must be absolutely devastated.'

Mary rose to her feet, her expression one of deep sympathy. It broke Sally and she too stood up, flinging herself into her aunt's arms whilst giving vent to her feeling. She had tried to be strong, and with her mother constantly nagging her to pull herself together, the pain was trapped like a hard knot in her stomach. Now, feeling her aunt's arms around her, she found comfort in the contact as Mary's hand patted her back.

'Sally,' she murmured. 'I know this feels like the end of the world now, but please believe me, you *will* get over it.'

She drew in juddering breaths, but didn't want to leave the shelter of her aunt's arms, clinging on as if to draw strength from her. Finally she was able to bring herself under control; sniffing now she said, 'Oh, Aunty, I'm so glad that you're here.'

Sally was upstairs when Ruth came home that
148

evening, and seeing Mary she smiled with delight. 'Well, who'd have thought it? Both you and Denis Walters coming back on the same day. It's lovely to see you, and are you home for good?'

'Yes, I am. It was lovely in Spain, but my family is here and I missed you.'

'Christ Almighty, look at you. You're so brown, and what have you done to your hair?'

'I let my perm grow out.'

'Well, you should have done it years ago. You look amazing.'

'What's this about Denis Walters?' Sadie interrupted.

'Tommy collared me on the way home to tell me that his dad is back, and he looked as pleased as punch.' For a moment Ruth looked saddened. 'I doubt we'll see the lad this evening.'

'Huh, with Denis as bad as Laura, I doubt it,' Sadie said.

Ruth sighed as she sank on to a chair, kicking off her shoes. 'So, Mary, have you moved back into your flat?'

'Yes, and it wasn't a problem.'

'I doubt it'll be so easy to get your old job back, and I still can't believe that you became a waitress in a Spanish hotel.'

'It was fun and we'll talk more about it later, but for now my main concern is Sally.'

'I hope she pulls herself together soon,' Ruth said. 'She was like this after her miscarriage and I didn't think she'd ever snap out of it.'

'Yes, I remember you telling me in one of your letters. Poor Sally, she's been through so much, and now this. She looks awful, and is losing too much weight. This break up has obviously knocked her for six, but knowing how much she loves Arthur, isn't there anything we can do to get them back together?'

'Leave it out, Mary. Don't you think we've tried? Anyway, with Arthur moving a young tart in, I think Sally's better off without him.'

'Arthur's a good man and I still find that hard to believe.'

'Good man! Huh, I used to think so too, but not now, not after this.'

Mary frowned, determined to see Arthur. She had listened to the explanation of the break up, but none of it made sense. Something funny was going on, and no matter what they said, she couldn't accept that Arthur was living with another woman. She would go round there to see for herself, and if it *was* true, she'd have a few choice words to say.

Arthur stood up again and winced with pain. God, his stump was sore, but determination to walk without a stick carried him forward.

In an effort to distance his mind from the pain, he thought back to his first visit to the hospital gym. He had shown them all right. Shown them that he was quite capable on his new leg, and after about twenty minutes they had chucked him out, obviously in agreement. Now all he wanted was to manage without a stick, to walk like a man again and not be seen as a cripple.

He hadn't known what to expect when Joe drove him to the hospital for his fitting, but found it easier than expected. His stump had been covered with a nylon sock, and then a thick woollen one, before the artificial leg was attached. A leather, corset-like contraption was strapped around his thigh to hold it in place, with another strap to go round his waist or over his shoulder.

When he had first stood up with most of the weight on his good leg, it hadn't felt too bad, cumbersome, but bearable. He'd had no idea then of how sore it would become, and now grimaced.

Arthur's thoughts returned to the present as Joe walked into the room, carrying two cups of coffee. He shifted slightly to take one, unable to help a small wince of pain.

'Trying to do too much again, I see. Why don't you give yourself a break?'

'I'll show her,' he mumbled. 'I'll show her that I'm not a cripple.'

'I suppose you mean Sally. You're getting a divorce, so why do you care what she thinks?'

'I just do!'

'I know you didn't want to talk about it before, but what about now? Will you tell me why you let your parents think that Patsy has moved in with you?'

'Because they were so sure that we're shacked up, believing Sally over me. Sod them, if that's the sort of man they think I am, I'm not going to disillusion them.'

'So, it's your pride. *Now* it makes sense.'

'Patsy hasn't moved in, and I have no intention of letting her. Yet I was condemned without a hearing.'

'You're still seeing her though.'

'Yes, I am, and so what. Are you jealous?'

'No, I'm not. I only took Patsy out a few times and soon found she wasn't the girl for me. I still can't believe you prefer her to Sally.'

'Look, Sally doesn't want me, and I'm not a flaming monk. Now come on, let's change the subject.'

The two men went on to talk about work for a while, until at nine thirty someone knocked on the door. 'Stay put, Arthur,' Joe said as he went to answer it. 'You obviously need to rest that leg.'

Arthur listened. He could hear a woman's voice, and for a moment his heart leapt. Was it Sally? His feelings were immediately deflated when Mary walked into the room, and forcing a smile, he said, 'Hello, Mary. So you've come home.'

Another one stating the obvious, Mary thought, his words an echo of what everyone said as soon as they saw her. If she'd been in better humour she might have told Arthur that she wasn't an optical illusion, but instead, ignoring the other man in the room, she said, 'Can we talk?'

'Joe, this is Sally's aunt and she's just returned from Spain. Though I doubt she's called round to tell me about her adventures.'

'Pleased to meet you,' Joe said as he proffered his hand.

Murmuring a greeting, Mary shook it, but with Sally's heartbreak heavy on her mind she hadn't come here to socialize. She'd come to see for herself if Arthur had another woman, and so far there wasn't any sign of one.

'Arthur, I'd best be off,' Joe said.

'Yes, all right, mate. I'll see you in the morning,' Arthur replied, and as Joe left the room he added, 'Mary, do you mind sitting down? It's making my neck ache looking up at you.'

Involuntarily Mary glanced at Arthur's leg, but there was no sign that he was missing a part of one. Two shoes were visible, both looking the same. Taking a seat, she said without preamble, 'I can't believe what I've been hearing and I came round here to see for myself.'

'See what?'

'This young woman I hear is living with you.'

Arthur's lips drew back into a sneer, his annoyance obvious. 'As you can see there isn't a woman here. Yet even if there was, Sally has filed for a divorce so I don't see that it's any of your business.'

'Sally only sought legal advice after hearing from *your* solicitor.'

'Is that what she told you? Another lie – but of course everyone believes precious Sally.'

Mary was about to ask him what he meant when the door opened. With her back towards it, and rather hidden in the large leather chair, she heard a female voice.

'Thank God that stuffed shirt has gone and I'm fed up with him looking at me like something he's stepped on. Joe still doesn't approve of us, Arthur.'

'Patsy,' Arthur said, his voice holding a warning.

'What?'

Mary stood up, and, startled, the girl's eyes rounded as she said, 'Oh, I didn't see you there!'

'Obviously not. So, it's true, Arthur. You *have* got someone else living with you?'

His voice was thick with anger as he replied, 'So, just like the others, you've jumped to that conclusion.'

'What else am I supposed to think?'

'Think what you bloody well like. Now I suggest you leave.'

'I'm not going anywhere until I sort this out! What do you mean about Sally filing for divorce first? And is this girl living with you or not?'

'Now look here, I don't have to answer to you, and you needn't stand there looking like some sort of avenging angel. You've already had Sally's version of the truth, so like everyone else, I doubt you'll believe mine. Now as I said, I want you to leave.'

Mary ground her teeth, but there was no arguing with the finality of Arthur's words. She snatched up her handbag and marched from the

154

room, but not before giving Arthur's girlfriend a look of disgust.

It was only when she reached the end of Maple Terrace that she began to think logically again. Arthur was under the impression that Sally had filed for divorce first, but why? And what did he mean about Sally telling lies? Of course she hadn't, and anyway, she had seen Arthur's girlfriend for herself.

It didn't seem possible that so much had happened in such a short time. She had left for her cruise sure that Arthur would recover from his accident, and looking forward to seeing a bit of the world. And she *had* enjoyed her holiday. There were a lot of elderly people on board, but she had made friends, even flirted a little with a few single men of her own age. But the pain of losing Leroy was still fresh and none of them had touched her heart, while one soon lost interest when he found out that she wasn't a rich widow. Mary smiled at the memory of seeing him moving on to another woman, this time one at least ten years older.

She remembered the sights she had seen, falling in love with each port of call. Italy had touched her heart, but then they had sailed through the Suez Canal and on to the beauty of the Maldives. There had been so many places that enchanted her and held special memories, each captured on film.

When the cruise was almost over, she hadn't wanted to return to England. She felt alive, invigorated, and wanted to do something outrageous, something new. And if the truth be known, she wanted to do it before she became too old.

As they had neared Spain, a chance conversation with one of the crew led her to apply for the job in a hotel, and she had been amazed to get it. The life enchanted her for a while, the people, the culture, but gradually homesickness had set in, enhanced when she saw guests coming and going, returning to England after their holiday.

Finally she was unable to resist the pull of home, and gave in her notice, finding herself joyful at the thought of her return.

Mary frowned. And what a return! She had come down to earth with a bump when she saw Sally's unhappiness. She felt helpless, and in the face of Arthur's intransigent attitude, she doubted there was any way to save her niece's marriage.

Thirteen

'I want to see my daddy!'

'Well, you can't,' Sally said tiredly.

'I hate you, Mummy.'

With her arms akimbo and hands on hips, Angel glared at her with indignation and Sally closed her eyes against the sight.

'You should let her see her father,' Sadie said.

Sally's eyes widened. 'What?'

'You heard me,' Sadie said and then exhaled loudly. 'Listen, Sally, as I've said before, I know you think you're punishing Arthur by keeping them apart, but Angel is suffering too and it isn't right.'

'But he doesn't deserve to see her.'

'Maybe not. However, it's Angel who concerns me. I'm not condoning what Arthur has done, but he *is* her father.'

'Mummy, pleeeease,' Angel appealed.

'Go on, Sally. Let her see him, if only for a little while,' Ruth urged.

They were both nagging her now, Sally thought, and wondered angrily whose side they were on. 'I said no.'

'I hate you, Mummy!' Angel cried again, running into Ruth's arms.

There was a moment of startling clarity as Sally watched the scene. God, what sort of mother was she? In her desperation to punish Arthur, she had used the only weapon she had – her daughter. Worried that Angel might try to go to Maple Terrace again, she kept her in whenever she thought that Arthur would be at home, and Angel was chafing at the restriction. Sally swallowed, sickened by her self-centred behaviour. She held out her arms. 'Angel, come here, darling.'

'No, don't want to,' the child said, burrowing into her grandmother.

'Oh, Angel, I'm so sorry, darling. Of course you can see your daddy.'

The child lifted her head. 'Really?'

'Yes, really, and I'll give him a ring now to make the arrangements. It's Sunday so he'll be home, and if you like you can go to see him after dinner.'

'Yippee,' Angel cried, pulling away from Ruth and doing a little jig.

As Sally rose to her feet, her gran touched her arm. 'I'm glad you've come to your senses at last.'

'I've been awful, Gran.'

'You're hurting, love, and it's understandable, but I knew you'd come round eventually.'

Sally heaved a sigh, her feet dragging as she went into the hall where she hesitated before picking up the receiver. She didn't want to talk to Arthur, didn't want to hear his voice, but for Angel's sake she had to. Yet despite knowing now that she had used Angel as a weapon, and hating herself, she still didn't think the child was ready to see her father with Patsy. With this in mind she dialled the number.

'Hello.'

On hearing Arthur's voice, Sally froze for a moment, the pain of his betrayal still unbearable. 'Arthur,' she said quietly.

'Is that you, Sally?'

'I've just rung to say that I've decided to let you see Angel.'

'Huh, that's big of you, especially as you had no right to keep us apart. She's my daughter too.'

'I know that and she's missing you. However, I don't want her to see you with Patsy.'

'Really – and why not?'

'I should have thought that was obvious. Angel is already upset that we're living apart, and it would only add to her confusion if she sees you with another woman.'

There was a silence and then she heard a loud sigh. 'At some point, she'll have to get used to it, but for now I'll make sure that Patsy stays out of the way.'

Sally's stomach twisted, still unable to bear the thought of them together. She took a deep breath, steadying her voice. 'Our Sunday lunch is almost ready, so how about I fetch Angel round for an hour afterwards? Say at three o'clock.'

'An hour! Surely she can stay longer than that?'

'All right, two hours, but then I'll return to pick her up.'

'Fine.'

Sally's goodbye was clipped, finding as she dropped the receiver back into the cradle that she had to fight her feelings. She wouldn't cry, she wouldn't. As she returned to the kitchen, Angel looked at her expectantly. Sally forced the parody of a smile. 'I'll be taking you to see Daddy after dinner.'

Angel ran a little circle around the room, cheering loudly, until Sadie snapped, 'For Gawd's sake, pack it in, child. You're giving me a headache.'

'Sorry, Gamma.'

'Why don't you go out to play?'

'Can I, Mummy?'

For a moment Sally hesitated, but Angel knew she would be seeing her daddy later so was unlikely to wander off. 'Yes, I suppose so, but stay in Candle Lane, or else.'

As the door closed behind the child, Sally sank on to a chair again. When she took Angel to see Arthur, she would have to look at him, to see him again, and dreaded it.

When Arthur walked into the living room, Patsy could see that he was fuming.

'What's the matter, darling?'

'That was Sally. She's agreed to let me see Angel at last.'

'Oh, that's nice.'

'You won't say that when you hear the rule

she's laid down. Rules, bloody cheek! She wouldn't be able to set terms if that bloody solicitor wasn't dragging his feet about access.'

'Calm down, love. What rule are you on about?'

'I can see Angel, but only if you're not around.'

Patsy hid her feelings, saying calmly, 'That's not a problem. I'll just make sure I'm upstairs while the child is with you.'

'Thanks, love.'

'Does Sally still think that I'm living with you?'

'Yes, I think so, and so do my parents, but I've no intention of putting them straight. If that's what they choose to believe, then sod them.'

Patsy lowered her eyes. She had tried every trick in the book to take the relationship further, but to no avail. Arthur wanted her for sex, and plenty of it, but he still wouldn't let her stay the night. She had a feeling that, despite his protestations, he wanted Sally back, and now Patsy's eyes narrowed. She'd have to think of something, some mischief to keep them apart.

Ruth watched as Angel picked at her food without appreciation and wondered if Tommy was getting anything to eat. Denis Walters said that he'd stopped drinking and that Laura had too, but Ruth doubted it. When she saw Tommy he still looked neglected, but when she questioned him he was tight-lipped, saying that his father said he shouldn't talk about family business. Poor Tommy looked dirty and underfed, and Ruth wished she could do more for him.

'Angel, eat your carrots,' Sally said.

'Don't want them.'

'There are starving children in the world who'd be glad of the food on your plate,' Ruth said.

'They can have it.'

'Angel, don't cheek your nanny,' Sally snapped.

Ruth was unable to help the comparison. When she'd fed Tommy he scoffed it, eating anything that was put in front of him. Angel on the other hand was picky, but with a small shake of her head Ruth knew it was their fault. They had all spoiled the child, but now as her granddaughter gave her a heart-stopping smile, Ruth grinned back. Well, she *was* adorable.

Sadie smacked her lips. 'That was smashing, Ruth. I love a nice bit of lamb with mint sauce.'

'I'm glad you enjoyed it,' she replied. Her mother was so much happier since Mary had come home. She was less moody, though there were still odd occasions when she got out of her pram. There was no doubt that the stroke had changed her, but it was less noticeable nowadays.

Ruth was happier too, though she had to hide the fact. When Sally and Angel had moved to Maple Terrace, she missed them so much, the house feeling empty and desolate without them. Now, though, they were back, and though she played the part of being sympathetic at the breakdown of Sally's marriage, secretly she was hoping there would never be reconciliation. Ruth frowned now. She had supported her mother in persuading Sally to let Angel see her father, but now hoped it wasn't a mistake. She didn't want Sally anywhere near Arthur, not if there was the slightest chance of them getting back together. Ruth lowered her eyes. She shouldn't think like that, it was selfish, but then with her next thought, she justified her attitude. After what Arthur had done, he didn't deserve Sally.

At three o'clock, Sally took Angel's hand and walked her to Maple Terrace. The early June day was warm and if she hadn't been so tense she might have enjoyed the walk; instead her teeth were gritted as she rang the doorbell. It was some time before it opened, and despite everything, her heart leapt when she saw Arthur. He stood straight and tall, with no crutches, his hand loosely holding a stick.

'Daddy, you've got a new leg!' Angel cried.

Arthur smiled down at his daughter, and then moving sideways he beckoned her inside. 'Yes, I have, princess. Come on in?'

'Mummy too?'

Sally bent over, ruffling her daughter's hair. 'I'll be back to pick you up in a couple of hours. Be a good girl.'

Angel looked bewildered, but stepped inside, and as Arthur closed the door, the tears that

163

threatened welled in Sally's eyes. Oh, he looked wonderful, and despite everything she still loved him. She turned, her shoulders hunched as she walked along Maple Terrace, and with her eyes down she didn't see Patsy until almost on top of her.

'Hello, Sally, and thank you for letting Arthur see Angel. He's been missing her.'

Sally said nothing, only fighting to hide her feelings.

'He's been working so hard to walk without a stick,' Patsy chirped, 'and all because he doesn't want to walk with a limp when we get married.'

'Married! You're getting married?'

'Well, yes. Didn't he tell you?'

Sally shook her head, her voice a murmur. 'No.'

'Men!' Patsy exclaimed. 'Still, no doubt he'd have got round to it eventually. Of course we'll have to wait until the divorce comes through and I know all the legal stuff takes ages. Oh well, I'll just have to be patient, and at least in the meantime we're together. From what Arthur said, it seems you want me to stay out of the way whilst Angel's with him, but don't you think it's a bit daft? Arthur and I are living together, and if you ask me it would make more sense for Angel to get used to the idea. After all, you can hardly expect me to disappear every time she comes round.'

Sally felt sick, but forced her head high as she tried to sound unconcerned. 'Yes, you're right, and as you're obviously on your way home now, I suppose this is as good a time as any.'

'Thanks, Sally. Must dash and it will be lovely to see Arthur and Angel together.'

Sally continued on her way, feeling a sense of unreality. It was hard to believe that at one time she thought they had the perfect marriage – thought that Arthur loved her as much as she loved him. Now, of course, she realized that his love was just a shallow thing – something easily pushed aside. So much so that he could propose to Patsy before their divorce had come through.

The finality of it hit her. It was over, her life with Arthur was over, and somehow she didn't think she could bear it.

'Ann,' Sally cried, surprised to see Arthur's sister on the doorstep.

'Mum said you're coping all right, but I wanted to see for myself. She's looking after the kids for me and Dad dropped me off here for an hour or two.'

'Come in,' she said, forcing a smile. Her heart was still aching, and she just wanted go to her room, be alone to nurse her wounds until she had to pick Angel up again.

Sadie looked up as they went into the kitchen, her eyes widening in surprise. 'Hello, love, it's been a while since we've seen you.'

'Yes, I know. I'm afraid I don't get to London as often as I'd like. I keep nagging my husband to learn to drive and at last he's going to take lessons. It'll make all the difference, and with Dad's back playing him up he'll be able to have a rest on his day off instead of driving to Milton Keynes.'

Sally listened to this exchange whilst studying her friend and sister-in-law. Ann was looking frumpy, matronly, all traces of the young girl who'd been mad on the latest fashions gone. As a child she'd had a weak eye, one that nestled in the corner of the socket. It had caused her no end of problems at school; name calling, jokes, but Ann had weathered it all. When Sally's healing gifts had begun to develop, she had focused on Ann, sensing it was a muscle weakness.

Elsie had listened to her, devising a series of exercises to strengthen the eye. She held a pencil up in front of Ann's face, making her follow the movement for hours on end. Up, down, side to side, but it had done the trick and Ann's eye had gradually straightened. Nowadays there was only a small sign of the cast if she was overtired, the eye slightly leaning towards the corner again.

Ann turned to her now, 'Where's Ruth and Angel?'

'Mum's having a nap, something she always does after Sunday dinner, and Angel is visiting her father.'

'So, you've agreed to let him see her at last.'

'She was missing him,' Sally said bluntly.

Ruth came into the room now, stifling a yawn. 'I thought I heard a knock on the door. It's nice to see you, Ann.'

'Hello, Ruth, and I'm sorry I woke you. I've come to have a chat with Sally.'

'Good for you. She needs all the support she can get at the moment. Your brother has a lot to answer for and should be shot for what he's done.'

Sally saw the pain that crossed Ann's features and rose to her feet. 'Come on, let's go for a walk,' she suggested.

Ann agreed, and soon they were walking along Candle Lane, neither speaking for a while, but then Ann broke the silence. 'I still can't believe that you and Arthur have broken up.'

'Well, we have.'

'I know we've talked on the telephone, but I had to see you. I can't imagine how you're feeling, and when Mum told me that Arthur's got that girl from upstairs living with him, I just couldn't believe it. I went round to see him, but Patsy was there and I lost my temper when Arthur refused to speak to me alone. I'm afraid I stormed out and since then we haven't spoken.'

Sally said nothing, only reaching out to gently squeeze her friend's hand, Ann squeezing back as they walked in silence for a while.

'Mind you, Sally, I'm not really sure that Patsy is living with Arthur. I was only there for a short while, but there was no sign of her things.'

'Oh, she's living with him all right, and don't

forget, Arthur isn't denying it. In fact, from what Patsy told me, they're getting married when the divorce comes through.'

'No! My God, I can't believe it.'

'It's true,' Sally said, her voice thick with tightly reined emotion.

'What time are you picking Angel up?'

'In about half an hour.'

'I'll come with you,' Ann said, her expression taut.

Sally bit on her lower lip. 'Please don't make a scene or anything. I don't want any nastiness in front of Angel.'

Ann turned, their eyes meeting, then, exhaling loudly, she nodded. 'All right, but it will be hard to keep my mouth shut.'

They continued to walk, until finally they headed for Maple Terrace. Sally knocked on the door, dreading seeing Patsy's smug face again, but it was Arthur who opened it.

He looked surprised to see Ann, but quickly recovered. 'Are you both coming in?'

'No thanks,' Sally said.

'If that tart's in there, I'm not coming in either.'

'If you're talking about Patsy, she isn't a tart, and I won't have you calling her one,' Arthur snapped. 'I'll get Angel.'

'Hold on a minute,' Ann said. 'I hear congratulations are in order.'

'What are you talking about?'

'Sally tells me that you and Patsy are getting married.'

Arthur seemed to stretch, his neck rising out of his collar like a tortoise. 'Oh, and of course, you believe her.'

Ann looked puzzled for a moment, but as she opened her mouth to speak, Angel appeared, grinning as she ran forward. 'Hello, Auntie. Are them boys with you?'

'If you mean your cousins Jason and Darren, no, I'm afraid not. Nanny Elsie is looking after them.'

'Come on, Angel, it's time to go home.' Sally said.

'But I want to stay with Daddy.'

'You can see him again next week,' Sally cajoled, anxious to be away. It was hard to look at Arthur and her fists were clenched into balls, nails digging into her palms.

'Well, Ann, it was nice to see you, and thanks for the congratulations, even if they are misplaced,' Arthur said, a hint of sarcasm in his tone.

Ann's lips curled, but she kept her voice even, 'For the sake of you know who, I'm saying nothing.'

Arthur's eyes went to Angel. 'Off you go, princess, and I'll see you next week.'

Angel hugged him, but then he gave her a gentle push in Sally's direction. She took her daughter's hand, urging, 'Come on, sweetheart.'

As they walked away Arthur remained on the doorstep, and Ann waited until they were out of earshot before saying quietly, 'Don't you think it was funny the way Arthur reacted when I congratulated him? It was rather like he was hinting that you were telling lies. Are you sure you haven't got the wrong end of the stick?'

'Yes, I'm sure, but if you don't believe me, why don't you ask Arthur for yourself?'

'I'll do that,' Ann said.

They were quiet then, Angel skipping beside them, and had only just reached Candle Lane when Bert turned up. He said a quick hello, adding, 'Sorry I can't stop, but the boys are running Elsie ragged. Come on, Ann, we'd better get back before your mother reaches the end of her tether.'

They said goodbye and as they drove away, Sally's eyes were shadowed. Arthur's reaction had been strange, and he'd implied that she was lying about the marriage. But why?

When the telephone rang that evening, Arthur unwrapped his arms from around Patsy and went to answer it.

His sister's indignant tone rang down the line. 'Arthur, what's going on? Sally tells me that you're going to marry Patsy, but you made out that she's telling lies. I don't know what you're playing at, but after what you've done, don't you think Sally has suffered enough?'

'Huh, I can see where your sympathies lie. Well, Ann, if you choose to believe everything Sally tells you, that's up to you. Now, if you don't mind, I'm busy,' he snapped, slamming down the receiver.

His face was grim as he went back into the living room, and though Patsy looked inviting with her top off and skirt up round her thighs, his passion had died. It had been great to see Angel that afternoon, but it served to emphasize how much he was missing her, and, if truth be known, Sally too. He'd blown it, blown his marriage, but why did Sally have to turn everyone against him?

'What's the matter, darling?' Patsy asked and, as he sat beside her, she reached out to stroke his inner thigh.

'That was my sister. It seems that Sally has told her another cock and bull story.'

'Really! What has she said this time?'

'She's told them that we're getting married, and it seems that everyone believes her.'

'Did you tell your sister that it isn't true?'

'No, and if they want to believe everything Sally tells them, sod them. Sod the lot of them.'

'Never mind, darling,' Patsy said, her voice honey soft. 'They'll come round in time, I'm sure of it, and in the meantime . . .'

Her lips covered his, warm and moist, and wanting to send his pain to oblivion, Arthur gave himself up to the sensations she aroused. Patsy too gave herself up to the passion, relief coursing through her body that the plan had worked.

Telling Sally that she and Arthur were getting married had been a risky thing to do, but desperate times called for desperate measures. It could have gone badly wrong, but thank God for Arthur's pride. Instead of denying it, he had reacted as she'd hoped, and now she had put a further wedge between him and Sally.

Thankfully there was a wedge between Arthur and his family too, one that she hoped would stay in place for a long time. Yes, his pride was something she could use against him, and with any luck it would cause him to propose soon. Oh, she wasn't stupid and knew he didn't love her, but what did love matter? If he asked her to marry him to get back at Sally, that was fine with her, and she'd say yes like a shot.

Fourteen

A week later, on a lovely clement day, two things happened in quick succession in Candle Lane. The postman delivered a letter to every door, and before he had reached the last house on one side, street doors were opening as neighbours converged.

Nelly Cox, her face white with shock, hurried to number five, and as Sally answered the door she bustled inside.

'Ruth, have you had a letter?'

'Yes, so I can guess why you're here.'

'I don't care what they say, I ain't leaving Candle Lane.'

'As they're pulling all the houses down, you

172

won't have any choice.'

'They can demolish mine around me, but I ain't shifting.'

'You might get offered something better.'

'What, in one of them matchbox blocks that are going up! No thank you, I ain't going in one of them. If they want me out, they'll have to bleedin' carry me.'

'We've been scheduled for redevelopment before and it didn't happen,' Sadie said. 'Maybe the council will defer it again.'

'I doubt it,' Ruth murmured, but then Nelly swayed on her feet. 'Sit down, love. You look fit to drop.'

Sally too saw the agitated state Nelly was in, her mother now urging, 'Quick, Sal, shove the kettle on to boil again. I think Nelly's in shock and a cup of sweet tea might help.' She then gently touched the old woman's shoulder. 'I'm sorry, love, but I've got to leave for work or I'll be late. We'll talk again when I come home this evening.'

'Yes, get yourself off,' Sadie urged. 'We'll look after Nelly.'

Sally called goodbye to her mother as she hurriedly made the tea, and making sure that it was good and strong she added three teaspoons of sugar, saying as she handed it to Nelly, 'Don't worry. It might be ages before they can rehouse us all. The letter only says that we're now scheduled for redevelopment again, but not when.'

Nelly's hands were shaking as she lifted the

cup to her lips, and Sally found that for the first time her lethargy was lifting as she too began to worry about leaving Candle Lane. Would her mother be rehoused in a place large enough for all of them? If not, she'd have to find a flat, but with rent to pay she'd have to be sure of a weekly income from Arthur. So far she had drawn what cash was needed from their bank account, but was worried that Arthur would close it soon. If he did, until she received some sort of financial settlement, she'd have no money.

Nelly swallowed the last of her tea, colour now returning to her cheeks. 'You could be right, Sally. We could be here a long time before they try to move us out.'

'Yeah, maybe,' Sadie said, 'but our turn will come round eventually. The lane is going to be demolished, and that's that.'

'Over my dead body,' Nelly cried. 'I don't care what they say. I ain't going nowhere. I'm staying put.'

'Don't be daft,' Sadie retorted. 'When that huge ball starts swinging and knocking down the walls, you'll be out of your place like a shot.'

'No I won't! If we all refuse to move, what can they do? In fact, I think I'll go and have a word with everyone in the lane. If we stick together, we might be able to beat the buggers,' Nelly said forcefully as she rose to her feet, and now with something to act on it seemed she had regained new strength.

'Dream on, Nelly Cox,' Sadie called, but the door had already closed behind the old woman.

'Gran, do you think the council will offer us a three bedroom flat?'

'Blimey, I dunno, love. There's only your mum and me down as living here now, so I doubt it. Mind you, she could inform them that you're staying with us and it might make a difference. Have a word with her when she comes home.'

'I'll do that, but I'll take Angel to school now or she'll be late. I won't be long, Gran,' and as she left the house with her daughter, Sally saw that Nelly was already knocking on doors.

In the Walters house, the second traumatic event was unfolding.

'Dad! Dad!' Tommy shouted.

'Wh ... what?'

'Dad, wake up! There's somefing wrong with Mum.'

Denis Walters' eyelids felt like they were stuck together with glue as he forced them open. He had worked late, coming home to a house that looked like a bomb had hit it. He'd searched in all of Laura's usual hideaways, even finding empty bottles hidden in the boy's room, and presenting her with the evidence, they'd had a stinking row. The stupid woman denied that she was drinking, yet she stank of booze, and he was just about ready to give up. Unable to face sharing her bed that night he'd fallen asleep on the sofa, but now his neck felt stiff as he struggled to sit up. 'All right, son, I'm coming. Just give me a minute to get dressed.'

'Hurry up, Dad. I can't wake her up.'

Tommy's words had him shooting to his feet and, quickly pulling on his trousers, he clutched them unfastened as he took the stairs two at a time, bursting into the bedroom. Denis blanched when he saw his wife's face, knowing instantly that she was dead. With his stomach turning he said quickly to Tommy, 'Run to the doctors, son. Tell him to come right away.'

'Is Mum all right?'

'Do as I say,' Denis yelled, and as soon as his son had scampered downstairs he sank on to the side of the bed. Oh, Laura, Laura! If he hadn't slept downstairs, would he have been able to save her? Had she died in pain, calling for him? Please, no, he thought, let her have gone in her sleep.

Denis stood up and, taking a shirt from the wardrobe, he dressed before sitting at Laura's side again. The house felt strangely silent and he had no idea how long he sat there, gazing at his wife, his eyes burning, but dry. Eventually there were sounds in the hall of his son returning, and shortly after Tommy walked into the room, the doctor behind him.

'Tommy, go back downstairs,' Denis ordered.

'No, I want to see me mum.'

'Do as I say!'

The doctor pushed past the boy, shaking his head as he looked at the bed. 'Close the door,

Mr Walters,' he said, eyes flicking behind him to make sure that Tommy was safely out of the room.

Denis did as he asked, and after a quick examination the doctor spoke again. 'I'm sure you've realized that your wife is dead, Mr Walters, and it was probably another heart attack. I'll arrange for her body to be moved, but in the meantime I suggest you find someone to look after your son.'

His mind in a blur, Denis thanked the man and then grimaced. Christ, he'd thanked the doctor for telling him that his wife was dead. How bizarre was that? His mind jumped. Tommy, yes Tommy, the boy would have to be told, and then got out of the way while Laura's body was taken out of the house. Now though he followed the doctor downstairs, dreading the task ahead of him as he showed the man out.

'What's wrong wiv me mum?'

'Tommy, come here,' Denis said. He had hardly ever put his arms round his son, and now bending down he placed his hands on the boy's shoulders. 'I'm afraid your mum has passed away.'

'What's passed away? Did she faint?'

'No, lad, your mother's dead.' Denis hated the brutality of the words, and as Tommy's face crumbled he ineffectually pulled him into his arms. The boy smelt musty, of unwashed clothes and an unwashed body.

As the child sobbed, Denis wondered how he was going to cope with him now. How could he work and look after a child? Christ, what was the matter with him? His wife had just died and here he was fretting about the future when she hadn't even been buried yet. Bloody hell! How was he going to pay for a funeral? They had no life insurance, no savings – he closed his eyes in despair.

Sally was on her way back from taking Angel to school when she saw the doctor leaving the Walters house. She wondered if Laura were ill again, and had only been indoors for a few minutes when someone knocked.

Denis stood on the step, his expression agonized. 'What is it?' she asked. 'Has something happened to Laura?'

Tommy shot out from behind his father, throwing his arms around Sally's legs. 'Me mum's dead. Where's Ruth? I want Ruth!'

'You'd better come in,' Sally invited, her arm automatically going around Tommy's shoulders.

Denis shook his head, leaning forward to whisper, 'The doctor is arranging for my wife's body to be taken away. Can I leave Tommy with you until she's gone?'

'Of course you can, and if there's anything else I can do, please let me know.'

'Thanks,' the man said and, as though unable to cope with his son's grief, he quickly left.

'Come on, Tommy,' Sally said, leading him into the kitchen.

As soon as Sadie saw the boy she asked

sharply, 'Why ain't you in school?'

'Me ... me muvver's dead,' he cried, throwing himself on to the sofa as his thin body shook with sobs.

'Blimey, Sal, the poor little sod. His mum was so young too.'

Sally sat beside Tommy, pulling him into her arms, finding that her own tears were mingling with his. What an awful day, she thought. First they had all been told that Candle Lane was to be demolished, and then poor Laura Walters had passed away. The tragedy of the second event overrode the first, and for the first time in ages Sally forgot her own pain as she gently rocked Tommy back and forth.

When Ruth arrived home from work, Tommy was back with his father but, on hearing the news, she was knocking on Denis Walters' door only minutes later.

The man opened it, his eyes shadowed with grief. Then, hearing her voice, Tommy scooted in front of his father, throwing himself at Ruth. She crouched down, holding him tightly, her heart aching for this child that she had come to love.

'Come in,' Denis said.

Ruth stood up and, holding Tommy's hand, she followed Denis into the kitchen. It was a mess again and her nose wrinkled with distaste. It wasn't right. Tommy shouldn't have to live like this. 'Denis, would you like Tommy to stay with me until you get things sorted out?'

'I can't ask you to do that.'

'I don't mind. He's no trouble, and no doubt you have arrangements to make.'

'What do you think, son?'

Tommy looked from one to the other, his face wet with tears. 'I don't 'spect you want to be on yer own, Dad. If you like, I'll stay with you.'

Denis gulped, obviously touched by his son's words. 'There's no need, son. I've got things to do, and you might be better off with Mrs Marchant.'

Ruth too was amazed at Tommy's sensitivity, the child then saying, 'All right, I'll go with Ruth, but you will come to see me, won't you, Dad?'

'Of course, and when I've sorted things out you can come home.'

'You'd best get yourself a few things, Tommy,' Ruth urged. 'Some clean clothes and underwear.'

'I ain't got any clean clothes.'

'Then bring your dirty ones and I'll wash them.'

As Tommy ran from the room, Denis said, 'Laura loved the boy, she really did, but when she was drinking she wasn't capable of doing anything and I'm afraid she let the place go. I did try to get her off the booze, but I had to work and couldn't watch her for twenty-four hours a day.'

Ruth nodded sympathetically, but her mind was elsewhere. With Laura gone, what was going to happen to Tommy? Was Denis capable of looking after the boy? And as though Denis was aware of her thoughts, he spoke again.

'I don't know how I'm going to cope with him now.'

Tommy came back into the room, clutching a bundle of clothes to his chest. Rags, Ruth thought, they all look like rags, but she smiled gently as she took them. 'Right, come on, love, let's get you next door. Say goodnight to your dad and you'll see him tomorrow.'

'Night, Dad,' Tommy said, surprising them both when for a brief moment he threw his arms around his father.

Denis impatiently pushed him away, 'Off you go, son.'

Ruth's lips tightened as she led Tommy out and, unbeknown to him or his father, there was one thought that kept going round and around in her mind. She doubted Denis would be able to cope, and that was fine with her. She loved the boy, and if Denis would agree she'd welcome Tommy into her home, and her heart, permanently.

Fifteen

Joe sat in his car, a little further along Battersea High Street, and watched the house. He was determined to check up on Patsy, sure that she wasn't all she pretended to be. There were plenty of single blokes around, but when he'd given her the elbow she had set her cap at Arthur, and he wanted to know why.

He was sure that she'd deliberately set out to break up Arthur's marriage and suspected that the girl was looking for a ready-made meal ticket, but once again he wondered why she had chosen a married man.

He'd hoped that the break up would be short-lived and that Sally and Arthur would get back together again, but instead they had grown further apart. Arthur was so angry with Sally now, saying that she had caused a rift with his parents and sister. She had lied to them, told them that he was going to marry Patsy, and they had believed her.

Joe sighed, unable to believe it of Sally. He wanted to talk to her, to get her side of the story, but when he'd suggested going to see her, Arthur went potty. Once again he hinted that there was something going on between them, but Joe told him that he was mad. He'd pretended that he had no interest in Sally, but knew it wasn't true. He loved her, would always love her, but even if she and Arthur didn't get back together, he could never act on his feelings. It would destroy his friendship with Arthur, and their business partnership.

When Sally had walked out, it hadn't taken him long to work out that Arthur's attitude to the break up was all bluff. Yes, he was sleeping with Patsy, but he had no deep feelings for the girl. It was just that his pride had been badly injured and Patsy made him feel like a man again. Arthur loved his wife, Joe was sure of it, and there had to be a way to get them back together.

Joe glanced at his watch. Patsy had been in there for over half an hour, but with no idea how long it would take to do this client's hair, he settled back to wait.

Only ten minutes later the street door opened, and with his side-mirror angled to watch the house, Joe stared uncomprehendingly at the man who was seeing Patsy out. He was bald – totally bald, and at least seventy years old. He'd intended to follow Patsy, but now waited until she was out of sight before getting out of the car. Maybe Patsy had been doing someone else's hair in the house, but there had been something strange in the old chap's attitude towards the girl – something almost intimate.

Joe straightened his tie and buttoned his jacket before approaching the house. He then knocked on the door, wondering what on earth he was going to say to the man when he opened it.

However, as soon as the old chap saw him standing on his step his face showed alarm. 'Yeah, what do you want?'

'I'd like to ask you some questions about the young lady who just left.'

'Blimey! Are you CID?'

Joe blinked, wondering what made the man think he was a police officer, but quickly realized he could use it to his advantage. 'I'm investigating the young lady's activities and as I said, I'd like to ask you some questions.'

'I won't have to come down to the station, will I?'

'I could interview you in your own home, but it depends on how cooperative you are.'

'Come in,' the man invited, obviously eager to avoid a trip to the police station.

Joe followed him down the narrow hall to a room at the back, and as the man sat down he indicated another chair. Joe took the seat and trying to look official, said, 'Can you tell me why the young woman was visiting you?'

The man's face flushed crimson. 'If you're investigating her activities, surely I don't have to spell it out.'

'I'd still like you to tell me.'

'She ... she's a prostitute. Look, I don't know anything else about her. I've got her phone number, passed on to me by a mate, but that's all.'

Joe felt the colour drain from his face and

fought to hide his shock, only managing to murmur, 'I see.'

The man's eyes narrowed suspiciously. 'Here, hold on, I'm not sure that you're a copper. Show me your warrant card!'

Joe rose quickly to his feet and before the man could react he dashed down the hall and out of the house. Then, almost leaping the last few feet to his car, he jumped in and drove off, his hands moist with sweat as they gripped the wheel. Christ, he thought, speeding around the corner, that had been a close call.

As he reached the High Street Joe chuckled, berating himself for running off like that. After all, it was unlikely that the old man would complain to the real police, not after entertaining a prostitute.

Bloody hell, Patsy was a prostitute! Who'd have thought it? And somehow he had to break the news to Arthur. God, he'd go bloody mad!

That same evening, Nelly Cox stood on her doorstep, leaning against the stanchion, and deep in thought. She had tried everyone in Candle Lane, but other than two or three people, none of the others were interested in mounting a protest. The young couples welcomed the demolition, saying they'd be glad to get out of this dump and were hoping for a decent place to live.

Nelly looked up and down the lane. There were no trees, no front gardens, just flat-fronted terraced houses. She didn't care. It might not be

185

a pretty place, but it was her home and all her memories were here. Her life with George, her old friends, and though most of them had moved away, a few still remained.

There had been sad times, but none of these came to the front of her mind as she looked back on the years. She recalled street parties, and would never forget the dancing in the lane at the end of World War Two. Another had been arranged for Queen Elizabeth's Coronation, and though it couldn't compare to the end of the war celebrations, she had vivid memories of doing a knees-up with her neighbours.

Mrs Edwards, who once lived in number seven, made her husband push their old piano into the lane, and along with someone else on a mouth organ, the music had been lively as they danced the night away. Booze had been flowing, the men drinking beer from barrels and the women sipping sherry or port.

Nelly glanced along the lane again, her eyes resting on the Walters' door. She'd been saddened to hear of Laura's death, and in the old days all the neighbours would have banded together to help. A collection would have been arranged for flowers, and food organized for the funeral. Those days were gone, and instead of popping in and out of each other's houses for a good old gossip, doors were locked and families sat in front of their little boxes, watching television for hours on end.

Had anyone been to see how Denis Walters was coping? Yes, maybe Ruth and Jessie Stone,

186

but there wouldn't be many who'd take the trouble. A small voice whispered in Nelly's conscience. 'What about you?' She frowned, quickly making her way to Denis Walters' door.

'I'm sorry to hear about your wife,' she said as he opened the door, saddened to see the pain in the man's eyes. 'I've come to see if there's anything I can do.'

'Thanks, do you wanna come in?'

She followed Denis into his dirty kitchen, remembering when hers had looked the same. Nowadays though it was as shiny as a new pin, and she was determined to keep it that way. 'How's Tommy?' she asked.

'He's taken it badly and is next door with Mrs Marchant.'

'Ruth's a lovely woman. She'll take good care of him.'

'I know.' A small silence fell but then Denis blurted out, 'I don't know what I'm gonna do. I ain't even got the money to bury my wife, and how can I work with Tommy to look after?'

'Haven't you any family who can help?'

Denis shook his head, 'My parents are dead, and I've no brothers or sisters. Laura's parents may still be alive, but they severed all connection with her. She's got a brother, but he's a lot older than her and it's years since she contacted him.'

Nelly's interest was piqued. 'Did they fall out?'

'Yeah, he was upset when he saw our kids.'

'But why?'

'Because Laura had been told not to have children. She had a bad heart defect and was told that a pregnancy would be dangerous. As a child she'd been fiercely protected, her parents constantly worried about her health. Laura hated being treated like an invalid, and when old enough she ran away from home. Years later her brother came to see her, but seeing the kids he questioned her about her health. That was like showing a red rag to a bull with Laura. They had a row and parted on bad terms.'

'You'll have to let him know that his sister has passed away and, if they're still alive, her parents too,' Nelly said gently. 'Who knows, they may be able to help.'

'You're right. They ain't short of a few bob.'

'Is the brother married?'

'Yes, with one grown-up kid, and you're right, I'd better ring him. Though God knows where Laura put his letter. I know it's got his telephone number on it.'

'I'll leave you to it, and don't forget if there's anything I can do, you only have to ask.'

'Thanks,' Denis said and as Nelly bustled out, he started to search for his brother-in-law's telephone number.

It took Denis an hour but at last he found the number and, clutching the piece of paper, he hurried to the phone box.

Nelly Cox was right, Laura's family had to be told, and they might offer to help. Would they stump up money for the funeral? God, he hoped

188

so. Laura deserved a better send off than one the National Assistance might provide.

'Hello,' a voice said, the soft Scottish burr making Denis gulp with pain. When he'd first met Laura, she too had had those soft tones. She'd been working as a chambermaid in a hotel, but wanted to be a receptionist. To gain promotion she had worked hard to remove all trace of her Scottish ancestry, but then Denis had proposed and Laura left the job to get married.

'Hello,' Denis choked. 'Is that Andrew?'

'Yes, and who's this?'

Denis stumbled his explanation, his voice a croak, finally saying, 'She, er, she had a heart attack.'

For a moment there was silence, but then Andrew said, 'I'm so sorry, Denis. I'll tell my parents straightaway and then I'll get the first train to London in the morning. Are you still at the same address?'

'No, we live in Battersea now,' and after giving him the new address, they said their goodbyes, Denis feeling a sense of relief as he replaced the receiver.

Laura and her brother may not have kept in touch, and though he had only met Andrew once, he'd liked the man. Laura's parents were still alive, and surely they, or Andrew, would pay for the funeral? Surely they'd help with sorting out Tommy's future too? The boy was family after all, and deserved a better life than this.

As Denis walked home he admitted where his thoughts were taking him. He'd been a useless father and knew he wouldn't be able to cope with the boy. He'd taken no interest in his son since losing his daughter, drowning out his pain with drink. Yes, he'd stopped boozing recently, but what good had it done? He hadn't been able to save Laura.

When Denis arrived home he went into the kitchen, immediately taking a half bottle of whisky he'd bought earlier out of the cupboard. So far he'd resisted opening it, but now he stared at the liquid before raising the bottle to his lips. When Andrew arrived, he'd see what a useless drunk he was, and with any luck he'd take Tommy back to Scotland with him. The boy would have a good life and be well provided for, which was more than he could offer.

Now, as Denis drank deeply, he was sure it was the best thing for all of them.

Sixteen

Early the next morning Arthur opened his front door to Joe, surprised when the man said, 'We need to talk.'

'Is there a problem on the site?'

'No, but I need to tell you something before we set off.'

'Sounds serious, and anyway I'm not ready yet so you'd better come in.'

Arthur was proud of himself that morning, but so far Joe hadn't noticed, and walking in front of him now he waited for some reaction. There was none. Impatiently he said, 'Haven't you noticed anything?'

'No, but I've got a lot on my mind so it isn't surprising.' He glanced around the sitting room, adding, 'What am I supposed to have noticed?'

'Me, you daft bugger. Can't you see something different?' Arthur stood straight as he walked across the room.

'You're not using a stick! Well done, and if I didn't know differently, there's no sign that you have an artificial leg.'

Arthur grinned, pleased at Joe's comment. It had taken him longer than he'd anticipated to ditch the stick completely, but he could sense that his friend was agitated. 'Something's obviously worrying you, so sit down and spit it out.'

Joe took a seat and for a moment he seemed to gather his thoughts. 'Arthur, I've got something to tell you about Patsy.'

'How many times have I told you to stay out of it?'

'She isn't all she pretends to be, Arthur.'

'What's that supposed to mean? Oh, never mind, it doesn't matter anyway. If you must know I'm getting fed up with her. It was great at first but now it's wearing a bit thin. I keep telling her that I don't want to take things further, but she won't listen and is constantly pressuring me to move in. It's getting on me wick, and I don't know why she's in such a hurry. She's got a decent flat upstairs and we see a lot of each other, but she's getting more and more possessive.'

'I think I know why,' Joe murmured.

'Do you? All right, tell me.'

Arthur's jaw dropped as he listened to Joe, at first unable to believe what he was hearing. Of course Patsy wasn't a prostitute. 'Don't be stupid. You're talking rot!'

'No, I'm not. I've told you I spoke to one of her clients, and believe me she wasn't cutting his hair.'

If Arthur had any strong feelings for Patsy, he might have been deeply upset, instead he only felt bewildered and angry. Christ, he'd been sleeping with a prostitute and now felt a wave of sickness. Blimey, how many blokes had been

192

there before him? He stood up abruptly, and forgetting that he no longer needed a stick, he snatched it up. 'I'm going up to see her, and you'd better cover your ears, Joe.'

Arthur banged on Patsy's door, glowering at her when she opened it. 'I want to talk to you.'

'What's wrong?'

'I've found out what you do for a living,' Arthur spat.

Her eyes narrowed. 'Look, you'd better come up.'

'What's the matter? Don't you want the neighbours to hear?' Arthur said, but she was already on her way back to her flat and he was forced to follow her. It was difficult, and un-used to tackling stairs he found he had to cling to the banisters.

'Right, what's all this about?' Patsy asked as they reached her living room. 'I can see you're annoyed about something, so spit it out.'

'Annoyed! I'm more than annoyed, I'm bloody fuming. A prostitute, you're a fucking prostitute!' Arthur spat, uncaring of his language.

'How dare you! I'm no such thing.'

'Yes, you bloody well are. Joe followed you, spoke to one of your clients, and you weren't there to cut his hair!'

'Who the fuck is he to spy on me?' The veil dropped, the real Patsy in evidence now, her coarse language matching his. 'What I do is none of that sanctimonious bastard's business.'

'Joe is a friend, and a good one. He had his suspicions about you and decided to check you out.'

As though stuck for words, for a moment Patsy just stared at him, but then she sneered, 'Friend, you call him a friend! You must be mad, especially as he's fucking your wife!'

'You lying cow. Just because you're a tart, don't tar my wife with the same brush. Christ, to think I've slept with you! How many men have been there before me, eh, tell me that!'

'Enough, and most of them are better at it too. Now get out of my flat, you bloody cripple.'

Arthur's face blanched. Patsy's mask had slipped to show a hard and embittered woman, one who he couldn't believe had fooled him into thinking that she loved him. Christ, what a mug he'd been! He turned away from her, stumbling as he went back downstairs.

'Are you all right, mate?' Joe asked as Arthur walked into the room.

'Yes, but it wasn't pleasant. Shit, Joe, I can't believe I've been sleeping with a prostitute.'

'Yeah, well, I nearly fell for her act too. Look, I'm sorry, mate, but there's stuff to sort out on the site and we should be leaving for work. Are you up to it?'

'Huh, it would take more than that floozie to bring me down. Come on, let's get out of here,' Arthur said, wanting only to get out of the house and away from the stench of Patsy Laurington. Arthur looked out of the window as the car sped towards Reading, Patsy's words

194

repeating over and over in his mind. Cripple, she had called him a cripple.

'You're a bit quiet, mate. Are you upset about Patsy?'

'No, she's just a tart and I'm well rid of her.'

'You sure are, mate.'

Arthur only nodded. He was well rid of Patsy, and Sally too for that matter. Women, he was sick of them. Patsy had turned out to be a prostitute, and his wife a bloody liar. Sally had turned his parents and sister against him, but now he groaned softly. She had probably done it for revenge, and he could have told his family the truth. Instead he'd let his stubborn pride get in the way, playing into Sally's hands

'Nearly there,' Joe said.

Arthur nodded, his thoughts still turning. Once he had licked his wounds, he'd put his parents straight, his sister too, and then tell them that it was over with Patsy. He was still upset that they had chosen to believe Sally's lies, and wondered how they'd react when they found out the truth.

Nelly Cox was deep in thought too. She had finally accepted that a sole protest against the demolition would be a waste of time, but still couldn't bear the thought of leaving Candle Lane. She had moved here straight after her marriage, and other than her parents' house, it was the only home she'd known. What if the council wanted to stick her in one of those tower blocks? She'd heard that when the lifts broke down you had to climb hundreds of stairs to get to your front door. No, she didn't fancy being stuck in a flat miles from the ground. What sort of life was that!

It had been a while ago when that young Social Worker had knocked on her door, offering her a place in Osborn House, an old folks home. She had told her in no uncertain terms to bugger off. Old folks home indeed! But now Nelly was rethinking that decision. Would living in Osborn House be better than living in a tower block? Nelly doubted it, but there was only way to find out, and that was by going to have a look at the place before she made any decisions.

With her mind made up, she combed her hair and grabbed her battered handbag. Osborn House was a bus ride away, close to Battersea Park, but she'd only seen it on the outside. Now though she intended to see inside.

When she reached the stop in Long Street, Nelly found a bus pulling in, but being short and tubby she had difficulty climbing on to the platform.

When the young bus conductor saw her plight he jumped down to give her a hand. 'Come on, old girl,' he said, taking her elbow.

'Ta, love,' Nelly grinned, but then sobered. Old girl! Yes, she *was* getting old, but that didn't mean she was ready for the knacker's yard.

As the bus reached Battersea Park Road, Nelly frowned when she saw the huge council estates. So much had changed in the area, so many of the old streets gone, replaced by huge tower blocks, with tier after tier of windows, reaching up into the sky. They looked soulless, empty, and without streets there were no women to be seen chatting on doorsteps, no children playing games outside.

Nelly continued to gaze sadly at what had once been streets of terraced houses, knowing that Candle Lane would soon go the same way. She fought tears. Her old life was dying, along with her neighbourhood.

They were at the park now, and nearing her stop, Nelly rose to her feet. The conductor smiled at her, again coming to her assistance and holding her elbow as she got off. She thanked him and only a few steps further along the road, Osborn House loomed in front of her. She paused for a moment to wipe beads of perspiration from her forehead then, taking a deep breath, she stepped through the gate and into the grounds. They looked nice, she had to admit that, with pretty flowerbeds, planted out with petunias that were just starting to bloom, and benches scattered around.

Nelly saw an elderly lady sitting on a bench close to the path and hesitantly approached. If she could talk to a resident, she would hear from the horses' mouth what the place was like. 'Excuse me, dear. Can I have a word?'

The woman looked up and when their eyes met, Nelly's jaw dropped. 'Blimey, Peggy Green!'

'Gawd, stone the crows! Is that you, Nelly Cox?'

'I ain't an apparition, love. What are you doing here? When you were moved from Candle Lane I thought you'd been given a flat.'

'Yeah, that's right. But when me old man died the kids didn't like me living on me own. They said I couldn't manage, and I suppose they're right. I've been living here for six months now.'

'Couldn't you have moved in with one of your boys?'

'No, they ain't got room, but they come to see me every week.'

'Are you happy here?' Nelly asked as she plonked herself down beside Peggy.

'It's all right. I've got me own room and was allowed to bring some of me own furniture with me. I've even got me canary, but he's getting old now and doesn't sing anymore.'

'I've been offered a place here too, Peggy, though I'm not sure I want to take it.'

'I wasn't sure either. When I first moved in and saw the other residents, it felt like I'd been plonked here while waiting to pop me clogs.'

'Blimey, Peggy! I don't like the sound of that.'

'Nah, it's all right, Nelly. I soon found out I was wrong. We're well looked after, and we have occasional trips out. There's bingo twice a week and sometimes we have entertainment laid on. We even have dances.'

'Do you? That sounds all right.'

'It's better than living alone. There's always

someone to chat to, and though some of the residents are a bit doddery, there's others like us with a bit of life left in them.'

'I'm still not sure, Peggy.'

'Why don't you come inside and have a look round. I'll show you me room too.'

Nelly agreed, and in another hour she was on her way home again, her mind made up.

Seventeen

Denis Walters didn't call to see his son in the morning. Shaking her head with annoyance at his insensitivity, Sally took both children to school. She hadn't long been back when Mary called round.

'You're early, Auntie.'

'Yes, I know, but I've got a bit of news.'

'Oh yeah, and what's that?' Sadie asked.

'I've got my old job back at the surgery, and I can't tell you how pleased I am.'

'I thought you liked working at the hospital.'

'It's all right, but I don't like the shifts, especially being on Casualty Reception late at night.'

'Will you be on reception again in the surgery?'

'Yes, but unlike the hospital, I know the patients, and they know me.'

Sadie chuckled, 'Yeah, but I seem to remember that some called you an old dragon.'

'Yes, they did, but then some patients don't seem to realize how busy the doctors are and expect to see them straight away. It isn't always possible, especially if they get called out. Anyway, enough about me. How are you feeling, Sally?'

'I'm all right.'

'You still look dreadfully thin. Are you eating?'

'Yes,' Sally murmured.

'I know it's only been a couple of months, but you *will* get over it. It took me a while to get over breaking up with Leroy, but I'm all right now.'

Sally was glad that her aunt had moved on, but her own pain had hardly diminished. She made them a drink and listened to her gran telling Mary about the goings on next door.

'The boy's sleeping here until his father gets the funeral sorted out, and though he's a little hooligan, you can't help feeling sorry for him.'

'It's awful that he's lost his mother at such a young age.'

They continued to chat, but then an hour later, Mary said she had to leave. Sally walked with her to the door where her aunt gripped her hand. 'Oh, Sally, I wish there was something I could do, some way to get you and Arthur back together.'

'I don't want him back, Auntie. Anyway, he's got someone else now.'

Mary nodded sadly and Sally kissed her cheek, watching for a moment as her aunt walked along Candle Lane, her stance as usual upright and dignified. She looked every inch a lady, her head held high, and Sally was struck by how different she was from her mother, the two sisters like chalk and cheese.

The rest of the day passed slowly and now Sally was picking the children up from school. Poor Tommy looked so sad, his shoulders slumped as he walked along beside her, and for a treat Sally took them into the corner shop for some sweets.

Both children made their selections, one of Angel's being a sherbet fountain, and Tommy's a gobstopper. Now they were walking along Candle Lane and as they drew level with Tommy's street door he darted forward and rattled the letter box. 'I'm gonna see me dad.'

'He may not be in,' Sally warned, but the words had hardly left her mouth when the front door opened and they saw Denis Walters swaying on the step.

'I thought you were Andrew,' he slurred. 'I eshpected him to be here by now.'

'Yer drunk,' Tommy said, his mouth set in a scowl as he looked up at his father.

'Just drowning me shorrows. You can't blame a man for that.'

'Come on, Tommy. Leave your dad for a while.'

'Yeah, go with Shally,' Denis said. 'I'll be round later.'

'Who's Andrew?' Tommy asked.

'He's yer uncle and you'll see him later, but first he and I have things to talk about.'

'I don't remember him.'

'Course you don't. He hasn't been to see us for years.'

'Come on, Tommy,' Sally insisted. 'I don't like leaving Gran for long.'

The boy reluctantly turned away, following her into number five. Sadie was snoozing, and indicating that they be quiet, Sally sat both children at the kitchen table with crayons and colouring books.

Sally then began to prepare the vegetables for dinner, her thoughts drifting to Arthur as another potato joined the pot. Why couldn't she put him from her mind? Her marriage was over, and she had to accept that. There were times when she thought of Mary's words, her aunt somehow sure that there had been a misunderstanding about the divorce, but always her thoughts came back to the same thing. What did it matter? Arthur had someone else now. Yet despite the pain there was no hiding away from her feelings. She still loved him, would always love him, and once again tears flooded her eyes.

The quietness was short-lived as the children began to squabble, fighting over the same colour crayon, and then Sadie's voice rang out.

'For Gawd's sake, Sally, sort these kids out. They're giving me a bleedin' headache.'

'All right, Gran,' she placated, hiding her tears. 'Now that's enough, you two. If you don't behave yourself there'll be no telly later on and you'll miss *Blue Peter*.'

'Can we go out to play?' Angel appealed.

'Yes, all right, but don't dare leave Candle Lane. And that goes for you too, Tommy.'

'But I wanna see my gang.'

'You can do without your gang for once. I'm relying on you to keep an eye on Angel.'

His lower lip stuck out belligerently. 'I ain't a bleedin' babysitter, you know.'

'I'm not a baby!' Angel protested.

'Out!' Sally shouted.

'But he called me a baby,' and marching up to Tommy she shoved him in the chest. 'I don't like you, and I ain't playing with you.'

'Good! Yer a girl and I don't play wiv girls.'

'Now listen, you two,' Sally snapped. 'If you don't stop arguing I'll put the pair of you to bed.'

'He started it!'

'I ain't staying here. I'm going home.'

Sally heaved a sigh and put a hand on the boy's arm. 'Listen, love, you can't go home until your dad comes to fetch you. Now how about the two of you make up and play outside for a while until dinner's ready.'

Tommy looked rebellious for a moment, but as Sally widened her eyes in appeal he said, 'Yeah, all right,' and going up to Angel he held out his little finger. 'Pax.'

Angel hooked hers around it. 'Yeah, pax.'

'Right, off you go, and don't forget. Stay in the lane.'

When both children had left a blissful silence fell on the kitchen, only to be broken by a loud knock on the door.

'Christ, ain't we gonna get any peace,' Sadie snapped. 'Who the bleedin' hell is that?'

'I can't see through walls, Gran,' Sally replied. When she opened the door she found Nelly Cox on the step.

'Come in,' she invited, trying to put a welcoming smile on her face. In truth she felt like her gran and would have welcomed a bit of peace, but there was no way she'd turn this lovely old lady away.

'Wotcher, Sadie. How are you?' Nelly asked as she followed Sally into the kitchen.

'Fine, and what are you looking so cheerful about?'

'I'm moving out of Candle Lane in a couple of weeks.'

'What! Have you been offered a place already?'

'You could say that, Sadie. I've decided to move into Osborn House.'

'Are you mad! It's an old people's home.'

'I know, but I've been to see it and would rather be in Osborn House than stuck in a tower block. Peggy Green has been in there for a while and she likes it.'

'Nelly, start at the beginning,' Sadie urged. 'You've lost me.'

Sally listened to the conversation, surprised at Nelly's decision, but maybe the old lady was right. Perhaps it would be better for her to live amongst people of her own age, than to live alone.

Angel and Tommy were watching a man who had turned into the lane.

'Do you fink he's me uncle?'

'He might be,' Angel replied, 'but he's a bit old. Come on, let's ask him.'

The two children ran up to the man, Tommy saying, 'Are you me Uncle Andrew?'

'I might be, lad. Now I knew a baby called Thomas many years ago, but surely this big strapping lad in front of me can't be him.'

'Thomas,' Angel spluttered, liking this man with his funny way of talking. 'He ain't Thomas. His name is Tommy.'

The man smiled, but there was a tinge of sadness in his eyes. 'And what is your name, lassie?'

'I'm Angel.'

'And a bonny angel you are too.'

Tommy tugged on his arm, asking again, 'Are you me uncle?'

'If you're Tommy Walters, then yes I am. Now, how about we go and have a word with your father?'

'He's in there,' Tommy said, pointing to his front door.

'Aren't you coming in with me?'

'Nah, me dad's pissed. I'm staying next door.'

For a moment the man looked shocked, but then he crouched down in front of Tommy. 'I'm sorry to hear about your mother, lad.'

Tommy lowered his head, his little teeth biting on his bottom lip. Seeing this Andrew drew the boy into his arms. 'There's no shame in tears,' he murmured.

Angel hovered as Tommy settled against his uncle for a while, but then the man said, 'I must talk to your father, lad.'

Tommy cuffed his face, both children watching as his uncle knocked on the door. Denis Walters opened it, and after inviting the man in, the door closed abruptly again.

'He seems nice,' Angel said.

'Yeah, and he's got ginger hair like you. Anyway, don't you dare tell me mates that I cuddled him.'

'Why not?'

''Cos I don't want them to think I'm a cissie.'

Angel looked a bit bemused, but said, 'All right, I won't tell them, but I want a suck on your gobstopper.'

And with the resilience of the young Tommy sprinted off, shouting, 'You've got to catch me first.'

'Well, Denis,' Andrew said, 'I didn't expect to find you in this state, but I suppose I can understand you having a drink or two. I didn't take it well when I lost my wife.'

'I didn't know, and I'm shorry to hear that,' Denis slurred.

'I did write to Laura but she never replied. Mind you, I wrote to your old address so she may not have got it.'

'Yesh, that's probably it. Do you want a drop of whisky?'

'No thanks. I just met Tommy outside and he's a nice looking lad.'

'He ain't a bad kid, but he's had it rough for a while.'

'Rough! What do you mean?'

Andrew listened as Denis began to speak, the man often stumbling over his words, and found he had to fight his growing anger. The man was moronic, bemoaning his life, and it soon became obvious that he was after money. Maybe it was the drink talking, but when he insinuated that he couldn't look after his own son, Andrew didn't want to hear any more. 'Listen, man, let's try to sober you up. We can't talk while you're in this state.'

'I'm all right,' he said, his hand reaching for the bottle again.

'No,' Andrew said sharply, 'you've had enough and I think you had better sleep it off. Come on, show me where your bedroom is.'

Denis protested, but the drink overcame him and he allowed himself to be led upstairs. When he saw the bed he backed away, 'No! No.'

Andrew ignored his protest, pressing him down, Denis mumbling as he fell on his side, 'Laura, Laura,' and then clutching a pillow he almost immediately passed out.

Andrew looked around the spartan room and shook his head. God, who'd have thought his sister's life would have come to this? The kitchen had been bad enough, but this room was even worse. Guilt flooded him and he cursed himself for not keeping in touch with Laura. She may have run away, may have married a useless waster, but she deserved better than this.

He'd been saddened when Denis had told him that their little girl had died, but also angry. The man knew that Laura had a heart defect, and knew that she shouldn't have children. Why hadn't he done something to prevent it? The strain on his sister's heart must have been enormous, and God knows how much extra damage had been done.

He looked briefly at his brother-in-law and his mouth pursed in distaste. Laura had survived two pregnancies, only to land up in a filthy hovel like this. He remembered the young, pretty girl Laura had been, a girl who, despite her health, was determined to live a full life.

Three hours passed and still Denis slept on, snoring loudly. Andrew checked on him then trailed back downstairs, his stomach rumbling with hunger, but looking in the kitchen cupboards there was little food to be seen. With nothing else for it, he decided to find a local café or restaurant, and without keys to get back in, he hoped Denis would be awake by the time he returned.

There wasn't much activity as Andrew stepped on to Candle Lane, just a few children playing with marbles in the gutter, and glancing swiftly at the house next door he wondered when he'd get a chance to see his nephew again. The little girl who'd been with him was cute, with red, unruly hair and a cheeky smile. He frowned, thinking that she reminded him of someone, but then his tummy rumbled again, the thought of food once again becoming uppermost in his mind as he made his way to the main road.

It had been a long time since he'd been in London and, eyeing the huge factories that lined the road, he hoped it would be a long time before he was here again. Scotland beckoned, the green hills calling, and for a while his thoughts dwelled on his late wife. He'd known Moira all his life, her family living close by, and they married six months before the war. She became pregnant almost immediately, but then he'd been called up, his son nine months old before he was given leave.

His mind shied away from the intimate side of his marriage and the farce it became, focusing now on his son. Donald was a grown man now, married to a lovely girl, and with his first grandchild on the way, Andrew hoped he'd soon be able to return to Scotland.

There was a café a little further along and, as Andrew approached it, he hoped his parents were all right. They were both elderly, and though he'd asked his son to keep an eye on them, he hated being so far away. How long would it take to arrange Laura's funeral? At least a week, he decided, his heart sinking.

Eighteen

'Oh, Arthur,' Elsie cried, 'why didn't you tell us this before?'

'You all chose to believe Sally, and I was angry, Mum. You condemned me without a trial.'

'What do you expect?' Bert snapped. 'You'd hardly been home for five minutes when you slept with that girl, and you can't deny that.'

'I'm not denying it, Dad, but despite what Sally told you, I didn't move her in, and I had no intentions of marrying her.'

'You carried on sleeping with her though.'

Arthur knew that what his father said was true and lowered his eyes. The sex with Patsy had become like an obsession, and for a while he couldn't get enough of her, but he could hardly tell his parents that. She had consumed him, doing things to him that aroused him to fever pitch, things that he'd never done with Sally. A wave of nausea had him gulping. Christ, she was a prostitute, but he couldn't face telling his parents. Instead he'd just said that they'd broken up as they weren't getting on any more.

'I still can't believe that Sally lied to us,' Elsie said. 'It's so unlike her.'

'Well, she did, and it was her idea to get a divorce, not mine.'

Elsie ran a hand through her hair. 'None of this makes sense. I think your father and I need to talk to Sally.'

'Why? Don't you believe me?'

'Oh, son, I don't know what to think. Until now you never denied that Patsy was living with you, or that you were going to marry her.'

'But I've told you why. Listen, Mum, if you don't believe me you can ask Joe. He knows that Patsy didn't move in, and that I had no intention of marrying her.'

Elsie gazed at Arthur's face, sure that her son was telling the truth. 'So why do you think Sally lied to us?'

'I think, by causing a rift between us, it was her way of getting revenge.'

'Well, you can't blame her for that,' Bert snapped.

'Maybe not, but if she'd been a proper wife, none of this would have happened.'

'Arthur,' Elsie said, reaching forward to lay a hand on his arm, 'let's go back to the beginning. I know you think that Sally was repulsed by your leg, but she assured me she wasn't. I think you may have been oversensitive and imagined it. She might have kept a distance between you in bed, but that was because she was afraid of knocking your stump.'

Arthur shook his head, 'That's not how I remember it.'

'Well, son, it's how Sally remembers it, and it

211

seems to me that the two of you got your wires crossed.'

'Maybe,' Arthur conceded.

'Why don't you talk to her?' Elsie urged.

'No, Mum. Not after the lies she's told.'

'For Christ's sake,' Bert snapped. 'All right, Sally may have told a few fibs, but that's nothing in comparison to what you've done. She was by your side the whole time you were in hospital, and despite what she went through, culminating in a miscarriage, she pulled herself together for your sake. Whilst you, Christ, you hadn't been home for more than five minutes when had it off with that bloody slut.'

'Don't be crude, Bert.'

'Sorry, love, but he makes my blood boil. If it happened once it would have been bad enough, but he's been carrying on with that girl since Sally left him. When she caught him with that tart, he didn't go to see her, didn't once try to get her back, but now he's got the cheek to sit there full of self-righteousness because Sally told a few lies.'

'Listen, Dad, at first there wouldn't have been any point in going to Candle Lane. As Patsy said, Sally needed time to cool down, and I took her advice. Then, when Angel sneaked round here and Sally came to fetch her, she made her feeling plain. According to Patsy, she didn't want to see me, or talk to me, and said that she was going to file for a divorce.'

Bert's eyes narrowed, 'So, it was Patsy who told you that Sally wanted a divorce?'

'Yes, that's right.'

'And you believed her.'

'Why shouldn't I? And not only that, Patsy also told me that Sally was going to deny me access to Angel.'

'Is that why you went to see a solicitor?' Elsie asked.

'Well, yes. Sally didn't leave me any choice.'

'Arthur,' Elsie said, and unlike his father, her voice was soft, 'according to Sally, *you* were the one who put in for a divorce first – not her.'

'But that isn't true. It's another one of her lies.'

'Christ, son, that slut has been leading you around by the nose and I can't believe you've been so gullible,' Bert snapped.

'What do you mean?'

'Arthur,' his mother said, 'can't you see that it isn't Sally who's been telling lies. It's Patsy. She's been stirring it, adding fuel to the fire, and worse, you let her.'

At his mother's words, Arthur hung his head, his thoughts racing as he looked back at all the things that Patsy had said and done. They were right, of course they were, and he felt sick inside at his own stupid gullibility. He hadn't tried to talk to Sally, but instead he'd been led on by everything Patsy said.

'Arthur, why don't you go to see Sally?'

'No, it's too late. Dad's right, if it had been just once with Patsy, I might have had a chance, but not now.'

'Does Sally know that you've broken up with

213

Patsy?'

'No, Mum.'

'Don't you think you should tell her?'

'I'll mention it when she next brings Angel round, but it won't change anything.'

Elsie sighed and then said, 'Well, son, we've got to go, but why don't you come to dinner on Sunday, and in the meantime, I'll have a word with Sally.'

'It'll be a waste of time, but I'd love to come to dinner with you,' Arthur said and, after hugging his mother, he walked with them to the door, pleased that there had been a reconciliation.

However, his mood was still low as he returned to the living room. His mother said she would talk to Sally, but he doubted it would do any good. She'd never forgive him, and he couldn't blame her.

Elsie climbed into the car, waving at Arthur as they drove off. 'Come on, Bert,' she said as the car turned the corner. 'Let's go and have a word with Sally.'

'All right, but it's Arthur who should talk to her, not us.'

'Maybe, but at least we can even the ground.'

Bert nodded, and it was after nine thirty on that Friday evening when they pulled up in Candle Lane.

Elsie knocked on the door and a startled Sally opened it, but she soon recovered, saying, 'Hello, come on in. I'm afraid Angel's in bed and asleep.'

'It's you we've come to talk to.'

They followed Sally through to the kitchen, Ruth looking surprised to see them too. 'Hello, love,' Elsie said, then she added, 'Where's Sadie?'

'She's a bit under the weather with a cold and has gone to bed. What brings you here at this time of night?'

'We've just come from Arthur's and there's something Sally should know.'

'Is he all right?' Sally asked, her eyes wide.

'Yes, he's fine,' Elsie said, gratified to see Sally's concern as she flopped down on to the sofa. 'But he's broken up with Patsy.'

'Broken up with her? Why?'

'Apparently they weren't getting on.'

'It seems a bit sudden. They're supposed to be getting married when the divorce comes through.'

'No, Sally, that isn't true, and we don't know where you got that idea from.'

'Arthur told me.'

'Did he, Sally? Think about it. Did Arthur actually say that he and Patsy were getting married?'

Sally frowned and was quiet for a moment before answering. 'Well, no, it was Patsy who told me, but Arthur didn't deny it.'

'You've both been taken for mugs,' Elsie said, her voice growing animated as she gripped Sally's arm. 'That Patsy's been telling lies all along. She told Arthur that you were going to file for a divorce and were going to stop him from seeing Angel.'

'But that isn't true.'

'Yes, we know that now, but that's why Arthur sought legal advice,' Elsie said, going on to tell Sally that it had been Patsy causing all the mischief. 'She was obviously out to get Arthur, but he didn't let her move in with him, despite what she told you. Please, won't you talk to him? It isn't too late to save your marriage.'

Once again Sally was quiet, but then she shook her head. 'It is too late. All right, Patsy told lies, stirred things up, but at the end of the day, Arthur still slept with her. Not once, not twice, but many, many times. I can't forgive him, Elsie.'

Ruth had been quiet, but now she spoke, 'She's right, Elsie. If it had been just once, it would've been bad enough, but he's been carrying on with that tart for ages.'

Elsie's eyes flashed as she turned to Ruth, 'What about Angel? Surely the marriage is worth saving for her sake?'

'Angel's fine. She sees Arthur once a week and is perfectly happy living here with us.'

'Now you listen to me, Ruth—'

'Leave it, Elsie,' Bert said. 'Sally's made her decision, and as far as I'm concerned, it's no more than Arthur deserves. Now come on, it's late and time we left.'

Elsie knew by her husband's tone that it would be useless to argue. She'd leave it for

216

now, but she wasn't going to give up. Some-how, she was determined to get Sally and Arthur back together.

After giving her in-laws a hug, Sally saw them out, and when she returned to the kitchen it was to find her mother stiff with indignation.

'I can't believe that Elsie expects you to take Arthur back.'

'I know, Mum.'

'Well, don't listen to her, my girl. And how come she's doing all the talking for Arthur? It strikes me that he should be the one to come round here, begging on his hands and bloody knees for your forgiveness. But he hasn't, has he? No, he's left it to his mother to act as spokesperson.'

Sally nodded tiredly. Her mother was right, and sadly she said, 'I think I'll have an early night too.'

'All right, love. Sleep tight.'

Sally kissed her and then feeling drained she disconsolately climbed the stairs to her bed-room. Angel was asleep, thumb in her mouth as usual, and for a moment Sally gazed down on her daughter wondering about their future. The lane was to be demolished, and they could be rehoused anywhere, assuming of course that it would be in a place big enough for them all. If not she faced living alone, without her mother and gran, and dreaded it.

Slowly she undressed, climbing into bed, hugging the pillow as tears welled. She couldn't forgive Arthur, she just couldn't, and even now, still etched in her memory, was the sight of the ecstasy on his face when she had caught him making love to Patsy. The betrayal was like a knife in her heart, and despite time passing, the wound still felt fresh. She sobbed, knowing that she could never take him back, but also knowing that despite everything, she still loved him.

Nineteen

Sally was still feeling low the following morning, but managed to hide it. Poor Tommy had just lost his mother, and needed them. She made breakfast, and then took a tray through to her gran's room.

'Are you feeling any better?'

'Yeah, it's just a cold. You didn't have to bring me a cup of tea in bed. I'll be up soon.'

'Trust you to catch a cold in June, Gran. Still, it's Saturday and there's no harm in having a lie in.'

'Yeah, it's all right for some,' Ruth said as she came into the room, 'But I've got to go to work. I'll see you later.'

'Yes, see you,' Sadie said, propping herself up on one elbow.

Sally left the room with her mother, and when they went back to the kitchen Ruth grabbed her handbag before crouching down to give Tommy a cuddle. He clung on, not wanting her to leave, his eyes wet with unshed tears.

For a moment Angel looked sulky, her jealousy obvious, but then Ruth let go of the boy and cuddled her granddaughter, whispering, 'Tommy's just lost his mum and he's a bit upset. Be nice to him, love.'

Angel looked confused. 'Lost her? But I thought she was deaded.'

Ruth looked to Sally, who, taking her cue, said, 'Come on, you two. Breakfast is ready.'

The children went to the table and Ruth was able to slip out, but just as they'd finished eating someone came to the door. Sally opened it to see Denis Walters, accompanied by an older man with red hair and, as she invited them in she wondered why the man was giving her such a strange look. 'Er ... can I get you anything.'

'No thanks,' Denis said. 'We're going to sort out the death certificate, and then to see the undertaker. Do you mind looking after Tommy?'

'Of course I don't mind."

'Thanks, love, it's good of you.'

Tommy ran up to his father, clinging to his trousers. 'I want to come wiv you and me uncle.'

'It's no place for you,' Denis said sharply, pushing the boy away.

Tommy's uncle tousled the boy's hair, his voice placatory, 'We won't be long, lad, and when we come back you and I can get better acquainted.' He then turned to Sally. 'Hello, I'm Tommy's uncle, and it's kind of you to look after him.'

'Hello,' Sally murmured, taken by this man's kind demeanour.

'There's one more thing, Sally,' Denis said. 'Would it be all right for Tommy to sleep here at night until after the funeral? Andrew has come down from Scotland and needs the boy's bed.'

'No,' Andrew protested. 'There's no need to put the lad out of his bed. I can find a hotel.'

'There's no need for that,' Sally told him. 'Tommy is welcome to sleep here.'

'Thanks, it's good of you,' Denis said. 'Come on, Andrew, we'd best be off. And you, Tommy, see that you behave yourself.'

Sadie came into the room, her eyes flicking from one man to the other before she focused on Denis. 'I'm sorry to hear about your wife, and she was so young too.'

'Thanks,' and remembering the introductions this time he added, 'This is Laura's brother, Andrew.'

Sadie cocked her head to one side, her eyes puzzled as she looked at the man. 'Have I met you before?'

'No, I don't think so, Mrs ... er ... .'

'Mrs Greenbroke, but you can call me Sadie.'

'Well, Sadie, it's nice to meet you.'

'Come on, let's go,' Denis urged.

Angel had been quiet the whole time the two men were there, but as they left she said, 'I like

220

Tommy's uncle. Nanny likes him too.'

Sally frowned, wondering why her mother hadn't mentioned that she'd met the man, but then hearing a small sob she turned to find Tommy sitting on the floor, his head low.

She crouched down beside him, pulling his skinny body into her arms and as his head burrowed into her chest he choked, 'I want me mum.'

For a short while the only sounds to be heard were Sally's gentle murmurings and the boy's sobs, but then Angel ran across the room and squatted down beside them. 'Tommy,' she said, 'you can share my mummy if you like.'

Sally smiled at her daughter over Tommy's head. Yes, she could be impossible. Yes, she could be captious and spoiled, but there was also this gentle and sensitive side to her nature. It also seemed that she had an intuitiveness about people, and once again her dislike of Patsy came to mind. Her ears pricked up as Tommy answered.

'Fanks, Angel, and you can share my uncle wiv me.'

'Oh, good,' Angel said. 'He's nice.'

As Andrew walked along the road with Denis, the man was once again bemoaning his life. He felt sorry for his brother-in-law, but even so felt his anger mounting. The man was a drinker, a heavy one, and it was obvious he had no time for his son.

'I ain't got the money to pay for Laura's

funeral,' Denis now said. 'I don't know what I'm going to do.'

'I'll pay for it,' Andrew snapped.

'I can't let you do that,' Denis protested.

'If you're broke, what choice is there?'

'None, I suppose, but believe me, I'm not proud that I haven't the money to bury my wife.'

'Laura's my sister, and as I said, I'll pay. I'm only sorry that I didn't do more for her when she was alive.'

Denis nodded slowly, then said, 'I don't know what I'm gonna do about Tommy. He's a good kid, but I don't know how I'm going to look after him.'

Andrew's lips tightened. 'If you stopped drinking it might help!'

'Look, I know I ain't been the best father in the world, but now I only want what's right for the boy.'

'Then as I said – stop drinking.'

Denis scowled. 'I'll need to work to pay the rent, and how am I supposed to do that with a kid to look after?'

'You could pay someone to look after him while you're at work.'

'Yeah, maybe, but it would cost a pretty penny.'

Andrew said nothing, sensing that the man was after money again. Yes, he could offer financial help, but Denis would just blow it on drink. The boy needed stability, yet he doubted he'd get that from his father. He would've liked to offer Tommy a home, but it was impossible. He lived alone, and his job as a surveyor sometimes entailed long hours. His parents, even if they had wanted to, couldn't help. Nowadays they could barely look after themselves, let alone a small boy.

The problem continued to play on his mind, but many hours later he still hadn't found an answer.

At five thirty, Ruth was glad to make her way home from work. It had been a busy day and her feet were aching. Poor Tommy had been on her mind all day and she hoped he was all right.

Once again she worried about his future, but she'd been giving it a lot of thought and as far as she was concerned there was only one answer. Denis was incapable of looking after his son, and surely he would see the sense of letting Tommy live with her. It wouldn't be easy, but with Sally's help it would work out all right, and at least the boy would have a better life than being brought up by that no good drunk Denis Walters. She would wait until the funeral was over and then have a talk with the man. Surely he'd see things her way?

At last she turned on to Candle Lane, her feet throbbing, but with home in sight she picked up her pace, smiling with delight when Tommy ran full pelt to greet her, Angel in his wake.

As Tommy reached her, Ruth held out her arms. 'Hello, darling. Are you all right?'

'Yeah,' he said. 'I've seen me uncle and he's nice.'

Angel joined in the circle. 'Did you get me any sweets, Nanny?'

'Yes, darling, some for Tommy too,' she said, digging into her bag and pulling out two small paper bags.

'Fanks!' Tommy said, avidly clutching his.

'Are you coming in now?'

'Not yet. Mummy said we can play out until dinner's ready.'

Ruth nodded and, after ruffling both children's hair, she went indoors, glad to sit down and kick off her shoes.

'Tommy said his uncle's nice. Have you met him, Sally?'

'Yes, he came round with Denis this morning.'

'What was he like?'

Sally eyes widened. 'Why ask that when you've already met him?'

'I haven't.'

'That's odd. Angel was taken with Tommy's uncle and said that you like him too.'

'Think about it, Sally. What chance have I had to meet the man?'

'It's about time that kid was sleeping in his own home,' Sadie interrupted. 'But now he's going to be kipping here until after the funeral.'

'Mum, he hasn't been any trouble, and anyway you might have to get used to seeing more of him.'

'What's that supposed to mean?'

224

'I want to take him on. He'd have a better life with me than with his father.'

'Huh, you think you can move him in here, do you? You're forgetting something, Ruth. The lane is coming down and we're to be rehomed. We might only be offered two bedrooms, so how are we all going to fit in? There'll be you and me, Sally and Angel. Two bedrooms might not be enough for the four of us, let alone Tommy Walters.'

Ruth sank back in her chair, the breath leaving her body in a rush. Christ, she hadn't thought of that! Annoyed she said, 'Don't gloat, Mum. I know you don't want the boy living with us, but you never know, if I explain things to the council they might give us a bigger place.'

'Yeah, and pigs might fly. Anyway, you're off your head wanting to take that kid on. You ain't getting any younger, you know.'

'Thanks, Mum, it's kind of you to point that out, but I'm still quite capable of looking after a small boy.'

'With you at work it strikes me that it'll be Sally who gets lumbered – not you!'

'Sally won't mind, will you, love?' Ruth asked as she looked at her daughter.

'Mum, as I told you before, even if the council gives you a two bedroom place, there still might not be enough room for me and Angel. I might have to find somewhere else to live.'

'But what about your gran?'

'I'll have to make sure it's close by, and then it will be the same arrangement as before.'

Ruth sat quietly for a moment, hating the thought of her daughter moving out again and going over the logistics, she shook her head decisively. 'There'll be no need for you to move out. As long as our new flat has a decent sized kitchen, we can use the living room for Mum as we do now. Then you and Angel can have one of the bedrooms, and if I get custody of Tommy, we can share the other one.'

'Yes, that would be all right for a while, but once the kids get older, they can hardly share our bedrooms.'

'We'll worry about that when the time comes. Sufficient unto the day, as the saying goes.'

'All right, Mum, I suppose it could work, but I wouldn't count your chickens about Tommy yet. I have a feeling his uncle might sort something out.'

'What sort of feeling?' Ruth asked sharply 'Is it one of your funny psychic ones?'

'I'm not sure, but something tells me that Tommy won't be living here.'

Ruth felt her heart sink and standing up she stuffed her swollen feet back into her shoes. 'Christ, Sally, I hope you're wrong. In fact, I'd better meet this uncle.'

'All right, but dinner's nearly ready so don't be long.'

Ruth nodded and as she left the house Tommy and Angel came running up to her again, their mouths full of sweets, and it was Angel who managed to speak, 'Where you going, Nanny?'

'I'm just popping next door to Tommy's

house. You two stay out here.'

'All right,' Angel agreed, both children running off to play with a few other children again.

Ruth watched them for a moment, a soft smile on her face, and then knocked on Denis's door. 'Hello,' she said when he opened it. 'Can I have a word?'

'Yeah, come on in,' he said.

Ruth could smell the alcohol on his breath, and now began to worry. Was Laura's brother as bad? Was he a drinker too? Huh, if he was, there was no way she was going to leave Tommy in their care. 'I see you've been drinking, Denis,' she said, unable to keep the note of disapproval from her voice.

'Yeah, but don't look at me like that, Ruth. I've had enough of that from Andrew. He doesn't approve either, but the pair of you seem to have forgotten that I've just lost my wife.'

'And Tommy has just lost his mother,' Ruth snapped.

'Tommy's all right.'

'Did you manage to get the funeral sorted out?'

'Yes, nearly everything's been arranged, and thankfully Andrew is going to pay for it.'

'That's good,' and flicking her eyes around the room she added, 'I was hoping to meet him.'

'He's just popped down to the corner shop, but he'll be back soon. Do you want to wait?'

Ruth nodded. 'Is he close to Tommy?'

'Not really. He hasn't seen the boy since he

227

was a baby.'

'Oh, I see,' Ruth said, her mind racing. Surely Denis would see that even if the boy's uncle offered him a home, it would be like living with a stranger. Should she make her offer now? What if the man left soon? What if he took Tommy with him?

She was about to speak when there was a knock on the door, Denis saying, 'That's probably Andrew now. I'll go and let him in.'

Blast, Ruth thought. She had missed her opportunity. Denis came back into the room, a man behind him, and even after all these years the recognition was instantaneous. 'No! Oh no,' she gasped, 'it can't be!' The room began to tilt and she had a vague notion of him moving towards her, his voice barely reaching her ears as blackness descended.

'Ruth. My God! Ruth!'

Twenty

When Ruth opened her eyes she saw Andrew leaning over her, his voice concerned as he asked. 'Are you all right?'

Her vision cleared, and then her mind, the question bursting from her lips, 'How ... how did you find me?'

'Ruth, I wasn't trying to find you. I'm here for

228

my sister's funeral and had no idea that you lived in this area.'

Denis now spoke, his expression puzzled. 'How do you two know each other?'

'It's a long story,' Andrew said, 'but for now would you do me a favour. Would you go out for a drink or something? Ruth and I need to talk in private.

'I suppose so, but I've no money.'

Ruth saw a flicker of annoyance in Andrew's eyes, but then he pulled out a few notes, thrusting them into Denis's hand. Her mind was still confused. Andrew said he was here for his sister's funeral. Laura! Surely he didn't mean Laura? It seemed impossible to comprehend – a chance in a million. Of all the places in London, Andrew's sister had ended up living in Candle Lane.

When Denis left, Andrew turned to face her again and Ruth's breath caught in her throat. My God, no wonder she had been so taken with Tommy. It was so obvious now, the family resemblance plain.

'This has been a shock for both of us,' he said, sitting down beside her and smiling faintly. 'Do you know you've hardly changed, yet how long has it been? God, it must be about twenty-four years!'

'You haven't changed much either. Maybe a bit less hair, but I knew you instantly. You said you were here for your sister's funeral. Surely you don't mean Laura? She was only in her late twenties or early thirties.'

229

'My parents had her late in life and there a huge age gap between us.'

Ruth still couldn't believe that Andrew was sitting beside her. She took in most of what he said, but her own thoughts were racing. He'd seen her. How could he not know? God, should she tell him?

As Ruth continued to listen to his voice, the soft Edinburgh tones bringing back memories, another part of her mind was still floundering. Andrew was married, he had a son, and when Laura's funeral was over he'd go back to Scotland. Perhaps it was better to let sleeping dogs lie. If she told him it would have a profound effect on his life – on *all* their lives.

'As you can see,' Andrew now said, 'there's a lot to sort out, and I may be here for another week or so.'

'A ... a week,' Ruth squeaked. It seemed he hadn't twigged yet, but if he saw her again, surely he'd put two and two together.

'Yes, but don't look so worried. Denis doesn't need to know about us, and surely after all this time you're not worried about your husband?'

'Husband!' Ruth blurted out, 'But I haven't got a husband. We divorced many years ago.'

Andrew frowned. 'But you looked almost frightened when I said I'd be here for over a week.'

God, she couldn't think straight, couldn't get her fuddled mind in order and now kicked herself. 'No ... no, I didn't. You must be mistaken.'

His look was doubtful for a moment, but then he smiled. 'So, you're divorced. I'm on my own too. I lost my wife just over a year ago.'

'I'm sorry to hear that,' Ruth said, her mind jumping again. Andrew was on his own. Did that make a difference? It was too much to take in and her head was beginning to thump. She needed to be on her own, to have time to think. Andrew's closeness was having an effect on her, one that after all these years, she was surprised to feel.

She rose to her feet. 'I must go, but if you're going to be around for another week or so, perhaps we can talk another time.'

'I'd love to see you again. How about I take you out to dinner? In fact, how does tomorrow sound?'

Ruth gulped. How would Andrew feel when he found out? Would he be angry? Yes, probably. 'Tomorrow, I ... I'm not sure,' she stammered.

'Tell me where you live and I'll pick you up at seven o'clock.'

'Live? But I thought you knew. I've been looking after Tommy. I live next door.' Ruth saw him frown again and kicked herself again. Why couldn't she think straight? She had to keep them apart or he'd make the connection. Before he could speak she hurried to the door, calling as she left, 'I must go now. I ... I'll let you know about dinner.'

Ruth almost burst through the door, Sally saying, 'Mum, you've been ages and dinner's

231

almost ruined.' She then cocked her head to one side, adding, 'Are you all right?'

'Yes ... yes I'm fine,' she said, desperately trying to hide her feelings. 'Sorry I was so long. Come on then, let's get this dinner dished up.'

Sally looked at her a bit strangely, but started to drain the vegetables. Ruth took a pan from her and spooned potatoes on to plates, relieved when her daughter called the children in.

'So, what did you think of Tommy's uncle?' Sally asked as they sat down to eat.

'Wh ... what?'

'You're miles away, Mum. I asked you what you think of Tommy's uncle.'

'I like him,' Tommy interrupted.

'Yes, and Nanny does too,' Angel said.

'Yes, that reminds me, Mum,' Sally said. 'As I said before, Angel seems to think that you already know the man. Is she right?'

'For God's sake,' Ruth blustered, fear making her voice loud, 'can't I eat my dinner in peace without being asked stupid questions?'

'What's stupid about it?' Sadie asked. 'Either you know the man or you don't, and there's no need to shout at Sally.'

'Whether I know the man or not is my business and I've a right to a bit of privacy!'

Sadie's forehead furrowed. 'Privacy! What's privacy got to do with anything?'

Ruth shook her head, 'As I said, that's my business,' and for the rest of the meal she refused to say another word. Her mind was racing, her stomach churning, so much so that most of her dinner remained on her plate.

If Sally found out, how would she react? Oh God, what was she going to do?

And at seven thirty that evening when she was putting Tommy to bed, Ruth still had no answers.

At the same time in Maple Terrace, Arthur sat gazing into space. Since his parents had been to see him, he'd had to face the truth and it wasn't pleasant. He knew now that Patsy wasn't just a prostitute, she was a mischief maker too, and he'd been too wrapped up in anger and pride to see it.

Christ, what had happened to him since he'd come out of hospital? What sort of man had he turned into? He'd let Patsy manipulate him, fool him, and it was only now that he was thinking straight. She still lived upstairs, and he still heard her going in and out, but so far he hadn't laid eyes on her.

Arthur stood up and walked across the room, his leg still a little sore, but he wasn't going to give in and use his stick again. For God's sake, he thought, continuing to berate himself. His mother said that Sally had kept a distance between them because she had been afraid of hurting his stump, and now he realized that it explained everything. He should have talked to her, told her that his wound wasn't giving him any pain. Instead he'd believed the worst.

He walked to the window, just in time to see Joe's car pulling up outside and felt a sense of relief. They were going out for a drink, and he welcomed it, glad to be out of the house and away from his brooding. He waved to Joe, indicating that he'd be straight out, and saying as he got into the car, 'Hello, mate.'

'Wotcher. What pub do you fancy?'

'Any one will do me, and I intend to have a skinful.'

'Really, and what brought this on?'

Arthur told Joe about the reconciliation with his parents, then going on to admit that he'd been wrong about Sally, finally saying, 'I thought she saw me as less than a man."

'Yeah, I suppose I can see why you got the wrong end of the stick about Sally, but it doesn't really excuse you for sleeping with Patsy.'

'I know that but, despite my bravado, I came out of hospital on the defensive, looking for things that weren't there, and I realize that now—' Arthur's eyes narrowed. Joe had turned into Candle Lane.

He pulled up outside number five, and then turned, smiling faintly, 'Arthur, it isn't me you need to tell, it's Sally.'

'No, mate, she won't want to talk to me, and I don't blame her.'

'Listen, maybe she'll shut the door in your face, but she still deserves an apology and the least you can do is to offer one.'

Arthur bit his lower lip. It was true, Sally did deserve an apology, but she'd be bringing Angel to see him tomorrow and he'd talk to her then. 'Not now, Joe. It can wait until tomorrow.'

'You won't be able to speak openly with Angel around. Go on, we're here now,' Joe urged. 'I'll wait for you.'

Arthur took in a great gulp of air. Joe was right; he wouldn't be able to talk freely in front of Angel. He climbed out of the car, standing tall as he knocked on the door, at the same time hastily trying to rehearse what he was going to say.

Sally stood in front of him, at first looking shocked, but it quickly turned to anger. 'Go away!'

She was about to close the door when his hand reached out to stop her. 'Please, Sally, I've come to apologize.'

'Huh, you've left it a bit late.'

'Sally, I've been a fool and realize that now. I know my mother's been to see you, and she's told you what Patsy was up to. She was making trouble between us, but I was too daft to see it. Please, Sally, can't we put it all behind us. I want you back.'

'What? You must be mad. Patsy may have been making mischief, but it doesn't change anything. You still slept with her.'

He lowered his eyes, fighting to find words, but knew he had no defence. 'Sally, please, I'm sorry. I really did think that you couldn't stand the sight of my leg, and well, Patsy threw herself at me.'

As soon as he saw the expression on her face,

Arthur knew he'd said the wrong thing and braced himself as her lips curled.

'How dare you say I couldn't stand the sight of your leg? You know that isn't true! It's just an excuse, a lie, and as for Patsy throwing herself at you, why didn't you say no? You may have lost part of your leg, but you've still got your tongue! Now go away!' she yelled, and at this Arthur was unable to react quickly enough to stop the door slamming in his face.

For a moment he stood motionless, but then he turned, climbing back into the car.

'I take it that didn't go well,' Joe said.

'You could say that,' Arthur ground out, the truth hitting him with such force that it felt as though he'd been kicked in the guts. He'd lost Sally – lost the only woman he had ever really loved.

She would never forgive him and had made that plain, and as the car sped along Candle Lane, he knew once again, with sickening clarity, that it was no more than he deserved.

Ruth heard the street door slam, and seeing that it hadn't disturbed Tommy, the lad still fast asleep, she left her room, just in time to see Sally dashing upstairs and into hers. With her brows raised she poked her head round the door, asking, 'What's up, Sal?'

'Keep your voice down, Mum,' Sally hissed. 'I don't want Angel to wake up. Anyway, I don't want to talk about it.'

'But—'

'Mum, please, just go.'

Ruth shook her head but did as her daughter asked. Closing the door quietly she went down to the kitchen, saying to Sadie as soon as she walked in, 'Here, Mum, what's the matter with Sally?'

'Arthur's been round to see her.'

'What? He had the bloody cheek to knock on my door.'

'He came round to say he was sorry.'

'It's a bit late for that.'

'Yeah, maybe, but he sounded like he meant it.'

'Oh, and how do you know that? Were you listening?'

'Yeah, I must admit I snuck into the hall, and it's made me think. All right, he made a mistake, but maybe we should encourage Sally to go back to him. I think she still loves him and surely the marriage is worth saving?'

'You must be mad. After what he's done you can't expect Sally to take him back.'

'Angel adores him, Ruth, and little girls cling to their fathers.'

'Sally did all right when Ken left. In fact, we were better off without him.'

'You can't compare that bastard to Arthur, and anyway he wasn't Sally's real father.'

'Maybe not, but Arthur was the one who decided to sleep around.'

'It was only *one* girl so don't exaggerate. Anyway, before you condemn Arthur, think about the old saying. Those who live in glass

237

houses shouldn't throw stones.'

'What's that supposed to mean?'

'Are you forgetting that you had an affair?'

Ruth blanched. She couldn't believe her ears. It was almost as though her mother knew who Andrew was, but no, it wasn't possible. She gulped. It was just a fluke, it had to be, and she stammered, 'But ... but that was different. It was during the war and I thought Ken had been killed in action.'

'Nevertheless, it was still an affair and therefore I don't think it gives you the right to judge Arthur.'

'You haven't had a kind word to say about him either, so why change your tune now?'

'I told you, it was hearing how sorry he sounded. He still loves Sally, I'm sure of it.'

'Huh, if he loves her, how could he have slept with that whore? Anyway, there's no way Sally will take him back.'

At that moment there was another knock at the door and Sadie snapped, 'Christ almighty, it's getting like Piccadilly Circus in here.'

Sally was coming downstairs and called, 'I'll get it.'

She opened the door to see Nelly Cox and forced a smile, 'Come in, love.'

As they walked into the kitchen Sadie said sharply, 'Christ, Nelly, you're down here so often that you might as well move your bed in.'

'You won't 'ave to put up with me for much longer,' the old lady said. 'I'll be leaving the lane soon.'

'Sorry, Nelly, take no notice of me. It's just that Arthur's been round and we're all a bit upset.'

'Has he?' Nelly said, her eyes alighting on Sally. 'Does he want you back?'

Sally gestured Nelly to a chair. 'Yes. He came round to apologize, but it's too late.'

Nelly sat quietly for a moment, but then said, 'I felt like that too, but I'm glad I forgave George.'

'What!' Sadie spluttered. 'You're not saying that George had another woman!'

'Yes, he did, Sadie. We'd been married for about six years at the time and he had it off with the barmaid in the George and Dragon.'

'Never! I can't believe it.'

'It nearly broke us up, but I'm glad it didn't. It was my old mum that talked some sense into me.'

Sally listened with amazement. Nelly had been married for over forty years and her husband had been devoted to her. It seemed impossible to believe that he'd been unfaithful. 'What did your mum say, Nelly?'

'She said I had two choices. I could chuck him out, or I could take him back. Then she made me look at the alternatives. I loved George, but if I chucked him out I'd be miserable, my marriage over. On the other hand, George had made one mistake, and if I could forgive him we could go on to have a happy marriage.'

'I don't think it's as simple as that,' Ruth said.

239

'No, of course it wasn't. George was so ashamed and when I took him back he promised he would never do it again. Despite that it was a long time before I could trust him again, but I never regretted my decision. My mum was right – I'd have been as miserable as sin without him.'

'Well I never, Nelly Cox. You're full of surprises,' Sadie said.

'I've never told anyone until now, but I thought it might help Sally to know that she isn't the only one whose husband has strayed.'

'A lot of them do, including mine,' Ruth said. 'Mind you, I was glad to see the back of him.'

'Yeah, but as I said, I loved George. He made a mistake, one that made me sick to my stomach at the time, yet if I hadn't forgiven him we wouldn't have gone on to have over forty years together.'

Sally took in Nelly's words. Could she forgive Arthur? Once again the scene she had walked into flooded her mind. Most vivid was the look she had seen on Arthur's face and her stomach turned. No, she couldn't forgive him, she just couldn't, and feeling tears flooding her eyes she rushed from the room.

All three women watched her rapid departure, Ruth saying, 'I don't know about your husband, Nelly, but I could kill Arthur.'

'I thought telling Sally about George might help,' and then her eyes heavenward she added, 'Sorry, George, but I know you'll understand.'

'Nelly Cox,' Sadie said, her eyes narrowing

suspiciously, 'I think you made it up. Your George was never unfaithful.'

'Well, not as far as I know.'

'Nelly, if this brings Arthur and Sally back together, I'll kiss you, I really will.'

'Steady on, Sadie,' Nelly said, smiling happily, neither of them seeing Ruth's scowl.

Sally only had one foot on the stairs when the telephone rang. Turning she took a deep breath before picking up the receiver. 'Hello.'

'Sally, it's me.'

Her stomach did a somersault. Her voice cracking, she said, 'What do you want, Arthur?'

'Joe pulled up at a phone box so I could ring you. I had speak to you again, Sally. You ... you won't stop me from seeing Angel again, will you?'

'No,' she said shortly.

'Oh, thank God. Can I pick her up in the morning?'

'In the morning – why?'

'To take her up to my mother's. Ann and the boys are coming down for the day.'

Sally clutched the receiver, her knuckles white. Only a short while ago they had been a happy family and the gatherings at Elsie's were something she'd always looked forward to. Now, because of Arthur, those days were over. For a moment she was tempted to say no, to punish him, but then swallowed, understanding that once again she was considering using her daughter as a weapon. She couldn't do that, and no matter how much pain she was in, Angel had to come first.

'Are you still there, Sally?'

With a start she said, 'I'm still here, and yes, you can pick Angel up in the morning.'

'Thanks, Sally. I'll see you at about eleven.'

'Yes, all right,' she said, and then quickly replaced the receiver. Arthur still had the power to affect her, and she wondered if her love for him would ever die, but every time she saw or spoke to him, the memory of him with Patsy stood like a spectre between them. Nelly Cox may have been able to forgive her husband, but Sally found she just couldn't forgive Arthur.

Twenty-One

Unable to sleep comfortably in his nephew's lumpy bed, Andrew was up early on Sunday morning. He doubted Denis would show his face yet. The man had arrived home drunk again but he hadn't been surprised, only annoyed that *his* money had provided the booze.

He made some tea and toast, finding his thoughts dwelling on Ruth. He'd been amazed to see her, and equally amazed to find the old attraction still there. Over the years he'd occasionally thought about her, and though their time together had been short, her face remained vivid in his memory. Compared to his wife,

Ruth had been full of fun, her laughter infectious as they had danced the night away.

Now, though, something was troubling him. Something he couldn't put together. He'd be in London for over a week and it had worried Ruth. No, it was more than that. She had looked almost afraid and he couldn't understand why.

As he munched on his toast, Andrew's eyes roamed the kitchen, hating the conditions his nephew lived in. So far he hadn't had a chance to get better acquainted with Tommy, but that was something he hoped to remedy today. The poor lad had just lost his mother, and no matter how good Ruth was in taking him in for a few days, he must feel abandoned.

Andrew finished his breakfast and then went over to the fireplace, absent-mindedly fingering his sister's few cheap ornaments on the mantelshelf. An old biscuit tin, the lid depicting a Highland scene, caught his eye, and opening it he saw it contained photographs, the top one of his sister's wedding.

Andrew carried the tin to the table and sitting down he took the photograph out of the tin. Laura looked so happy and he felt a surge of pain. She was his sister, yet they had become like strangers. He put the photograph to one side and took out another one, this of a tiny little girl. Andrew felt his eyes moisten. She looked so cute, this niece he had only seen once. Once again he felt a surge of guilt. He should have kept in touch with Laura, should have checked on her now and then.

As he continued to rummage Andrew came across a very old sepia photo, cracked with age, and saw it was his parents. He looked at his mother's face, smiling to see her looking so young and pretty, but then his eyes widened in shock. He had seen that face before, and recently. How was it possible?

Comprehension dawned, along with anger. Why hadn't she told him? How could she keep it from him? He jumped to his feet, grabbed Denis's keys, still seething as he left the house to thump loudly on the door of number five.

Ruth awoke with a start, finding her arms wrapped around Tommy. She was glad that she'd decided to put him in with her, the boy finding comfort in being cuddled. But what had woken her? Had someone knocked on the door? She glanced blearily at her bedside clock, saw it was only just after six thirty and frowned when there was another loud knock. Who the hell was calling this early on a Sunday morning?

She eased herself away from Tommy and threw on her dressing gown, still cursing as she went downstairs to open the door. 'Andrew!' she cried, stepping back from the anger on his face.

'Why didn't you tell me? I had a right to know!'

Ruth shot a look over her shoulder. 'Please,' she begged, 'keep your voice down. You'll wake everyone up.'

'I asked you a question and I'm waiting for an answer.'

'I don't know what you're talking about. Tell you what?'

'Don't act the innocent. I can't believe I didn't see it immediately. Does she know?'

'We need to talk, but please, not ... not here,' Ruth stammered, eyes wide with fear.

His face suddenly softened, 'Ruth, don't look at me like that. I'm not a monster and I'm sorry for shouting, but this has knocked me for six. Look, Denis isn't up yet and I doubt he'll surface for some time. Why don't you get dressed and come next door.'

'All right, give me about ten minutes.'

Ruth closed the door quietly and crept upstairs, relieved that she was the only one awake. It was amazing that her mother hadn't heard the racket, but so far there wasn't a sound from anywhere in the house. She dressed quickly, snuck back downstairs again, and dashing off a note she left it on the kitchen table in case anyone got up before she returned.

At her soft knock, Andrew opened the door immediately, and following him into the kitchen, he handed her a photo. 'My mother,' he said. 'And as you can see, the resemblance is remarkable.'

Ruth studied the face, her voice quaking, 'I'm surprised you didn't notice straightaway.'

'Something niggled at me as soon as I saw her, but I just couldn't figure out what it was until I saw that photograph. Why did you tell me you'd miscarried, Ruth?'

She did her best to explain, her words often

stumbling. 'When my husband came home on leave and found me pregnant with your child, he ... he begged me to stay with him, and promised to bring her up as his own. I didn't know what to do, Andrew. Ours was a brief affair, and though I thought the world of you, Ken was my husband.'

'You still could have told me the truth, Ruth.'

'Oh, Andrew, I did what I thought was for the best. You had a wife and child of your own, and whether I was having your child or not, you'd still have gone back to them after the war.'

'Yes, you're right. Despite my feelings for you, I couldn't have left my wife and son, but I still had a right to know about my daughter. I could have seen her occasionally, watched her grow up and been a part of her life. She's beautiful, Ruth.'

'Yes, she is, and I can only say I'm sorry again. I did what I thought was for the best, but it turned out to be the biggest mistake I ever made.'

'Why, Ruth?'

'Ken never accepted Sally as his own, and he made both our lives a misery.'

'My marriage wasn't happy either.'

'Wasn't it? I'm sorry.'

His face softened a little, and he said quietly, 'Does Sally know that your ex-husband isn't her father?'

'She does now, but not for many years. I didn't tell her the truth until he left me.'

'And when she found out, did she ask about

me?'

'Yes, but I told her very little, making it impossible for her to trace you.'

'Why did you do that?'

'How would your wife and son have felt if she'd turned up on your doorstep?'

Andrew nodded slowly. 'Yes, you have a point, and I doubt my wife would have taken it well. However, things have changed now and there's no reason why I can't get to know her. Please, Ruth, tell her who I am. I think you owe me that much.'

Ruth stared into Andrew's eyes, saw his plea, and knew she owed it to both him and Sally. 'All right, come on then. There's no time like the present and I'd like you to be there when I tell her.'

Sally was the only one up when they walked in and, seeing them together, she looked puzzled. Ruth felt her stomach fluttering with nerves, but glancing at Andrew she saw his reassuring nod. For a moment she still hesitated, but then took a deep breath. 'Sally, I have something to tell you. This is Andrew Munro ... your ... your father.'

For a moment there was only silence as Sally stared at them, astounded. Then she spoke, her voice a squeak, 'My ... my father?'

Sally found herself dumbstruck as she continued to stare at Andrew Munro, waiting to feel something, but she just felt numb. Ever since she'd found out that Ken Marchant wasn't her real father she had dreamed of this moment –

dreamed of finding her dad and being swept into his arms.

Why couldn't she react? Why couldn't she move? He was looking at her, his expression soft, and a spark of recognition ran through her. Yes, she could see it now – see this man's resemblance to both her and Angel, and it wasn't just his red hair. My God, he's Angel's *grandfather*!

She stiffened as he began to walk towards her, but then his eyes seemed to fill and with a watery smile he held out his arms. Sally didn't know how, but the next minute she was in them, being held tightly as his soft voice murmured in her ear, words that made her own tears fall. 'Hello, my bonny lass.'

'Why are you cuddling Sally?'

They pulled apart, both now looking at Tommy. His hair was standing up like a brush, and suddenly the family connection and all it entailed, hit Sally. Laura Walters had been her aunt, and this little boy, one she had once rejected, was her cousin!

As if sensing her thoughts, Ruth said, 'Sally, don't say anything for now. There'll be time enough later.'

Sally still couldn't take it all in, and finding she was gripping her father's hand she turned to look at him, his smile making her heart leap.

His kindness became obvious too as he released her hand and squatted down in front of Tommy. 'Now, lad, you can't blame a man for cuddling a beautiful woman. Tell me, how are you?'

'I'm all right, but where's me dad?'

'He's still asleep, but you'll see him soon. How about getting dressed, and then you and I can become better acquainted.'

Tommy nodded, and as he ran from the room Ruth shook her head worriedly. 'I'm only just beginning to see how difficult this is going to be. There's going to be a lot of explaining to do.'

'Yes, but for now I'd like to concentrate on my daughter. Are you all right, lassie?'

'It's been a bit of a shock, and my head is still spinning.'

'Well, like me, Sally. I hope it's been a pleasant one. You and I have a lot of years to catch up on.'

'I'll have to tell my mother,' Ruth said, 'and no doubt she'll be up soon. In fact I'd better go to her room and tell her now.'

She was about to leave the room when Angel burst in. 'Mummy, tell Tommy! He won't let me in the bathroom and I want to pee!'

There was a stifled, choking sound, but then Andrew's laughter rang. Sally found it infectious and grinned, whilst Angel stood hopping, her face indignant as she said, 'Mummy, it's not funny. Tell Tommy!'

Sally took her daughter's hand, still hearing Andrew's laughter as they went upstairs. My father, she thought. That man's my father, and suddenly it was wonderful.

* * *

When Andrew finally stopped laughing, he and Ruth looked at each other, she saying, 'You do realize that Angel is your granddaughter?'

'What did you say?' a voice boomed.

'Mum! I was just coming to see you.'

'Did I hear you say that this is Angel's grandfather?'

'Yes, he is. Sit down before you fall down, Mum, and I'll tell you all about it.'

Ruth only just had time to tell her mother before Tommy dashed back into the room, and hoping that Sadie would have the sense to keep quite, she said hurriedly, 'That was quick, love. Are you ready for your breakfast?'

'Can me uncle have some too?'

Andrew shook his head. 'I think Ruth has enough mouths to feed. Have your breakfast, lad, and then come next door. I'm sure your father will be up by then.'

'Can't I come now?'

Andrew looked at Ruth and seeing her quick nod he said, 'Yes, all right, and I'm sure I can rustle you up something to eat.'

Ruth accompanied them to the door, whispering, 'Thanks, Andrew. My mother's still in shock and I don't trust her to keep her mouth shut.'

'They'll have to be told.'

'Yes, and soon, but give me time to draw breath first.'

'Told what?' Tommy asked.

'Little pigs have big ears,' Ruth said, smiling down at the boy.

'I ain't a pig!' Tommy said indignantly.

'I know you aren't. Now go on home with your uncle and I'll see you later.'

'Ruth, we'll talk again soon,' Andrew said.

'Yes, all right,' but as she closed the door, her face straightened. It had gone well, and Sally had taken to Andrew immediately. Yet as she had watched their burgeoning closeness, her mother's words came back to haunt her. She was right – girls did cling to their fathers.

Ruth remembered her own father, her devastation when he died, and now shivered. Andrew would be going back to Scotland soon, his home a long, long way from London. Had she set Sally up for more heartbreak?

Twenty-Two

Andrew managed to rustle up beans on toast, chatting to Tommy as the boy cleaned his plate. He was a nice lad, a bit rough round the edges, but his intelligence shone through. In some ways he reminded him of his own son at that age, both having the same quick minds.

He wondered how not only Donald, but his parents too, would take the news about Sally. Yet no matter what, he was determined to tell them. He wanted his daughter to be a part of his life, to make up for all the missing years, and

251

not only Sally, his granddaughter too.

Denis came into the room, scratching his head, his face showing the ravages of drink. 'Any tea in the pot?'

'It's probably cold by now.'

There were murmured grumblings as the man made a fresh pot, and as he sat at the table he burped loudly before saying, 'Did Ruth send you home, Tommy?'

'No, Uncle Andrew came and fetched me.'

'So, Andrew, how come you know Ruth?'

'It's a long story. We'll talk about it later.'

'What's wrong with now?'

'I said later,' and ignoring his brother-in-law's grunt of annoyance Andrew spoke to Tommy again, taking up the earlier conversation from where he'd left off. 'Well, lad, so you're seven years old?'

'Yeah, but I'm nearly eight. It's me birthday on Friday.'

Oh God, no, Andrew thought, his eyes shooting daggers at Denis. The man had arranged Laura's funeral on the same day as Tommy's birthday. What sort of father was he?

'Don't look at me like that! I'd forgotten, and with losing me wife, can you blame me?'

Andrew sighed heavily. Was he being too hard on Denis? Yet every word the man said grated on his nerves. Trying to keep his tone steady he said, 'You'll have to change it. We can't possibly have it on Friday.'

'Change what?' Tommy said, his eyes flicking from Andrew to his father.

252

'Mind yer own business,' Denis snapped. 'Go and play outside.'

'But I don't want to. I wanna stay wiv me uncle.'

'Do as I bloody well say!'

'It's all right, Tommy. I'm not going anywhere and we'll talk again later.'

'Can I go back to Ruth's?'

Andrew spoke quickly, 'Not just now, lad. Perhaps in an hour or so.'

'Why can't he go next door?' Denis asked.

'Trust me, this isn't a good time.'

Denis threw him a questioning look, but then shouted at Tommy to scarper, waiting until the boy had run outside before speaking. 'What's going on, Andrew? And how do you know Ruth Marchant?'

Andrew knew he'd have to tell Denis, but dreaded it. He took a steadying breath. 'I met Ruth many years ago, in fact during the war, but haven't seen her since.'

'Oh, like that was it? I've heard about the things that went on during the war. What was that little ditty? Oh, yeah. When their men were away, the wives went out to play.'

'Shut up! It wasn't like that. Ruth hadn't heard from her husband for a very long time and thought him killed in action. You have no idea what it was like. Bombs rained down almost every night and Londoners were going through hell. Many thousands were killed or lost their homes, and with strict rationing they were on near starvation diets. All right, Ruth

253

and I met, and yes, we had an affair, but those were desperate times. People lived for the day, knowing that it might be their last...' Andrew stopped speaking, annoyed with himself for justifying what happened to Denis.

'All right, keep your shirt on, mate.'

'That isn't the end of the story, and when you hear the rest I don't want any more derogatory remarks,' Andrew took another steadying breath. 'You see, Ruth's daughter is my child.'

'What! Sally Marchant is your daughter! Blimey...'

Andrew watched as Denis digested the news and waited for him to take on board the implications.

He didn't have long to wait as Denis suddenly leapt from his chair. 'Bloody hell! This means that Tommy is related to the Marchants. Sally's his cousin!' Denis flopped down again, his voice a mumble. 'I can't believe this. It's amazing.'

'Listen, I don't think Tommy is ready to hear all this yet. He's just lost his mother and it would be too much for him to take in. How about we leave it until after the funeral?'

'I dunno. He's very fond of Ruth and it might help him to know that he's a part of her family.'

'You may have a point, but do you mind if I consult with Ruth first? Angel will have to be told too, and maybe Tommy at the same time.'

'It's funny really. This makes me Sally's uncle and she must only be a few years younger than me, and Laura,' he said his face suddenly saddening, 'would have been her aunt. She missed her family and would have liked that.'

Andrew's stomach tightened with guilt. Once again he knew that despite their differences he should have kept in touch with Laura. Instead he now felt he'd abandoned her. There was only Tommy, his nephew, and his last link with his sister. 'Denis, you must try to change the date of the funeral.'

'Yeah, I'll have a go, but don't hold your breath. Blimey, I still can't get over this. Me and the Marchants are related.'

'Only by marriage,' Andrew said, and, seeing the calculating look in his brother-in-law's eyes, he wanted away from the man. It was about time he rang Donald and his parents to see how they were. 'I'm going to the telephone box on the corner, and then for a walk. I'll see you later.'

As Andrew left the house there was no sign of Tommy and he wondered where the lad had wandered off to. He walked slowly, trying to rehearse breaking the news to his family, and decided that he wouldn't do it yet. It had been hard enough to tell them of Laura's death, and though they had cut her out of their life, it had hit his mother and father hard. He knew that they regretted their decision, both realizing now that it was too late and they would never see their daughter again.

Sally got Angel ready, the child excited that she was going to Wimbledon with her daddy. Her mind was still churning, still trying to take it in that Andrew Munro was her father, and was distracted as she tied a ribbon in Angel's hair. With her daughter out of the way it would give her a chance to talk to him again and she couldn't wait.

On the dot of eleven there was a knock on the street door, and with so much on her mind she acted without thinking, standing aside to let Arthur in. 'Angel's ready but she's a bit over-excited at the thought of seeing her cousins,' and as he followed her into the kitchen, she added, 'Can you make sure that she's back before her bedtime?'

'Yes, of course.'

'Well, Arthur, isn't this civilized,' Ruth said sarcastically.

'Hello, Ruth.'

'Huh, if it was up to me you wouldn't have got over the doorstep.'

'I've only called round to collect Angel.'

'Yeah, well, you can bugger off out again,' she snapped.

'What's the matter, Nanny?'

'Arthur, you'd better go,' Sally said hurriedly. 'Angel shouldn't be hearing this.'

'Yes, you're right. I'll see you around six.'

Sally kissed her daughter, the child hugging Ruth and Sadie, but still looking puzzled as Arthur led her out. Sally waited until the door had closed behind them and then turned to her mother. 'My marriage may be over, Mum, but I don't think there should be any nastiness in

256

front of Angel.'

'Yeah, you're right and I'm sorry, love. I shouldn't have said anything, but seeing him made my blood boil!'

'I know, Mum, and I've been as bad, but from now on, for Angel's sake, we have to hide our feelings.'

'Here you two,' Sadie said, 'now that Angel's out of the way, is there any chance of meeting Sally's father?'

'You've already met him,' Ruth said.

'Yes, but I didn't know who he was then.'

'All right. I'll pop next door and invite him round.'

Sally found she was holding her breath until her mother returned. She couldn't wait to see her father again, to get to know this man who had just come into her life.

'Hello,' Andrew said, smiling gently as he came into the room. 'I'm glad Ruth asked me round. We have a lot of things to sort out.'

'You're telling me,' Sadie said. 'So, you're Sally's father, and seeing you again I can't believe I didn't guess.'

'She's very like my mother,' Andrew said.

'Have you told your parents?'

'Not yet. I rang them this morning, but I think I'd rather break it to them face to face.'

'Andrew, sit down,' Ruth invited.

Sally's thoughts raced. She had grandparents that she'd never met. What were they like? Would she ever meet them? Her father spoke, his words taking her breath away.

'I spoke to my son too. His wife is having a baby and it's due shortly.'

'Your ... your son,' she gasped. 'But that means he's my half-brother!'

'Sally, I'm sorry. Of course – you don't know about Donald. I should have thought before I spoke.'

'Stone the crows! This gets more and more complicated,' Sadie said. 'I'm beginning to lose track.'

'Andrew,' Ruth said, 'I think it would help Sally, and my mother, if you tell them about your family.'

'Yes, I think you're right.' He leaned forward, elbows on his knees and fingers steepled under his chin. 'Now, where shall I start? My father, Duncan Munro, was a surveyor and I took over the firm when he retired. My mother's name is Jane, and she was a McFarland before she married my father. They had two children, myself and Laura, and we grew up in a hamlet just outside of Edinburgh.'

'And – Donald?' Sally asked.

'I married Moira and we had one son. My wife died just over a year ago.'

'Is Donald older than me?'

'Yes, he was born in nineteen-forty.'

Sally rubbed her forehead and then said, 'Do we look alike?'

'No, not really. Donald takes after my wife, though he does have auburn hair. In fact, it's rather like Tommy's.'

'Blimey,' Sadie said. 'I wonder what your son

will make of having a skin and blister?'

'Skin and blister?'

'Yeah, it's cockney rhyming slang for sister. There are lots of them. Apples and pears for stairs and—'

Ruth broke in, 'Andrew, have you told Denis?'

'Yes, but Tommy doesn't know yet. I wanted to speak to you about that. The boy will have to be told and it's going to be a shock. He's just lost his mother and I'm not sure that he could cope with it yet. What do you think, Ruth?'

It was Sadie who answered. 'I don't think it would hurt. Kids are more resilient than we give them credit for. As you say, he's just lost his mother, but it might help him to know he's got other family.'

'I think my mother's right,' Ruth said. 'I'm very fond of the boy, and since Laura died he's clinging to me.'

'All right, if you think it's best I'll have a word with Denis.' A look of annoyance then crossed his face. 'The fool has arranged the funeral for Friday. Tommy's birthday.'

'What! Never!' Sadie spluttered.

'I'm afraid so, but I'm hoping he can change it. By the way, where's Angel?'

'She's out with her father. He came to pick her up a short while ago.'

'I did wonder why you're living with your mother, Sally. Does this mean that you're divorced?'

'Gawd, more explanations,' Sadie said.

259

Sally started hesitantly, telling her father why her marriage had broken up, the pain rising again when she spoke of Patsy. 'So you see, I can never forgive him.'

'Surely it's your husband who should move out of your home. Not you.'

'I couldn't live there again, not after seeing him with Patsy. When Mum gets rehoused, I'll find another flat.'

'Rehoused! What do you mean?'

It was Ruth who took over then, telling Andrew that Candle Lane was scheduled for demolition.

'When are you moving?'

'We don't know yet.'

'I just hope they don't stick us in one of them bleedin' tower blocks,' Sadie exclaimed.

Andrew had seen the council estates and nodded in agreement, 'I can't imagine anything worse. Have you ever been to Scotland?'

'You must be joking! I've never been out of London, not even during the war. What part of Scotland do you come from?'

'Edinburgh and it's a bonny place. It's full of history and the castle is a sight to see.'

Sally had listened with interest when her father had spoken of his family, but now her eyes widened as it hit her. Edinburgh! He lived so far away and soon he'd be returning to Scotland.

She had only just found him – only to lose him again.

Twenty-Three

They decided to tell the children together, choosing to do it when Arthur brought Angel back from Wimbledon.

Sally opened the door when he knocked, and seeing him standing so tall and handsome on the step, her insides jolted. Would it always be like this? Would she always feel this pain whenever she saw him?

'Hello, Sally,' he said. 'Here she is, safe and sound.'

Sally couldn't look at him again, instead focusing on her daughter, 'Hello, darling. Have you been a good girl?'

'Yes, but those boys were very naughty and Granddad was cross.'

'Ann's twins are a nightmare,' Arthur said, then with an appeal in his eyes added, 'Sally, can we talk?'

'No, we have nothing to say to each other.'

'Please, Sally.'

'I said no, and anyway we can't talk in front of Angel.'

'Why not, Mummy?'

'See what I mean,' Sally said, now forcing steel into her voice and eyes. 'Anyway, I'm busy.'

His eyebrows rose. 'All right, I'm going.' He then ruffled Angel's hair. 'See you next week, princess.'

'No, Daddy, don't go.'

'I have to, darling,' he said, hugging her to him for a moment.

'But, Daddy...'

'Bye, sweetheart,' he said, abruptly turning and striding off.

Angel made to run after him, but Sally grabbed her. 'You'll see him again soon,' she placated. 'Now come into the kitchen as we have something to tell you.'

'No, don't want to.'

'Come on, darling,' Sally urged.

Angel dragged her feet, but when they walked into the kitchen and she saw Andrew, along with Denis and Tommy, she brightened. 'Wotcher, Tommy, I've been out with my daddy.'

'Yeah, I know,' he said.

'You look upset, Sally. Are you all right?' Andrew asked.

'I'm fine,' she murmured, but in truth every time she saw Arthur it upset her. Oh, she didn't want to think about him, it hurt too much, and instead she sat down, pulling Angel on to her lap. She needed to distract her mind, and now looking at her father she said, 'Shall I tell them?'

'Yes, lassie, that's fine with me.'

Ruth could see that Sally was close to tears, and cursed Arthur. She listened now as her daughter began explaining things to the child-

262

ren, her words stumbling at first, but gradually gaining in strength.

Angel took it in a very matter of fact manner, almost as if she had already sensed the connection. She looked at Andrew, then at Tommy, smiling with satisfaction before saying, 'He's only your *uncle,* but he's *my* granddad.'

Ruth saw the crushed look on Tommy's face. 'That's enough, Angel!' she rebuked, holding out her arms and beckoning Tommy to her. 'Come here, love. We've got something else to tell you.'

She waited until the boy was in her arms and then turned to Denis. 'Do you want to tell him this bit, or shall I?'

'It'll be better coming from you.'

'Tommy, sweetheart, I'm very fond of you, we all are...' Ruth floundered, unsure how to explain things to the boy. 'And it isn't surprising that we're fond of you, because, well ... Sally is your cousin.'

'My cousin? My *real* cousin?'

'Yes, darling, and that makes me almost your aunty.'

He stared up at her, his eyes wide, and she gently hugged him. 'This means you're part of our family now.'

'Blimey!'

They all laughed and it broke the tension, but as Ruth looked at Denis she saw a calculating look in his eyes.

'Well, isn't this nice,' he said, smiling slyly. 'One big happy family. It's nice to know that

Tommy will always have someone to look after him when I'm at work.'

Ruth's smile was guarded. She still wanted to take Tommy on permanently, but this wasn't the time to broach the subject, and for now she'd pretend to go along with Denis's suggestion. 'Yes, Tommy has us now, and we'll make sure he's treated right.'

Arthur walked home. His father had dropped them off in Candle Lane, but he'd told him not to wait, hoping he'd get the chance to talk to Sally again. It had been a waste of time. She still wouldn't talk to him, and it was obvious she just wanted to get rid of him, her eyes hard and cold when saying she was busy. He'd lost her, and somehow he had to accept that his marriage was over.

The thought of going into the empty flat depressed him, and he decided to give Joe a ring. If he was free they could go out for a drink, and boy, he needed one.

There was a telephone box ahead and going into it Arthur fished out some coins, relieved when Joe answered. 'Do you fancy a drink, mate?'

'Yeah, all right. Do you want me to pick you up?'

'No, I'll come to Earls Court for a change. It's about time I saw your place.'

'How will you get here?'

'I'll get a cab.'

'Arthur, that's daft if you ask me. Surely it

would be simpler if I drive over to you.'

'No, I'll come there. See you soon,' Arthur said, and before Joe could argue he replaced the receiver. He was fed up with being beholden to Joe for lifts and intended to push ahead in his endeavours to drive again. His disability wasn't that bad, and once he'd proved he could still drive, he was sure permission would be granted.

It was a bugger finding a taxi, but at last, after walking to the main road, he saw one and hailed it. 'Earl's Court, mate,' he told the driver, giving him Joe's address.

He then sat back, watching the passing scenery and doing his best not to think about Sally. When they pulled up outside a tall house, one that looked imposing, his eyes widened. Blimey, fancy Joe living in a posh place like this. He pulled a face at the fare, thinking it astronomical, and after paying the driver, climbed the wide staircase to Joe's front door. He looked for a bell, but instead of one he saw at least eight. Finding one for Somerton, he rang it, and then waited ages before Joe appeared.

'Wotcher, mate, I'd invite you in, but I'm on the top floor and its five flights of stairs to get there.'

'Blimey, Joe, what sort of place are you living in?'

'It's a sort of bed-sit with a kitchenette. I like the area and it's fine for now. One day, when we've made a mint, I'll find something better.'

'I'm glad you said *when* we make a mint ... not if. Now, where's the nearest pub?'

'Just around the corner and by the look of you I think you need something stronger than beer.'

'What do you mean?'

'Come off it, Arthur, we've been friends too long for you to fool me. You're upset about something. Patsy hasn't been pestering you, has she?'

'No, she wouldn't dare. I hear her upstairs at times, and have seen her going in and out, but I haven't spoken to her.'

'So it's Sally then.'

'I tried to talk to her again, but she wouldn't have it. She'll never take me back, Joe, and I've got to accept that, but it doesn't stop me from wanting to drown my sorrows. In fact, when we get to the pub you can order me a double whisky.'

'Right mate, you're on.'

The two men matched each other drink for drink, until at ten thirty they staggered out of the pub, singing their heads off as they clung to each other, a lamppost, or anything else that came to hand as they weaved down the road.

Joe was the least drunk of the two and when he saw a taxi, he raised his hand to flag it down. 'Come on, Arthur, I've found you a cab,' but when the taxi driver saw the state of them, he drove off.

Joe grinned lopsidedly. 'Well, mate, it looks like you might have to kip down in my place for the night.'

'Yesh, all right,' Arthur said, reeling so badly that he ended up in the road.

'Whoops,' Joe said, grabbing his arm and pulling him back on to the pavement.

Arthur giggled inanely, unaware of the danger he'd been in as his voice rose in song.

It took a while, but Joe finally found his place, though he had a job to fit the key in the lock. 'Brace yourself, Arthur, we've got a lot of stairs to climb.'

Arthur looked up at the first flight, his eyes barely able to focus, and began to stagger up them. On and on the two men went, but luckily for Arthur he was so drunk that he couldn't feel any pain in his prosthesis. He began to sing again, an old Gracie Fields song, maudlin now, 'Sally ... Sally ... pride of our alley.'

Joe joined in, both men impervious to the shouts that rang out in the building for them to shut up. Arthur hung on to the banisters, unaware that the words of the song meant just as much to Joe as they did to him: 'You're more than the whole world to me.'

Twenty-Four

During the next four days, Andrew got to know his daughter, finding to his surprise that, like his mother, she had the gift of healing.

It hadn't taken him long to work out that Sally had no life of her own. He had wanted to take her out whilst Ruth was at work, but with Sadie to look after it proved impossible. It didn't seem right and he found himself increasingly annoyed. He knew Ruth had to work, understood her financial constraints, but even so he felt the burden shouldn't fall on Sally. If Ruth would accept his financial help, she could give up work and stay home, but though he'd offered, she'd refused.

Andrew's thoughts turned to Angel and he smiled. Since finding out that Tommy was her cousin, she now treated the boy as if she owned him. When she bossed him about, Tommy took it well, but Andrew could already see rebellion on his face. Tommy loved being part of the family and was obviously testing the water, but sparks would fly soon, he was sure of it.

Yes, Andrew thought, smiling softly, Angela was rather bossy and spoiled, but even so he was falling under her spell. She was a delight, and he was becoming very, very fond of her. Sally too was a wonderful young woman, and once again he found himself dwelling on her restricted life. Ruth worked full-time, and when Denis went back to work, Sally would have the added burden of looking after Tommy.

His thoughts now returned to his nephew and his approaching birthday. Thankfully Denis had been able to change the date of the funeral, and it was now being held on Monday.

With only one day left to buy the lad a present, he glanced at the clock. Denis was still in bed, and had the man got anything for his son? Somehow Andrew doubted it. With this in mind he decided to try to make it up to Tommy and buy him something a little bit special. He'd say it was from both him and his father, but with no idea what the boy might like, he decided to pop round to ask Sally if she had any suggestions.

'Hello, bonnie lass,' he said as she opened the door. 'I'm just off to find something for Tommy's birthday. I'm not sure what to get him so have you any ideas?'

'Come in, Dad,' Sally invited, 'and I'll put my thinking cap on.'

Dad! For the first time she had called him dad, and Andrew smiled with pleasure.

'Hello, Sadie,' he said, his smile still wide as he walked into the kitchen.

Sadie just grunted a greeting and Sally pulled a face. 'Gran's not in the best of humour today,' she whispered.

'I may be old, but I ain't deaf,' the old woman

269

snapped.

Andrew had come to recognize that Sadie could sometimes be testy, and though Sally said it was rare now, he didn't know how she put up with it.

'Dad, how about a train set?'

'What? Sorry, I was miles away.'

'I suggested a train set for Tommy.'

'Yes, good idea, and where will I find one?'

'There's a large department store at Clapham Junction. It's called Arding & Hobbs and is right on the corner so you can't miss it.'

'Right, I'll try there.'

Andrew kissed Sally on the cheek, called goodbye to Sadie, getting only a grunt in reply, and made his way to the bus stop, missing his car. It had made sense to travel to London by train, but nowadays he was unused to public transport.

As he stood waiting for a bus to arrive his eyes were once again scanning the area. He would miss his new-found family when he went back to Scotland, but seeing the huge factories belching out smoke, he certainly wouldn't miss the polluted air in this area of London.

At six thirty that evening, when Joe dropped Arthur off outside his flat, he stuck his head back in the car. 'You don't fancy a drink tonight do you, Joe?'

'No thanks, mate. I haven't recovered from last Sunday yet, and still can't remember getting home.'

Arthur managed a smile. 'When I woke up in your flat it gave me a bit of a turn. Christ, mate, it's a dump and I reckon you should find something better.'

'I will one of these days. Night, Arthur, see you in the morning.'

'Yeah, see you,' Arthur said, his mood low as he walked into the flat. After a day on site he hated coming home to emptiness, and even though he hadn't liked living with Sally's mother in Candle Lane, it was better than this. God, he missed Angel, missed the way she always ran to greet him, her cheeky little face lighting up in a smile.

As he flopped on to a chair Arthur's head sunk to his chest. It wasn't just Angel he was missing – it was Sally too. Memories of the happiness they'd once shared plagued him. Her joy when he came back from Australia, their wedding, and then the excitement of moving into their first home.

Things started to go wrong when Sadie had her stroke and they'd moved back to Candle Lane. There had been no privacy, and, with Angel in the same bedroom, no sex. Then there had been his prolonged stay in hospital, and the loss of his lower leg. He cursed himself for misjudging Sally, and now squirmed in his chair. She had always been intuitive and now he wondered if she'd picked up on his phantom pains, mistaking them for real ones. If that was the case, no wonder she had kept a distance between them in bed. Once again he kicked

271

himself for not speaking to her. He should have told her that his wound had healed and the stump was well-cushioned against knocks. But he'd been afraid – afraid in case she really did find him repulsive.

The telephone rang. It was his mother. 'Hello, Mum.'

'Hello, love. Tell me, when you took Angel back to Sally on Sunday, did she mention anything about her father?'

'No, we hardly spoke?'

'So you haven't heard the news. Ruth rang me last night and you're not going to believe this. Sally's father has turned up.'

'Huh, I bet Ruth soon showed him the door.'

'No, love, I don't mean Ken Marchant. I mean Sally's real father.'

'Really! I bet that was a shock for them. How did Sally take it?'

'According to Ruth, he's a lovely man and they hit it off immediately. The only problem is that after Laura Walters' funeral, he'll be returning to Scotland.'

'Hang on, Mum, you've lost me. What has Sally's father got to do with Laura Walters?'

Arthur listened to his mother's explanation and found his jaw dropping. It just sounded too fantastic to be true – a chance in a million. 'So this means that Sally is Tommy's cousin.'

'Yes, and I'm afraid for the first time in our friendship, I've fallen out with Ruth. She has no interest in trying to get you and Sally back together, and made that plain.'

'You can't blame her, Mum.'

'I don't agree, and anyway, it wasn't just that. She also said that when Denis goes back to work, Sally will be looking after Tommy.'

'Why has that upset you?'

'Isn't it obvious? Ruth wants to take the boy on, but with her at work, the burden of looking after Tommy falls on Sally.'

'If she doesn't mind, I don't know why you're getting so upset.'

'That girl has enough to do with looking after Sadie, and I told Ruth she should put her daughter first for a change. She didn't take too kindly to that and slammed the phone down. Anyway, let's change the subject. I still think you should talk to Sally again. If you love her, you can't just give up.'

'It'll be a waste of time.'

'How do you know unless you try?'

'I have tried, Mum.'

'Christ, son, can't you see that you'll have to put up more of a fight than this to get her back?'

'Don't keep on about it.'

'All right, I'll say no more, but will you bring Angel to see us again on Sunday? After falling out with Ruth, I don't think I'll be welcome in Candle Lane.'

'Yes, all right. Bye, Mum.'

As Arthur replaced the receiver he wondered if his mother was right. Should he put up more of a fight to get Sally back?

He went into the kitchen to make himself something to eat, and as he prepared a quick

273

meal, he decided to give it one more try. He'd go to see Sally again, and this time he'd make sure to properly rehearse what he was going to say.

Joe drove to Clapham Common. He was still sure that Sally and Arthur would get back together one day, unable to believe that two people who so obviously loved each other could remain apart. It had been a bit sticky when Arthur asked him out for a drink again, but he'd managed to fob him off, and was now on his way to meet Patsy. He doubted that Sally would ever return to Maple Terrace with the girl living upstairs, and that was something he hoped to remedy.

Patsy had been surprised to hear from him, and at first she'd been hostile, but he knew her now, knew what buttons to push, and finally she'd agreed to meet him.

He sat in the pub, eyes on the door, brows lifting when she walked in. There was no getting away from the fact that she was a stunner, her dainty innocent looks giving no clue to her occupation.

'Hello, Patsy. What would you like to drink?' he asked as she sat beside him.

'A vodka and lime, please.'

He went to the bar and was soon back, placing her drink on the table. 'Thanks for agreeing to meet me.'

'Well, I must admit I was surprised to hear from you.' And getting straight to the point she

274

added eagerly, 'You said something about a proposition?'

Joe's face and voice hardened. 'Yes, that's right. I'm proposing that you move out of your flat.'

'Move out of my flat! But why should I?'

'I should have thought it was obvious.'

'Not to me, it isn't.'

'Sally won't move back while you live upstairs.'

She shrugged her shoulders. 'That's just too bad.'

'Does your landlord know what you do for a living, Patsy?'

'What's that got to do with anything?'

'A lot, and I wonder how he'll react when I tell him that one of his tenants is a prostitute, using her flat to entertain men.'

'But I don't!'

'It would be your word against mine, Patsy, and what about the neighbours? When I tell them what you do for a living, I'm sure they'll complain too.'

'You bastard!'

'It takes one to know one, Patsy. Now I'll give you until the end of the month, and if you're not out by then I'll make it my business to spread the word.'

She jumped to her feet, her face livid. 'All right, you win,' and snatching up the glass of vodka and lime she threw it in his face. 'And you can stick your drink.'

As Patsy marched out of the pub, Joe pulled

out a handkerchief, hastily wiping him face. There had been moments when he'd felt sorry for her, moments when he wondered what had led her to a life of prostitution, but then he remembered the terrible trouble she'd caused. Patsy had gone out of her way to deliberately break up his friend's marriage, and now any feeling of regret he'd been feeling, died.

A few customers were looking at him, doing their best to hide their smiles, but Joe ignored them. As long as Patsy left the flat, that's all that mattered, and then he was struck by another idea. Yes, once the flat was vacant, he'd approach the landlord.

Twenty-Five

Andrew decided to take Ruth out to dinner, and called round to see her. He was determined to do something to help Sally, and hoped that this time he could persuade Ruth to accept his financial help. She wasn't the same woman he had met during the war, and he knew that life since then had knocked the fun out of her, yet even so, when he saw the love she showered on Tommy, he saw a warm and affectionate woman. Unlike Moira, he thought, remembering his late wife's cold and distant nature.

'Ruth, will you come out for dinner?' he asked as she opened the door. 'There's something important I'd like to talk to you about.'

She went pink, looking flustered as she said, 'Yes, I'd love to have dinner with you, but I need a few minutes to freshen up. Come on in.'

'Hello, Sally,' Andrew said as they walked into the kitchen. 'I've just popped round to invite your mother out to dinner.'

'You don't mind, do you?' Ruth asked.

'Why should I mind? The children are asleep,' and nodding in Sadie's direction she added with a wry smile, 'Gran too.'

'No, I'm not,' Sadie protested. 'I was just resting me eyes.'

'I wonder who was snoring then,' Ruth said, then turned to smile at Andrew. 'I won't be a tick.'

He nodded, looking at her legs with appreciation as she hurried from the room. Once again he was struck by how little she had changed physically in over twenty years. Her figure was still trim, her skin wonderful, and there were no signs of grey in her hair.

'How are the children?' he asked Sally.

'They're fine, but Angel is still bossing Tommy around.'

'Angel took it well that I'm her grandfather, and if anything it was more or a shock for Tommy to find out that you're his cousin. Once he gets used to the idea he'll find his feet, and woe betide Angel then.'

'Yes, I think you're right, but I doubt he'll pick on Angel. If anything he's always been protective of her. It's strange really, almost as if he sensed the connection between them.'

Andrew grinned. 'I don't know how you can say it's strange, especially with the gifts that you and my mother have.'

They continued to chat for a while, Andrew telling Sally more about his parents, but then Ruth came back into the room. 'Right, I'm ready,' she said.

In a flowery summer dress, topped with a lace cardigan, Andrew smiled at the pretty picture she presented. 'Come on, let's go,' he said, giving Sally a hug before they left.

As they walked along Candle Lane, Andrew impulsively took Ruth's hand, and as she turned to smile at him, her eyes were sparkling. For a moment he saw the happy young woman he remembered, one who loved to dance the night away. 'Do you recall doing the jitterbug with me, Ruth?'

'Oh course I do. We had a lot of fun in those days.'

'It was certainly fun when I flipped you over. I don't think I'll ever forget the sight of your frilly French knickers.'

'Andrew!' Ruth said, looking horrified, but then she giggled. 'It's just as well you weren't wearing a kilt or I'd have got my own back.'

'My goodness, woman. You'd have seen more than you bargained for. Scotsmen don't wear anything under their kilts.'

'Oh, I think you'll find I saw enough,' she said, going pink again.

Andrew squeezed her hand, remembering their lovemaking. It had been a passionate affair, their time together snatched, and little had he known that Sally would be the result. 'Our daughter's a lovely girl,' he murmured.

Ruth returned the pressure of his hand, and when they reached the restaurant they sat gazing at each other until the waiter brought the menu.

They chatted throughout the meal, at ease in each other's company, and often laughing at memories of their time together. They were on their final course before Andrew raised the subject that was heavy on his mind. 'Ruth, I'd like to do something to help Sally.'

'If you're going to offer financial help again – forget it. I can't accept your money.'

'But why? Sally is my daughter and I've provided nothing for her upbringing.'

'What is this – guilt? I decided not to let you know that you have a daughter, so you have nothing to feel guilty about. Sally is no longer a child, she's a grown woman, and I don't need your money for her upkeep.'

'I know that, but you're being selfish. If you'd accept financial help you could stay home to look after your mother. Instead you're laying the burden on Sally.'

'How dare you say I'm selfish? When Ken left I had to work full-time to earn enough to bring Sally up, and without my mother's help I don't know how I'd have coped. She contributed most of her pension, and looked after Sally while I was working my socks off. Now she's ill, and the role is reversed. Sally loves her grandmother and doesn't mind looking after her.'

'Are you sure about that? Have you asked her? She's a young woman, tied to the house all day, and if you ask me, it's *your* duty to care for your mother.'

Her eyes flashing with anger, Ruth said, 'I'm not listening to any more of this! You've been here for less than a week and think you can tell me how to run my life.'

'I'm not doing that. I'm just trying to help, and as I said, it's your duty—'

Her chair scraped back as Ruth got to her feet, face white with anger, 'Duty, you talk to me of duty, you sanctimonious sod! I've done well enough without you for over twenty years, and I can take care of my own affairs. In future I suggest you keep your nose out and ... and you can stick your money up your arse!'

With this Ruth stormed from the restaurant, the other customers trying to hide their amusement as Andrew threw down his napkin. 'Waiter,' he called, 'the bill, please.'

Ruth practically marched all the way home, seething with indignation. God, how dare Andrew call her selfish? She *had* worked hard to bring Sally up when Ken left her, with no further help from him, or any man!

Bloody hell, what an idiot she'd been. When Andrew asked her out to dinner, her heart had jumped, and stupidly she thought he was going to propose.

It was crazy, she realized now, crazy to expect that he still had feelings for her. He'd only been back in her life for a short time, and too many years had passed. She had imagined it – imagined his looks of affection. She'd been acting like a teenager, thinking herself in love, when all the time Andrew had only been interested in the welfare of his daughter.

As Ruth neared Candle Lane her steps slowed. It wasn't just Andrew who said she was selfish; Elsie had made the same suggestion. As with Andrew, she had lost her temper, falling out with her too. Was it true? Was she putting too much of a burden on Sally?

Bloody hell, anyone would think she enjoyed going out to work! When Sally was a child she would have loved to be a stay at-home-mum, but she'd had no choice. She had to work to pay the rent and feed them, yet Andrew had the cheek to talk about her duty.

As she arrived home, Ruth hesitated before putting the key in the lock, wondering once again if she was putting too much on to Sally. Was looking after her gran so bad?

No, she decided as she turned the key. Of course it wasn't.

Friday morning dawned clear and sunny and Sally crept downstairs earlier then usual. It was Tommy's birthday today and she was going to prepare a special tea for when he came home from school. The jelly would have to be made now if it was to set in time and she wanted to do it before the children got up.

There had been a debate about the birthday tea, Sadie saying it wasn't right when the boy's mother hadn't been buried yet.

Ruth argued that Laura would have wanted to celebrate Tommy's birthday. There would be enough tears on Monday, she insisted.

Sally had been torn between both points of view, but in the end had sided with her mother, much to her gran's disgust.

Tommy was still staying with them, and would be until Andrew returned to Scotland. Sally's face saddened. She didn't want to think about that.

Only half an hour later, Ruth appeared. As she came into the kitchen it was clear that her eyes were shadowed.

'Are you all right, Mum?'

'Yeah, why shouldn't I be?'

'You look a bit down in the mouth.'

'I'm fine,' she said shortly.

Her mother's moods were unpredictable these days and Sally heaved a sigh, deciding not to press her. 'I'll have to get the kids up soon, but before that I'll make you a cup of tea.'

She didn't answer and Sally's brow creased. Her mother was upset about something, she could see that, but it would be pointless to go on about it. With the star sign of Cancer the crab, when upset her mother would sink into her shell, and no amount of coaxing would get her to come out until she was good and ready.

Sally brewed the tea and then went to get the children up, knowing that Tommy was going to be a very excited little boy that morning.

It was a struggle, but Sally managed to avoid any spats between the children as she got them washed and dressed. Then, when they went downstairs, she smiled when she saw how Tommy's face lit up.

'Wow!' he yelled, looking in wonderment at the parcels. 'Can I open them?'

'Of course you can,' Sally said.

Tommy grabbed the largest, tearing off the paper, wonderment in his voice, 'Look, Angel. It's a train set from my dad and Uncle Andrew.'

'It's not fair. I want one too,' Angel scowled.

Ruth's smile was strained, but she spoke at last, 'Wouldn't you rather have a nice new doll?'

'I don't like dolls. I want a train set.'

'Now then, *miss*, it's Tommy's birthday to-day,' Sally admonished, 'and I don't want any sulks. When it's your birthday you can choose what you want, but until then I think you should wish him a happy birthday and give him our present.'

Angel ran to the dresser and taking the parcel she handed it to Tommy. 'I chose these, and you've got to let me play with them.'

Tommy took the package, eagerly tearing off the paper, his face lighting up when he saw the contents. There was a net bag of marbles, cigarette cards, the latest edition of his favourite comics, the Beano and Dandy, a jigsaw puzzle,

283

and a box of jelly babies. 'Cor, fanks.'

'And this is from me,' Ruth said, holding out another package.

'Blimey, this is me bestest birfday ever,' Tommy said, once again ripping off the paper. 'Cor, fanks!' he cried, pulling out six little boxes containing Dinky cars.

'I want some cars too,' Angel said, pouting.

After admonishing her daughter again, Sally spoke to Tommy. 'When you come home from school we'll have a birthday tea and I'll ask your father and uncle to join us.'

'Cor, fanks,' and grinning happily he went back to his toys.

As Tommy continued to play, Sally looked at her mother. She was still strangely quiet, and unusually she had hardly spoken to Tommy. 'Mum, are you sure you're feeling all right?'

'I've told you, I'm fine, but unlike some people, *I* have to get ready for work.'

Why had she said that, Sally wondered as her mother stomped from the room. She seemed annoyed that she had to go to work – but why?

That afternoon, Andrew found the birthday tea a success, with Denis sober and on his best behaviour. After the children had consumed copious amounts of food, including jelly and ice cream, he set up Tommy's train set, joining the children on the floor and regularly winding up the clockwork engine. After a while, unable to resist, Denis joined in too.

When Ruth came home from work the

atmosphere immediately changed. She was unsmiling, and her eyes barely met Andrew's as she took in the scene. He stood up, and walked over to her, saying quietly, 'Let's not spoil Tommy's party. Can we go somewhere and talk?'

'I suppose so,' she said, walking into the hall.

Andrew followed, and as Ruth went into Sadie's bedroom she kept her back to him, her arms folded defensively as she gazed out of the window. He had been cursing himself since last evening. Ruth was right – he shouldn't try to interfere in their lives. She had brought Sally up on her own, and had made a good job of it, but instead of praising her, he had called her selfish. In his desire to help Sally he had handled it badly, hurting Ruth in the process.

He went up behind her, placing his hands on her shoulders. 'I'm sorry. I had no right to call you selfish.'

She turned, eyes moist as she looked up at him. 'I've done the best I can, but I've been thinking about what you said all day. I took it for granted that Sally wouldn't mind looking after my mother, and she's never complained. Maybe you're right, maybe it isn't fair on her, but when my mother had her stroke I had little choice.'

'Please, Ruth, you don't have to justify yourself to me. If Sally is happy to look after her grandmother, that's fine. If she isn't, my offer of financial help, enabling you to stay home, stands.'

'I can't take your money, Andrew.'

'Why not? You've struggled on your own for years, and you'll be taking what you should have had when she was a child.'

'Let me talk to Sally, and then I'll think about it.'

'Fair enough, and as I said, I'm sorry for the way I spoke to you. Can we be friends again?'

She smiled up at him and Andrew's breath caught in his throat. Was he imagining it? Did her eyes now hold an invitation? His head bent and before he knew it, his lips were on hers, the kiss passionate.

When they finally broke apart, he held her tightly in his arms. God, how long was it since he'd kissed a beautiful woman? 'How about dinner again tonight?' he asked. 'And this time we won't talk about Sally.'

When her parents returned to the room, Sally saw her mother smiling happily. 'Andrew has asked me out to dinner again,' she said. 'Is that all right with you, Sally?'

'Of course it is. As usual I have nothing planned, but I'm thinking about offering healing at the hall again.'

'Good idea. It'll do you good to get out of the house.'

'Right,' Denis said, 'I'm off, and you Tommy, it's about time you packed that train set away. It's taking up too much room on the floor and someone might step on it.'

'No, leave it out, Tommy,' Angel protested.

'No, it might get broken.'

'Course it won't.'

'I'm putting it away,' Tommy insisted, beginning to pull the track apart.

Angel jumped up, kicking the engine in the process, and as it fell to its side Tommy glared at her, red-faced with anger. 'You did that on purpose!'

'No, I didn't.'

'Yes, you did,' and standing up he gave Angel a shove. As she fell backwards on to her bottom he stood over her. 'Don't touch my train set again!'

'Will if I want,' Angel cried as she scrambled on to her knees, and snatching the engine she was about to throw it.

'Angel!' Sally yelled. 'Don't you dare!'

'That's enough, lassie,' Andrew said as he swiftly picked up his granddaughter. He took the engine from her hand, handing it to Tommy. 'Now then, what sort of behaviour is this? Tommy was kind enough to let you play with his train set, and instead of thanking him, you try to break it.'

'I want a train set too.'

'I don't think you deserve one. Now say sorry.'

'No.'

Andrew sighed, and placed Angel back on to the floor. 'I'll leave you to sort this one out, Sally, but I think this little girl deserves a smack.'

'Yes, and she'll get one if she doesn't say sorry to Tommy.'

Angel's eyes flicked around the room, and seeing all their stern faces, she said, 'Sorry, Tommy.'

Tommy said nothing as he dropped to his knees, once again packing away the train set.

'Have you had a nice birthday?' Ruth asked as she bent to help him.

Tommy kept his head lowered, but Ruth noticed a quiver in his shoulders. 'Oh, love, it's all right. Angel didn't mean it,' she said, pulling him into her arms.

'I don't care about the train. It's me mum. It's me birfday and I want me mum.'

Ruth rocked the child and, glancing at Denis, she saw that he too looked distressed. He was a drunk, and she didn't have much time for the man, but when all was said and done, he had just lost his wife.

Once again she wondered how he was going to cope with Tommy. Yes, they would look after the lad while he was at work, but what about the evenings? Would the man give up drinking and take proper care of the boy? With a sigh she decided that when the time was right, she'd talk to Denis again, suggest that Tommy lived here with them permanently, but she'd wait until after the funeral.

At seven thirty, Sally put both children to bed whilst her mother got ready to go out, and at eight o'clock they had only just gone to sleep when Andrew called.

Sally watched them leave, thinking they looked nice together, but only ten minutes later there was another knock on the door. She went to answer it, her stomach twisting when she saw who was on the step. 'Go away, Arthur.'

'I want to talk to you. Please, just give me five minutes.'

'We have nothing to say to each other.'

'Please, Sally.'

'No,' she said, making to close the door.

His hand came out, holding it open. 'I won't leave until you agree to listen to me.'

Sally could see that he meant it and her mouth tightened. 'All right, but five minutes, and no more.'

'Can we talk in private?'

'My mother's out, so there's only my gran.'

'I'd rather talk to you alone.'

'All right, I suppose we can use her room.' She stood back to let him in, and in Sadie's room they stood facing each other, Sally with her arms folded defensively.

Arthur's eyes held an appeal. 'Sally, won't you give me another chance?'

'I can't. I could never trust you again.'

'It'll never happen again, I swear it won't. Please, don't throw our marriage away over one mistake.'

'One mistake! It was more than one, or are you now trying to tell me that you never slept with Patsy again?'

He flushed, lowering his head. 'It would only have been once if you hadn't left me.'

'Oh, so now it's *my* fault that you couldn't

keep your hands off of her!'

'No, I didn't mean it to sound like that, but when you left Patsy was there, throwing herself at me.'

'Huh, and you couldn't say no?'

'Sally, you know that she lied to keep us apart, and I was daft enough to believe her, but at the end of the day it was just sex with Patsy, that's all. It meant nothing.'

Sally found her fists clenched, nails digging into her palms. Whilst she'd been crying night after night, he'd been fine, sleeping with Patsy and obviously having a good time. At the thought of Arthur touching Patsy, of the intimacy they'd shared, she felt sick. 'The sex may have meant nothing to you, but as far as I'm concerned you betrayed me, and our marriage. Just go, Arthur.'

'Sally, please, I love you.'

'Love!' she screamed. 'You don't know the meaning of the word. Just get out. I'll never forgive you and as far as I'm concerned, our marriage is over.'

'What's going on?' Sadie said sharply as she came into the room.

'Nothing, Gran. Arthur is just leaving.'

'Sally...'

'I said get out,' she yelled.

Arthur shook his head, but then swung round to leave, and when Sally heard the street door closing behind him, she flung herself across her gran's bed, giving vent to her feelings, the pain of his betrayal still unbearable.

290

She felt the bed dip beside her, and then her gran's hand stroking her hair. 'Come on, love,' she cajoled. 'If you carry on like this, you'll make yourself ill.'

'Oh, Gran, I can't bear it.'

'It'll get easier,' Sadie consoled.

Sally cuddled closer to her gran, wishing it were true, that the pain would go away, but doubted it ever would.

Twenty-Six

On Monday, Laura's funeral was a sad affair, and to Andrew the bright, sunny, June day seemed incongruous. The sky should be grey, as grey as his mood. There were few in attendance, just himself, Denis, Ruth and a few neighbours. Now, as they left the small chapel, he walked across to the scant floral tributes laid on the ground.

'I'm sorry for your loss,' a woman said, and Andrew turned to look at her.

'Thank you, and thank you for coming. I'm sorry, I don't know your name.'

'It's Jessie, Jessie Stone. I was friends with your sister for a while, but then she started drinking again.'

Andrew's brow lifted, 'Are you saying you were only her friend when she was sober?'

'Yes, that's right.'

Andrew fought to keep his voice even. 'Well, Mrs Stone, it sounds as though you were a fair weather friend, but I'll say no more.'

The woman flushed, tutted, and then moved away, now offering her condolences to Denis.

Andrew walked over to Ruth, saying quietly, 'I still think that Tommy should be here.'

'It was his father's decision to send him to school, but I must admit it feels strange that the boy has no idea that his mother is being buried today.'

'Denis seems to think that he's too young to understand.'

'I doubt that. Tommy is astute for his age. Still, we'd best make our way back. Sally has laid on a little spread.'

Andrew took her arm, saddened that the funeral had seemed so short. His sister's life had been short too, but if she'd been happy her loss would have been easier to bear. His thoughts continued to turn as they journeyed back to Candle Lane. He'd be leaving tomorrow, but so much had been left undone. He was worried about Tommy and as Denis was drinking heavily, he wondered what sort of future his nephew would have. At least the boy had Ruth, he thought, turning to look at her profile as she sat beside him. Tommy clung to her, and in time he felt that she would become a surrogate mother.

'Ruth, will you have dinner with me again this evening.'

'Yes, of course I will.'

He squeezed her hand and then shortly after they were pulling up in Candle Lane, walking into the house to see a lovely spread on Ruth's kitchen table. Andrew looked at the neatly cut sandwiches, but found he had no appetite, despite going without breakfast that morning.

A hand touched his arm, and he saw that Sadie had come to his side, her voice soft. 'I'm sorry I wasn't there, love. I'm feeling much better nowadays and could have gone to the chapel.'

'It doesn't matter,' Andrew murmured.

Sadie exhaled loudly. 'I tried telling Ruth that I'd be fine, but she wouldn't listen.'

'She worries about you,' Andrew said in her defence.

'Yeah, and Sally over-worries too. I wish the pair of them would stop.'

His mood still low, Andrew forced a smile. 'They think the world of you and are bound to worry. I wish I'd shown more concern for my sister.'

'She's in a better place now, love.'

Andrew found no consolation in Sadie's words. Guilt still plagued him, and he suspected it always would. Once again he wished he'd done more for Laura, kept in touch, but now it was too late.

Two hours passed, and most people had left, only one neighbour remaining. She'd been introduced to Andrew as Nelly Cox, and he'd immediately taken to the kindly, chubby woman.

Nelly had volunteered to stay behind to help with the clearing up, and now Andrew urged Denis ahead of him as they left, 'I'll see you later,' he told Ruth, and then smiled at Sally. 'Thanks for all your hard work, lassie.'

She smiled at him, but the smile didn't reach her eyes. His daughter was unhappy, he knew that, but felt helpless. There were a few choice words he wanted to say to Sally's husband about his behaviour, but Sally adamantly refused to let him speak to the man. Her marriage was over, she insisted, and talking to Arthur wouldn't change that.

Ruth told him not to worry, saying that Sally would eventually get over it and he hoped that she was right. In the meantime he'd learned his lesson and was determined to stay in touch with his daughter, to be a part of her life, despite the difficulties and distance between them.

Sally was glad of the help as she cleared up, and in another half an hour she'd have to pick the children up from school. Heavy on her mind was her father's departure, and she was going to miss him so much. In the short time that he'd been in her life she had come to love him, Andrew being everything that she had dreamed of in a father. It was strange to think that she had paternal grandparents and a brother, and wondered if she'd ever meet them. She had wanted to ask her father, but in the burgeoning relationship, found herself a little reticent.

'Did you see the way Jessie Stone scoffed the

294

ham sandwiches?' Sadie said. 'If her mouth had been a bit bigger she'd had shoved them in two at a time.'

'Yeah, I saw,' Nelly said. 'She's a greedy cow, but enough about Jessie, I've got something to tell you.'

'Spit it out then,' Sadie urged.

'I'm moving into Osborn House the day after tomorrow.'

'Oh, Nelly,' Sally cried. 'Already!'

'Yes, love, it's all arranged. I can't take all me bits and pieces and I wondered if there's anything you'd like. What about me standard lamp, Ruth? It'd look nice in here.'

'Thanks, Nelly, I'd love it, but I'll be sad to see you go. Candle Lane won't be the same without you.'

'I'll be sorry to leave, but the lane won't be standing for much longer. Pop down tomorrow to see what else you'd like, you too, Sally. Anything that's left can go to the second-hand shop.'

'Nelly, I'm gonna miss you,' Sadie said, and reaching into her apron pocket she pulled out a handkerchief, dabbing at her eyes.

'Gawd blimey, yer never crying, Sadie.'

'Of course I ain't. I've just got something in me eye.'

'Yeah, right,' Nelly said, 'and pigs might fly. I didn't know you cared, Sadie.'

'Who said I do?'

Nelly chuckled and then flopped on to a chair. 'We go back a long way, you and me. If I

295

remember rightly, you moved into the lane just before our queen's coronation.'

'Yeah, that's right, and a lot of water has passed under the bridge since then.'

'It has, Sadie, it has,' Nelly said, the two women going on to reminisce.

Sally dried her hands, saying ten minutes later, 'It's time to collect the children.'

Nelly rose to her feet. 'I'm off too, and Ruth, don't forget to pop in and see what things of mine you can make use of.'

'I won't forget,' Ruth said. 'See you later, love.'

'Nelly, will you come to see me again before you leave?' Sadie appealed.

'Of course I will,' she said, lifting her hand in a wave before following Sally outside. Then saying, 'I know it's none of my business really, but I was hoping to see you and Arthur back together before I left.'

'There's no chance of that, Nelly. My marriage is over.'

'Are you sure, love? Are you sure that you really want to spend the rest of your life without Arthur?'

Sally's steps faltered a little, but she said nothing, and when they reached Nelly's house, the question remained unanswered.

It was nearly eight o'clock and Andrew was zipping his bag. He was packed, ready for his journey home in the morning, and now, glancing at his watch, he saw it was time to take Ruth

296

out to dinner. Denis was out, drowning his sorrows as usual, but still Andrew closed the street door softly behind him.

'Hello,' he said as Sally answered his knock.

'Come in, Dad. Mum's nearly ready.'

Andrew stepped inside, and then paused to lay a hand on Sally's arm. 'Listen, lassie. I know I'm leaving tomorrow, but I'm on the end of a telephone. If you need anything, just let me know. I'll ring you often, and as soon as I can I'll be back to see you.'

'You're coming back?'

'Of course I am. It won't be for a while as I have a lot of work to catch up on, but as soon as I get the chance I'll come down to London again.'

Sally was about to speak, but then Ruth appeared on the stairs. 'Hello, Andrew. I'm ready.'

Andrew smiled up at her, thinking how lovely she looked, and then turned to speak to Sally again. 'I'll be round to see you before I go in the morning.'

'All right. Bye, Dad,' she said, but Andrew could see the strain in her eyes.

As they left the house, Andrew took Ruth's hand. There was a growing intimacy between them, but so far she hadn't mentioned his offer of financial help. 'Ruth, have you spoken to Sally yet?'

'Yes, and she was adamant that she doesn't mind looking after her gran.'

'Are you sure?'

'Yes, I'm sure. Now can we *please* drop the subject?'

Andrew sighed heavily. He had done nothing for Ruth, or his daughter, and it weighed heavily on his mind. 'I feel I should be helping you in some way.'

'For goodness sake! Not again! As I told you before, I chose not to tell you about Sally. So will you stop trying to salve your flaming conscience.'

'That isn't what I'm trying to do.'

'Oh, Andrew, I'm sorry, I shouldn't have said that. Look, it's your last evening in London so let's not fall out.'

'All right, Ruth, but can I just say that if you need anything – anything at all – will you let me know?'

'If it will make you feel better, then yes, I'll do that.'

They reached the restaurant and after ordering their meal, Andrew said, 'I hate to see Sally so unhappy.'

'Me too, and I could kill Arthur for what he's done to Sally. She's still in an awful state, though she hides it well.'

'It's a shame the marriage broke up.'

'He was unfaithful, and worse, Sally caught him at it.'

'It must have been awful for her, but if you ask me, she still loves him.'

'I think you're right, but she'll never go back to him.'

The first course arrived and after a few

mouthfuls Ruth said. 'Are you still going to tell your parents about Sally?'

'Yes, of course; I'll tell my son too. Secrets have a way of coming out, and meeting you again has proved that.'

'How do you think they'll take it?'

Andrew paused in thought, his spoon poised. 'I don't know. My parents will be shocked, and I've no idea how they'll react. As for Donald, I'll just have to wait and see.'

'Have you any idea when you'll be able to see Sally again? I know she's going to miss you.

'My work has piled up while I've been away and I'll have a lot to catch up on. However, I'll come to London again as soon as I can, and it won't only be to see Sally.'

'Won't it?'

'I want to see you again too.'

'Do you?' she said, her face going pink.

'Yes, I do.' And as Andrew said these words, he knew he meant it.

Twenty-Seven

On the train to Scotland the next morning, Andrew felt torn in two.

It had been a difficult parting. He had hated saying goodbye to Sally, Angel too, both of them breaking down in tears as he left. He was amazed at how quickly he had come to love them both, and the pain of leaving them was heavy. Yet he had to return to Scotland; his life was there, his parents, and his son. Now, though, he felt that half of his heart was in London, the other in Edinburgh.

Andrew's thoughts turned to Ruth, and he examined his feelings. There was no doubt that the spark was still there, and he was sure she felt the same, but with him in Scotland, and Ruth in London, there was little chance of their relationship going any further.

The journey seemed endless; the sound of the wheels riding over the tracks was making Andrew sleepy and he began to doze. Hunger eventually drove him to the dining car, and as he ate he gazed at the passing scenery, his thoughts continually turning to London and those he'd left behind.

At last they reached Edinburgh, and leaving

the train Andrew grabbed a taxi, sinking back in the seat with a sigh. He looked out of the window, and as they left the city the rolling countryside came into view. At last his heart lifted. He was home.

The house felt damp and empty as he walked in and there was no one to greet him. However, the furniture shone and he eyed it with appreciation, pleased that his cleaner had kept the place up to scratch.

Leaving the hall he went into the large reception room, and after the small cramped house in Candle Lane, it seemed enormous. With a mental shake he went to the telephone, and dialling his parents' number he told them he'd be round to see them soon.

'Hello, son,' his mother said when he walked in an hour later. 'You look tired. Did ... did our flowers arrive for the funeral?'

'Yes, and they were lovely.' He saw his mother's eyes fill with tears, and going to her side he took her hand.

'Oh, Andrew, I can't believe I'll never see my daughter again.'

'How was Laura's husband?' his father asked.

'The man's turned into a drinker, a heavy one.'

'And ... and Laura's son?'

'He's a fine boy, Mother, and as bright as a button.'

The tears began to run down her cheeks. 'He's our grandson, but we've never seen him.'

'That can be remedied. I'm sure he'd love a

holiday in Scotland.'

Duncan Munro cleared his throat, his voice husky. 'Donald rang earlier, and when I told him you were coming to see us, he said he'd pop round too.'

As if on cue the doorbell rang, Andrew going to answer it. 'Hello, son, any sign of my grandchild yet?'

'No, Dad. I think he's so comfortable in there that he doesn't want to come out.'

'Oh, it's a boy is it?'

'I hope so, but then again,' he mused, 'a girl might be nice.'

As they walked into the sitting room, Andrew saw that his mother was dabbing her eyes. He wanted to tell them, to get it over with, but would the shock be too much for her? She brightened when she saw Donald, and it was then that Andrew made up his mind. 'I'm glad you came round, son. I have something to tell you all, and I might as well do it now.'

'You sound a bit ominous, Dad. Is it bad news?'

'I hope not, son.'

Though looking puzzled at this comment, Donald sat down, and after a pause Andrew began to speak, doing his best to keep it as brief as possible. There was a gasp from his mother, a grunt of annoyance from his father, and Andrew found he couldn't look at his son. It sounded terrible, he knew that. A wartime affair, a child he didn't know he had, and now a grandchild too.

The room was hushed as he finished speaking, but then his father's voice broke the silence, 'And you're telling us that Laura lived next door to this ... this woman!'

'Ruth, Father. Her name is Ruth.'

'Oh, Andrew,' his mother gasped. 'I can't believe you did such a terrible thing.'

'It was a wartime affair and those were extraordinary times. I was very young, away from my family for the first time, and well ... it happened.'

'Humph,' his father grunted. 'You were a married man, and Donald here must have been just a baby. You should be ashamed of yourself.'

'I'm not proud, especially when finding I had left Ruth pregnant.'

'Dad,' Donald said, speaking for the first time, 'this means I have a half-sister.'

Andrew braced himself and turned to look at his son. He dreaded the censure he would see in his eyes, but to his surprise Donald was smiling. 'Yes, it does, and as I said, her name is Sally. I ... I'm sorry, son.'

'Dad, you don't have to apologize to me. I loved my mum, but I knew you weren't happy.'

'Did you? I thought I hid it from you.'

'I know you tried, but I'm not blind. Anyway, you and Mum had separate rooms so it didn't take much working out. I also heard her talking to a friend once and she was making it plain that she found *that* side of marriage distasteful.'

'Donald!' Jane Munro snapped. 'I don't think

303

this is a subject for the drawing room.'

'Oh, Grandmother, this is the nineteen sixties.'

'Nevertheless, these things should not be spoken of so openly.'

'All right, I'm sorry.'

Andrew winked at his son, Donald then saying, 'Can I meet her, Dad?'

'Meet who?' Andrew asked, bewildered by the rapid change of subject.

'My sister.'

'Er ... yes, I suppose so. Perhaps when I next go to London you'd like to come with me.'

'If I can get away I'd like that, but in the meantime, tell me about her.'

'Well, like me, she has red hair, but facially she's a mirror image of your grandmother, and also has her healing gifts.'

'Does she?' Jane Munro said, her face softening. 'And – and her daughter?'

'Angel has red hair too, and again there's a resemblance to you.'

'Angel! What a strange name.'

'It's Angela really, but everyone shortens it.' Andrew said, smiling as he pictured his granddaughter. 'She's a little tomboy, but adorable with it.'

He saw his mother's eyes fill with tears again and with a small sob she said, 'If I have learned anything from Laura's death, it's that I was an unforgiving fool. I cut her out of my life, and now it breaks my heart to know I'll never see her again. Don't lose touch with your daughter,

304

Andrew. Go as often as you can to see her and perhaps bring her to Scotland to see us. I ... I'd love to meet her.'

'Things are a little difficult for Sally. She cares for her elderly grandmother and has little freedom.'

'She sounds a wonderful young woman.'

'She is, but don't worry, I'll find a way to bring her to meet you.'

His mother suddenly paled and Duncan Munro rose to his feet, shuffling to her side. 'I'm sorry, but I think your mother needs to rest.'

'Yes, come on, Dad,' Donald said. 'This has all been a bit of a shock for them and it's time we left.'

Andrew nodded, once again appreciating his son's maturity and common sense. His parents were elderly, and of course they were shocked, but thankfully they had taken it better than he'd expected.

'How about coming round to dinner tomorrow night, Dad? Maureen would love to see you.'

'Yes, I'd love to,' and as they parted, Andrew wondered how much longer it would be before his daughter-in-law gave birth to the baby.

In Candle Lane, the following morning, Nelly Cox was almost ready to leave, and now bustled along to number five to say goodbye.

'Oh, Nelly, are you sure you're doing the right thing?' Ruth asked. 'The council might have offered you something other than a tower block.'

'Yeah, maybe, but it still wouldn't be the same. I'd be living amongst strangers, and to be honest, I can't face it. At least in Osborn House I'll be amongst people of me own age, and they lay on a lot of activities.'

'We're going to miss you, Nelly,' Sally said, flinging an arm around the chubby old lady.

'Will you come to see me now and then?'

'Of course we will.'

'That's good, and you'll be able to keep me up with the gossip.' Her face was strained and it was obvious that she was fighting tears. 'I'd best be off. I thought I'd leave in style and a taxi is coming to pick me up.'

'What about the stuff you're taking with you?'

'It's already gone. That nice young chap at number twenty offered to take it in his van.'

'Oh, that was good of him,' Sadie said.

'Yeah, some of the newcomers to the lane ain't too bad.'

'Newcomers!' Ruth protested. 'They've been living here for five years.'

'That still makes them new,' Sadie said. 'Now then, Nelly, if I can make it I'll come to Osborn House to see you too.'

'I'd love that, Sadie, but after one look at you they probably won't let you out again.'

'You cheeky mare.'

The two old ladies grinned at each other, but then as Nelly turned to leave the room, Sadie's eyes became moist. 'Take care, love,' she croaked.

Ruth hugged Nelly, and Sally did the same, feeling a sense of unreality. It didn't seem possible that Nelly Cox was leaving the lane. She had been a part of their lives for so long, always there, and always ready to lend a hand to anyone in trouble.

'Please, don't see me out. It'd be my undoing,' Nelly begged.

'All right,' Ruth choked.

Nelly threw one last look at them over her shoulder, and then closed the door behind her, and as Sally let the tears flow it was as though a chapter had closed on their lives.

In Scotland, during the rest of the week, Andrew threw himself into his work. He dreaded going home, finding the house empty and unwelcoming, something he hadn't noticed before his trip to London. For the first time since his wife's death he found himself lonely, his thoughts often on Ruth, his daughter and granddaughter.

He saw his parents frequently and had dinner with Donald and Maureen again, his daughter-in-law impatient for the baby to be born. She was huge and walked around with her hand permanently cradling the small of her back, amused when he suggested a run round the block to start things off.

On Thursday evening, over a week since his return, he rang London. Ruth answered the phone and sounded pleased to hear from him. 'How are you?' he asked.

'Fine, we all are – well, except for Denis that is.'

'What's the matter with him?'

'He's drinking heavily and is hardly home.'

'But what about Tommy?' Andrew asked worriedly.

'Don't worry. He spends nearly all his time with us. In fact, if I can catch Denis when he's sober, I'm going to suggest that we have Tommy permanently.'

'Ruth, that's good of you, but now you really must let me help financially. I doubt you'll get anything from Denis for his keep.'

'There's no need. He's only one small boy, and will hardly eat us out of house and home.'

'Why do you have to be so stubborn? Tommy is my nephew and I want to help.'

'I'll think about it.'

Andrew sighed, knowing it would be a waste of time to push her. Even so he would see that he provided something towards Tommy's up-keep, if only his clothing, and now asked, 'Have you heard anything from the council about rehousing?'

'No, not yet, but I doubt it'll be long.'

'I just hope you get offered something decent.'

'So do I, but tell me, Andrew, how did your family take it when you told them about us?'

'They were upset at first about our affair, but they came round, and I know they'd love to meet both Sally and Angel. Maybe they could come up here during the school holidays.'

Ruth was quiet for a moment, but then said, 'Yes, I'm sure they'd love that.'

They continued to chat, but Andrew could sense something different in Ruth's tone and after a while reluctantly said goodbye.

With a heavy sigh he went to his study and picked up a folder to begin preparing a client's overdue structural report. The house was quiet, with only the chime of the grandfather clock in the hall, breaking the silence. With pen poised, Andrew tried to concentrate, but found his thoughts going back to Ruth.

Twenty-Eight

By the time another week had passed, Andrew had begun to catch up on his work. He'd spoken to Ruth on the telephone again, and then Sally, inviting her to Scotland to meet his family when Angel broke up from school for the summer holidays.

It hadn't been easy to arrange, Sally saying she couldn't leave her gran, but then he'd spoken to Ruth again, and she had agreed to take a week's holiday from work to look after Sadie. A date had been set for the first week in

August, less than a month away, and he could not wait.

When he'd told his parents that Sally and Angel were coming, they were thrilled, Donald too, all looking forward to meeting them.

Andrew flexed his arms, and stretched his back, feeling the stiffness easing. He'd had a lot to do since returning to Scotland and could do with a break, but then his secretary put another call through.

'Dad, it's a boy!' Donald cried.

Andrew could hear the excitement in his son's voice and grinned. 'That's wonderful, and is Maureen all right?'

'Yes, she's fine.'

'I'll be there as soon as I can.'

Andrew shouted a hurried explanation to his secretary before running out of the office. The hospital wasn't far away and he was soon in the maternity ward, staring down at a bonny, bouncing boy who had weighed in at nearly eight pounds.

His eyes grew moist as he looked at his new grandson. He had a shock of red hair, a screwed-up little face, and both parents were bubbling with happiness. 'Well, son, what are you calling him?'

'He's to be Andrew Duncan Munro, after you and grandfather.'

'Thank you,' Andrew said, his voice thick with emotion.

'Well, Dad, there's nothing to keep you here now. Your grandson finally decided to come into the world, and as you can see, he's a healthy wee lad.'

'What do you mean?'

Maureen smiled gently. 'Every time you've been to us for dinner, you have talked non-stop about Ruth.'

'Have I? I wasn't aware of it.'

'You've told us that she's a fine woman, warm and affectionate, not to mention attractive.'

'So what are you waiting for?' Donald asked.

'I don't understand.'

'Dad, I don't want you to spend the rest of your life alone, rattling round in that great empty house. We can tell you're fond of Ruth, maybe more than fond. If she feels the same about you, why don't you marry her?'

'Marry her! Oh, son, I don't know about that.'

'Don't let your marriage to Mum ruin the rest of your life. Ruth sounds nothing like her, and you deserve a bit of happiness.'

Andrew lowered his head. Yes, he was fond of Ruth, but at the thought of marriage he shook his head. 'It's too soon, and we hardly know each other.'

'Then go back to London and get to know her better.'

'I can't do that. I still have work to do, and anyway, Sally will be coming to Scotland with Angel soon.'

'Yes, Sally and Angel, but what about Ruth?'

'She has to stay behind to look after her mother.'

'Did you invite her to come at a later date?' Maureen asked.

'Well, no, but there'll be plenty of time for that.'

Donald laid a hand on his arm. 'Dad, you have a way of letting things slide, of burying yourself in work. If you leave it too long, Ruth will think you aren't interested, and if she's as attractive as you've told us, you could lose her to someone else.'

'Donald's right,' Maureen said. 'Work can wait. Your heart can't.'

Andrew gazed at his grandson again, a fine sturdy lad who would grow up in clean, fresh air. He thought about Angel, his lovely little granddaughter, living in totally different conditions, and it was then that he made up his mind. If he married Ruth it could solve all of their problems, and surely fondness was something to build on? 'Yes, you're right. I'll go back to London tomorrow.'

'And will you ask Ruth to marry you?' Donald asked.

'Yes, I think so, but she may say no.'

'I doubt it, Dad, but you won't know unless you ask.'

Andrew bent to plant a kiss on his grandson's head. 'Have you spoken to your grandparents?'

'Yes, after ringing you. They're as pleased as punch to have a great-grandson, and don't worry, we'll keep an eye on them whilst you're away.'

'Thanks, son, and now that you've both sorted out my life, I'd best be off. I'll be back as soon as I can.'

Andrew hugged both happy parents, and then almost ran from the hospital. It was already four o'clock and he had left work unfinished at the office, but with any luck, he'd be in London by tomorrow evening.

On Friday evening, Ruth's face was a picture when she opened the door. 'Andrew!'

'Aren't you going to invite me in?'

'Yes, of course, but why didn't you let us know you were coming?'

'It was a last minute decision and I thought I'd surprise you.'

Andrew found his heart thumping. Now that he was face to face with Ruth again, he began to recognize his feelings. Yet surely it wasn't possible? Surely it was too soon to know? She smiled at him and his stomach flipped. There was no denying it. He wasn't just fond of her – he loved her, and prayed she felt the same.

'Dad!' Sally cried as he walked into the kitchen. 'What are you doing here?'

'I've come to see you of course, but first I want to speak to your mother. Ruth, will you come out to dinner?'

'But you've only just arrived.'

'I know, but I have something important I want to talk to you about, and it can't wait.'

'Is something wrong?' she asked worriedly.

'No, nothing at all,' he said, smiling softly.

'Oh, Dad, Angel's going to be thrilled to see

313

you,' Sally cried. 'She hasn't stopped talking about you since you left and is so looking forward to our holiday. We didn't expect to see you before then. How long are you staying?'

'I'm not sure, and I hope Denis can put me up again.'

Ruth frowned. 'You'd be better off on our sofa. As I told you on the telephone, Denis is drinking heavily and rolls home all hours. Nine times out of ten, Tommy sleeps here, and that suits me fine.'

Andrew fought to control his annoyance. There'd be time enough later to sort Denis out, but for now he had other things on his mind. 'Well, Ruth,' he said, 'are you coming out to dinner?'

'Yes, but give me five minutes to get ready.'

'You look fine as you are.'

'At least let me put a bit of powder and lipstick on.'

Ruth was frantically looking for her compact, whilst Andrew turned to Sally. 'My daughter-in-law just gave birth to a bonny wee boy.'

As comprehension dawned, Sally's face filled with light. 'Oh, that means I'm an auntie.'

'Yes, it does, lassie, and your new nephew has red hair too.'

'Oh, I can't wait to see him.'

'I'm ready,' Ruth said, fluffing her hair as she looked in the mirror.

Andrew touched Sally's hand, saying goodbye to her and Sadie but, as he led Ruth outside, he found his stomach fluttering with nerves. It

314

wouldn't take long to reach the restaurant, and he was desperately trying to rehearse his words.

They sat at a small table by the window, and as he took the menu Andrew found his palms sweating.

'Are you all right?' Ruth asked.

'Yes, I'm fine. Now what shall we have to eat?'

They gave their order, and as the waiter walked away, Andrew gazed at Ruth. Should he ask her now, or perhaps wait until the final course? She was gazing back at him and was that affection he saw in her eyes?

Nerves held him back. For so many years his late wife had rejected him, scorned his affection, and he dreaded facing that again. Was he making the right decision? Was he ready to risk marriage again? He toyed with his napkin, remembering how lonely he had felt in Scotland, and berated himself. Of course he was ready, but later, he'd ask her later. God, what if she refused him?

'You're quiet, Andrew. Why don't you tell me what's on your mind?'

He grasped for something to say. 'Sally has Tommy to look after now, as well as her grandmother. How is she coping?'

'Oh – my – God!' Ruth cried. 'So that's why you came rushing back again. You're worried about Sally and want to tell me I'm a selfish mother again?'

'No, of course not. I understand that you have to work, but I think I have the perfect solution.

You see—'

Ruth cut in, hand up, the palm facing him. 'If you've travelled all the way from Scotland to offer me money again, you've wasted your time.'

'That wasn't what I had in mind. Please, let me finish,' Andrew urged, going on to say, 'I know you're to be rehoused soon, but I think I have a better suggestion. You see I have a large house in Scotland, left to me by my grandparents. It has six bedrooms and a small annex. There's room enough for all of us, Tommy too if his father will agree. You could give up work to care for your mother, and Sally could live in the annex with Angel.'

'What! You want us to move to Scotland?' Ruth stared at him in shock for a moment, but then her eyes narrowed. 'What are you asking, Andrew? Am I to be your servant – or your kept woman?'

'No – no! For goodness' sake, what do you take me for? Oh, hell, I've made a mess of this. What I'm trying to do is ask you to marry me.'

'Ma ... marry you?'

'Yes, darling, and as soon as possible. It would solve all our problems. I can't bear the thought of being so far away from you all, but I have to live in Scotland. As I said, you're due to be rehoused, and Sally has no home of her own. Can't you see it's the most sensible solution?'

Andrew watched the range of emotions that ran across Ruth's face. When he'd proposed he thought he saw joy, but now he saw doubt, consternation, and then worry.

'It isn't that simple, Andrew. I'm not sure that either Sally, or my mother, would agree to move to Scotland.'

'But why not? I live in a beautiful area with clean, fresh air, and plenty of space for Angel and Tommy to run around in. Surely that's better than the grim, dirty streets they play in now?'

'When you put it like that it sounds wonderful, but my mother is a born and bred Londoner and would never leave.'

'Ruth, it's *you* I'm asking to marry, not your mother. If your answer is yes and she wants to continue to live with you, she'll have to agree.'

'Oh, Andrew, I know you see my mother as a difficult woman, but before her stroke she was a different person and I owe her so much. Now though she's in bad health and such a big move might be too much for her.'

'Wouldn't Scotland be better for her than the possibility of being stuck in a council tower block?'

For a moment she just stared at him, doubt evident, and he reached out to grip her hand. 'Ruth, I'm comfortably off, so much so that I can support you all. Please say yes.'

She pulled her hand from his grasp. 'Andrew, you haven't mentioned one very important thing.'

'What's that?'

'You've asked me to marry you, and have pointed out how sensible it would be, but ... I

317

need more than that.'

Andrew gazed at her, saw her eyes lower, and then the penny dropped. God, he was a complete and utter fool. He'd forgotten the most important thing of all. He'd forgotten to tell her how he felt. 'Ruth, finding you again seems like a miracle to me, and though we've only just got to know each other again, I can't deny my feelings. I love you – in fact I don't think I ever stopped loving you. Please say you'll marry me.'

She smiled at him now, joy in her eyes, 'Oh, Andrew, I love you too ... and ... and my answer is yes.'

Andrew grinned with delight, but then his face sobered as Ruth said, 'I still don't think my mother, or Sally, will move to Scotland.'

'Well, darling, there's only one way to find out. As soon as we've finished our meal – we'll go and ask them. Don't worry, darling, I can be very persuasive.'

'I hope so,' she said, relaxing a little, and for the next hour they went on to discuss their wedding plans.

When her parents arrived home, Sally saw they were holding hands, but her breath caught in her throat when her father announced they were getting married. With hardly time to take it in, her mother then told them that they could all move to Scotland.

'Are you bleedin' mad!' Sadie spluttered. 'Scotland! I ain't living in Scotland.'

Andrew crouched down by Sadie's chair, speaking gently. 'Please, don't just dismiss it out of hand. I have a large house, in a lovely area, and Ruth will be able to give up work to look after you.'

'I don't need looking after and I'm sick of saying that. You go, Ruth, but I'm staying here.'

'Mum, don't be silly. You know you can't live on your own.'

'Sally,' Andrew said, moving from Sadie's side, 'what about you? Would you like to live in Scotland?'

'I ... I don't know. It's all a bit sudden.'

'Lassie, I've only just found you, and I hate us being so far apart. You're adamant that your marriage is over so there's nothing to keep you here. If you stay, I could travel down to see you, but it would only be for short weekend visits. I'd like you closer to me, both you and Angel. You have family in Scotland – grandparents, your brother. Please say yes, Sally.'

'Can ... can I think about it?'

'Of course, but when I travel back to Scotland, I'd like you all to be with me.'

'When are you leaving?'

'As soon as possible.'

'And when are you and Mum getting married?'

'I've told your mother that I'd like my family in Scotland to be at our wedding, and she's agreed to be married in Edinburgh. We haven't set a date yet, but I'd like it to be as soon as possible.'

Sally's mind was reeling. She was pleased that her parents were getting married, but moving to Scotland? A holiday, yes, but this was something else. Yet her father was right – there was nothing to keep her here. She would miss Elsie and Bert, but could travel to London to see them occasionally. Her mind jumped again. What about Angel? She would hardly see her father, and what would Arthur say? She needed time to think, but with Sadie still protesting loudly she couldn't get her thoughts into coherent order. 'Mum, Dad, I'm going to bed. I ... I'll try to give you my answer in the morning.'

Andrew placed an arm around her shoulder. 'Goodnight, my bonny girl. I'm sorry to spring this on you so suddenly, but if you decide to come, I promise you'll be happy in Scotland.'

Sally nodded, and after saying goodnight to the others she made her way upstairs. Yet hours later, as she finally drifted off to sleep, she still hadn't come to a decision.

Saturday morning dawned clear and sunny, but as Sally awoke her eyes felt sticky. She rubbed at them impatiently, and seeing that Angel was asleep she crept downstairs. 'Gran, you're up early. It's only six o'clock. Are you all right?'

'I'm fine, but I didn't sleep well.'

'I thought Dad might stay here last night, but he must have gone next door.'

'Yeah, he wanted a word with Denis.' Sadie shifted in her chair, then saying, 'You've had

320

time to think about it now, Sally. How do you feel about moving to Scotland?'

'I don't know, Gran. I still haven't made up my mind.'

'I tossed and turned all night, weighing things up, and then I came to a decision I didn't expect to make. Battersea ain't the same any more, and let's face it, Sal, we're always moaning about the stinking factories. Candle Lane is coming down, and we could be sent anywhere in the borough. I also know that despite saying the opposite, I can't live on my own. With this in mind I thought about you. I know that if I refuse to go, you'll insist on staying to look after me, and I ain't standing for that.'

'I don't mind looking after you. If you really don't want to move to Scotland, I'll stay too and we can live together.'

'No, girl! I've made up me mind. I'm going to Scotland and that's an end to it.'

'But...'

'No buts, Sally. Now let's talk about what you're going to do. Like me, you have to weigh up the pros and cons. If you go to Scotland, you'll still have us around, but this time Andrew tells me that you'd have your own little annex to live in.'

'I like the sound of that, Gran, but I'm still not sure.'

'Sally, without me to look after you'll have more freedom, and may even decide to get a little job. On the other hand, if you stay in London, it means you'll have to find somewhere to live, but once again, without the burden of me you may be able to get a little part-time job while Angel's at school. Either way, you'll have the freedom to make your own choices.'

Sally listened to her gran, but at the thought of being without her family she knew there was really only one choice. She was about to voice her thoughts when Sadie spoke again.

'Right, now let's talk about Arthur. I hoped you two would get back together, but I can see it's not going to happen. If you decide to move to Scotland he won't be able to see much of Angel, and may not like the idea. Mind you, as you're not leaving the country, I doubt he could stop you.'

'There's Elsie and Bert too. They'd miss Angel.'

'I know that, love, but Scotland ain't in Outer Mongolia. There'll be school holidays, weekends, so they'll still get to see her.'

'Gran, it sounds like you're trying to persuade me to go.'

Sadie grinned. 'Yeah, it does, and I promised myself I wouldn't try to sway you one way or the other. It would be different if you were still with Arthur. I'd miss you, but your place would be with your husband. Is there really no chance of you going back to him?'

'No, Gran. My marriage is over.'

'Well, love, if that's the case, I can't bear the thought of you living alone in London.'

'I'd still have Aunt Mary.'

'Christ, Mary! I wonder if your mum has told

her that she's getting married?'

'Yes, I rang her before I went to bed,' Ruth said, another early bird as she walked into the room, obviously catching the tail end of their conversation. 'She'll be down tomorrow to see us. Now tell me, have you two made a decision about Scotland?'

'Yeah,' Sadie answered. 'I'll go, but I don't like the idea of leaving Sally.'

'You won't have to, Gran. I've made up my mind and I'm coming with you.'

'Oh, that's wonderful,' Ruth cried. 'I'm going to get dressed and run next door to tell Andrew.'

She hurried from the room, and half an hour later they heard the street door close behind her. With a small shake of her head, Sadie said, 'She's as excited as a teenager and did you notice that she looks to have dropped years?'

'She's happy, Gran, and I think it's wonderful.'

Sally poured them both another cup of tea and then sat at the kitchen table, looking out on to Candle Lane. Slowly she shook her head, still unable to believe that they were really leaving.

It was ten minutes later when Ruth returned, Andrew with her and her eyes alight with pleasure. 'Denis has agreed,' she cried, 'Tommy can come too.'

Angel came into the room, her eyes sleepy, but they lit up when she saw Andrew. 'Grand-dad!' she cried, running up to him. 'You've come back.'

'Hello, my beauty,' and turning to Sally he

323

added, 'This one will have to be told too.'

'Told what, Granddad?'

Tommy appeared then, his eyes puzzled to see them all, and sitting both children down, Sally crouched in front of them as she tried to explain the move to Scotland as simply as possible, but doubted either her daughter, or Tommy, had any comprehension of the distance involved.

'My dad said that men wear skirts in Scotland. I'm not doing that,' Tommy scowled.

'They aren't skirts, laddie. They're kilts.'

'Don't care, I ain't wearing one.'

'Is my daddy coming with us?' Angel asked

'No, darling, but you'll still be able to see him. There'll be weekends, and school holidays.'

'What about my dad? Is he coming?' Tommy asked.

'No, love, but you'll see plenty of him. He'll come to Scotland as often as he can, and like Angel, you'll see him during school holidays.'

'That's all right then,' Tommy said, then asked, 'What's for breakfast?'

Ruth chuckled and went to pour out some cereal, whilst Sally, finding that her daughter had gone strangely quiet, gazed at her worriedly. Angel's eyes looked unfocused and strangely distant, but just when Sally was about to give her a little shake, her head tipped to one side as though she was listening to something. She then smiled and gave a little nod before saying, 'When are Nanny and Granddad going?'

'I told you, we're going too, but I'm not sure

when. You had better ask Granddad.'

'Well now, let me see,' Andrew said. 'It's Saturday today, so how about Tuesday?'

'Andrew, that's impossible,' Ruth spluttered. 'There's too much to do.'

'Like what? You'll have no need to bring any furniture and will only have to pack your personal things.'

'We'll have to do more than that. There's the house to close down, the meters to be read, and what about the children's school?'

'I live in a lovely little hamlet, with a good school for the children, and they can start there when the new term starts in September. As for the utilities, I can sort those out by telephone.'

'I ain't leaving my furniture behind,' Sadie protested. 'It's all I've got left of my home with Charlie. I've slept in the same bed since the day I got married, and I ain't going without it.'

Andrew smiled gently, 'In that case I'll lay on a small removals van.'

'Thanks,' Sadie said. 'That's settled it then. Tuesday it is.'

Andrew grinned with delight, and picking Ruth up he swung her round. 'Start packing your cases, woman. We're all going to Edinburgh.'

'I think you're forgetting that I have to work today. Oh, God, it'll have to be my last day too. It means leaving Sid without notice and that makes me feel awful.'

'Mum,' Sally placated, 'Sid's been talking about retiring for ages and maybe the time is right. You said he's hardly in the shop these days and leaves all the running of it to you.'

'Yes, you're right, he does, but I still dread telling him.'

'He'll be all right, Mum,' and as she said the words, Sally somehow knew they were true.

'Bloody hell,' Ruth exclaimed. 'Look at the time! I'd best get a move on and I'll have to ring Mary again before I go. Goodness knows what she'll say about us all moving to Scotland.'

'I'll get out of your way,' Andrew said, 'and I'll see you later.'

He gave them all a swift kiss, and urging Tommy to behave himself, he left the house. Sally saw that her tea had grown cold, but didn't move to pour another. It was finally hitting her. They were leaving on Tuesday, and she still had to tell Arthur.

Twenty-Nine

On Sunday things were already frantic. Ruth was in her bedroom, clothes strewn everywhere as she sorted her wardrobes, bemoaning having to discard things she had hoarded for years.

She thought back to yesterday, her last day at work, and it had been a relief to find that Sid didn't mind when she told him she was leaving.

Apparently a supermarket chain wanted to buy the premises, along with other shops in the road. Thanks to Sid's son the deal was lucrative, and it was obvious now why he had been so keen for his father to retire. With a sigh, Ruth held up a halter neck dress; the style was too young for her now, but she still hated to throw it away. With a last rueful look at it, she threw it on the pile of rejects, and then began to empty her chest of drawers.

In the room next door, Sally was also starting to pack, but every now and then she glanced nervously at the clock. Arthur would be calling for Angel soon, and she would have to tell him. This was a meeting she wasn't looking forward to and was dreading his reaction.

Soon after, when she heard Arthur's knock, Sally purposely straightened her shoulders, but despite the pretext of bravado, she was still trembling as went downstairs to let him in. 'Er ... I need to talk to you in private. Would you come into my gran's room?'

He looked surprised, and as she stood aside to allow him to walk ahead of her, Sally saw no sign of a limp, no sign that he had an artificial leg. He turned to face her, looking tall and handsome, and her stomach flipped. Berating herself she fixed her mind on what he'd done, hardening her heart against her feelings.

Tommy was next door with his father and Andrew, whilst Angel was in the yard, absorbed in a game of make-believe shop, and hoping she'd remain that way for a while longer, Sally closed the door. She then turned to face Arthur, but found she couldn't look him in the eye, and head down she blurted out, 'I have something important to tell you. We ... we're all going to live with my father in Scotland.'

She looked at him at last, saw his puzzled frown, and then he said, 'Scotland! What are you talking about?'

'My father and mother are getting married,' Sally said, suddenly aware of how strange that sounded. 'He ... he has a large house with room for all of us, and ... and I've agreed to go. Angel and I will live in the annex.'

'Don't be stupid, Sally. You can't take Angel to Scotland. When would I get to see her?'

'Occasional weekends – school holidays.'

Arthur's face suffused with colour, his voice now rising in anger, 'I'll fight this, Sally. You have no right to take my daughter so far away.'

Sally found her own anger mounting. If she remained in London it would mean finding a flat to rent, and bringing her daughter up alone. Instead her father had offered her a home, a wonderful place to live with her family around her. 'I have every right! You were the one who committed adultery and caused the break up of our marriage. If you want to try to stop me, go ahead! I'll see you in court!'

The high colour now drained from Arthur's face, and instead of anger she saw pain. 'One mistake, Sally, I made one mistake.'

'We've been over this before. You slept with Patsy more than once, and that's something I can never forgive.'

'Oh, Sally, please. I've told you it'll never happen again, I swear it. Please, don't go to Scotland. Come back to me and let's make a fresh start.'

There was the sound of footsteps, then Angel's voice, the door opening as she ran into the room. 'Daddy!' she cried, running up to him. 'I thought I heard you.'

Arthur swept her up, but his eyes were still on Sally. 'Please,' he whispered.

Sally hesitated, but then shook her head saying decisively, 'No. Never.'

His face crumbled in defeat, and as he lowered Angel to the floor his voice sounded strangled. 'Come on, let's go to see Nanny and Granddad.'

After kissing Angel goodbye, Sally found that once again she was unable to meet Arthur's eyes. Every time she saw him, the memory of his adultery was like a knife to her heart, yet despite this she was unable to deny her feelings. She still loved him.

She walked with them to the hall, and as they left the house, questions whirled in her mind. Was she making the right decision? Could she go back to him?

God, what should she do? Sally went back upstairs. She needed advice, someone to talk to, and went into her mother's room. 'Mum, Arthur's just been to collect Angel and he's asked me to go back to him. What do you think?'

'What! After what he's done?'

Sally sat on the side of her mother's bed, her head low. 'I still love him, Mum.'

'Now you listen to me, my girl. Arthur had only been home from hospital for five minutes when he had it off with that tart. To top it all, when you left him, he didn't even bother to come after you. No, instead he carried on sleeping with Patsy. Christ, Sally, you'd be mad to trust him again.'

She took in her mother's words and the pain of Arthur's betrayal rose again. Yes, she still loved him, but what he'd done *was* unforgivable. She stood up and left the room with her shoulders slumped. 'Yes, you're right. I'd best get on with our packing.'

Had Sally looked back, she would have seen the look of triumph on her mother's face.

Arthur couldn't hide his feelings from his mother. As shrewd as ever, Elsie could see that something was wrong. She cuddled Angel for a while, but then suggested that she went into the garden with her grandfather.

'Right,' Elsie said as soon as her grand-daughter was out of sight, 'Tell me.'

And Arthur told her, seeing a devastation that matched his own. 'Scotland!' she cried. 'They're all going to Scotland! But it's so far away!'

'I tried to talk to Sally, but she wouldn't listen. I blew it as usual.'

'Arthur, start at the beginning. What have you said to Sally?'

'The first time I tried to talk her into coming back to me, I made a right mess of it. I said it was her fault that I'd slept with Patsy again and that it wouldn't have happened if she hadn't left me.'

Elsie could guess how Sally would have responded to that. She loved her son dearly, but he rarely took the blame for anything and always tried to find a scapegoat. He'd been the same as a child, but she'd been unable to make him face up to his own mistakes. Yet he had so many wonderful qualities, ones she felt made up for this one flaw in his character. Anyway, who was she to cast stones? Everyone had faults, herself included. 'Arthur, when are you going to take responsibility for your own actions?'

'Don't start, Mum. I know it was my fault, but when Sally told me that they're going to live in Scotland, you can't blame me for losing my temper.'

Elsie sighed. 'No, I suppose not. Don't give up though, Arthur. If you want Sally back, you must try again.'

'It's no good. Sally was adamant, and now that she's moving so far away, I'll only see Angel during school holidays.'

'Oh, God, this is awful. I'm going to miss Angel too, but not just my granddaughter, I'll miss all of them. I know I've fallen out with Ruth, but I'd hate us to part with bad feeling.' She rose to her feet now, pacing the room, and then came to a decision. 'I'll go to see them straightaway, and perhaps talk to Sally at the same time. She might listen to me.'

'I doubt it, Mum.'

Elsie ignored this and went to the back door, calling to Bert. When he came inside she said hurriedly, 'I want you to run me to Candle Lane.'

'What? Now?'

'Yes, it's important. I'll tell you all about it in the car.' She then turned to Arthur again, 'Make some sort of excuse to Angel, and stay here until we come back.'

Arthur nodded, rising to his feet and walking out to the garden. Elsie watched for a moment as he crossed the lawn towards his daughter. Angel was playing with the cat, pulling a piece of string and giggling as the animal tried to catch it. Her red curls were bouncing, the sun enhancing the fiery colour, and she saw Arthur sweep the child up into his arms. God, how must he be feeling? He had lost his wife, and now must feel that he was losing his daughter too. There had to be something she could do, there just *had* to. 'Come on, Bert, let's go,' she urged, anxious now to get to Candle Lane.

Ruth's bed was still strewn with clothes. When she heard the knock on the door she thought it was Mary and hurried downstairs to let her sister in.

'Elsie! Bert!' she said, startled to see them instead of Mary on the step.

'Arthur has just told me that you're all going

away and I had to see you.'

'Why? Do you want to tell me that I'm a selfish mother again?'

'Please, Ruth, don't be like this. I'm sorry, I really am. It was just my concern for Sally that made me speak out. We've been friends for years, since our children were small, and I don't want to part on bad terms.'

When Ruth saw the earnest appeal in Elsie's eyes, she stood to one side. She had a lot to thank Elsie for, and she too had hated falling out. 'Come in and let's forget all about it. It's all water under the bridge now.'

'I can't believe you're getting married,' Elsie said as they came inside.

'You could have knocked me down with a feather when I saw Andrew. He's wonderful and just as I remembered him.'

'I'm pleased for you, even though it seems a bit quick.'

'I know, it's amazing. If he'd lived nearer I think we would have taken things more slowly. Still, quick or not, I'm over the moon. This is the best thing that could have happened for all of us.'

Elsie stiffened. 'Except for Arthur! Sally's taking Angel such a long way away and he's in a terrible state.'

Ruth's stance also changed and her voice hardened. 'When my daughter caught Arthur with that girl, she was in a state too. It's his fault that the marriage broke up, and seeing what Sally has been through, I can't feel sorry for him.'

'Ruth, please, let's not fall out again. Arthur made a terrible mistake, but he still loves Sally. Isn't there something we can do to get them back together again?'

'No, I'm afraid not. She's made up her mind and is coming with us.'

'Is she in? Maybe I could try talking to her again.'

Ruth lowered her eyes. She was getting married, going to Scotland, and when Sally had agreed to go with them, her happiness had been complete. Sally's marriage was over, and the last thing she wanted now was a reconciliation. Earlier, she had seen that Sally was having doubts, but had managed to talk her round. She couldn't have Elsie putting a spoke in things. 'It would be a waste of time. Sally has told me that she will never take never take Arthur back and she's upstairs packing. She's been through enough and I don't want her upset again.'

'But—'

Another knock on the door cut off Elsie's protest. Ruth went to answer it determined that Elsie wouldn't get a chance to speak to Sally out of her hearing. 'Mary, come in.'

As they went into the kitchen, Mary greeted Elsie and Bert, and then asked, 'Where's Mum?'

'Like the rest of us, she's sorting out her bits and bobs.'

Bert's voice suddenly boomed. 'Ruth, we don't want to upset Sally again, but we'd like to see her before we go.'

'I heard your voices and was on my way down,' Sally said as she walked into the kitchen.

'Sally, we have to talk to you,' Elsie said. Her eyes flicking around the room she added, 'Maybe it would be better if we spoke in private.'

'Anything you have to say to Sally, can be said in front of us,' Ruth protested quickly.

A look of annoyance crossed Elsie's face, but before she could protest, Bert intervened. He walked up to Sally, taking her hand in his. 'I know you've been badly hurt, but I've seen the state my son is in. Can't you find it in your heart to forgive him?'

'Please, Sally,' Elsie urged.

Ruth held her breath, her heart thumping as she looked at her daughter. *Oh, please don't go back to him,* she silently willed.

'No, it's too late now,' Sally told them, and Ruth's breath left her body in a rush.

'Do you still love him?' Bert asked.

'Please, I don't want to talk about it any more,' she said, tears suddenly filling her eyes.

'I told you I didn't want my daughter upset again,' Ruth cried. 'She's been through enough. Now I don't want to be rude, but I think you should go.'

Sadie came into the room. 'What's going on?'

It was Elsie who answered. 'We just came to talk to Sally and to say goodbye to you all.'

'I hate goodbyes,' Sadie said grumpily as she shuffled across to her chair.

335

Elsie pulled Sally into her arms. 'I'm sorry we've upset you, and it's the last thing we wanted to do. We'll go now, love. I know you're leaving on Tuesday, so I doubt we'll see you again, but will you keep in touch with us?'

Sally dashed the tears from her eyes and with a watery smile, said, 'Of course I will, and ... and you'll still see Angel. I'll bring her down to see you as soon as I can.'

Elsie then turned to Ruth. 'Despite what's happened, will you keep in touch too?'

'I'll ring you, I promise.' Ruth said, and seeing the distress on Elsie's face she felt awful. This was her friend, a woman who had helped her so much. Yes, she wanted Sally with her in Edinburgh, but suddenly saw she had been putting herself first. Still, she thought, salving her conscience, Elsie had other grandchildren, and she would still see Angel occasionally. She ran across the room, wrapping her arms around her friend. 'I'm going to miss you so much.'

It was Elsie who pulled away first, sobbing as Bert led her from the room.

'God, that was awful,' Mary said, speaking for the first time. 'The poor woman was so upset. Mind you, I'm going to miss you all too.'

'You can come to visit us as often as you like. Andrew has a large house so there'll be plenty of room.'

'Have you set a date for the wedding?'

'No, not yet. Everything is happening so fast, but when we do have a date, you will come, won't you?'

'Yes, of course. Wild horses couldn't keep me away.' She then turned to Sadie. 'Well, Mother, when Ruth rang me again me this morning, I was surprised to hear that you've agreed to go.'

'Yeah, I surprised myself too. I never thought I'd leave London, and even when bombs were falling during the war, I stayed put.'

Mary turned again, now focusing on Sally, her smile kind. 'Listen, my dear, if you change your mind about going to Scotland, you'd be welcome to stay with me.'

'Don't be daft,' Ruth protested. 'You ain't got room.'

'I'd make room, but to be honest I'm just being selfish. You're all moving away and it feels like I'm losing my whole family.' And as though fighting her emotions, Mary's voice became brusque, 'Anyway, where's Andrew? I've yet to meet him.'

As if on cue there was a knock on the door. 'I expect that's him now,' Ruth said, hurrying to answer it, soon leading him into the kitchen. 'Andrew, this is my sister, Mary.'

'Hello,' he said, reaching out to shake her hand.

'So, you're going to marry my sister.'

'Yes, and I hope you'll come to our wedding.'

'As I told Ruth, I'll definitely be there.'

Sally was hardly listening, her mind drifting again and her head beginning to ache. 'If you don't mind, I'd best get back to my packing,' she said, glad to leave the chatter of voices in the room. Her heart was heavy as she went upstairs, and instead of packing she flung herself across the bed.

She had made her decision, she was going to Scotland, but now as Sally turned over to stare up at the ceiling tears flooded her eyes.

Thirty

Monday morning dawned bright and clear, but when Arthur climbed into the car, Joe could tell by his friend's face that something was wrong. 'You look a bit down in the mouth. Is your leg playing you up?'

As Arthur told him about Sally leaving for Scotland, Joe's jaw dropped. He too was shocked by the news, sure until this moment that eventually there'd be a reconciliation. He drove automatically, turning at the lights, feeling absolutely dumbstruck.

When Patsy had moved out, he'd gone to see the landlord, arranging to take over the flat. When Sally returned he just wanted to be near her, to watch over her, and to be there if she ever needed him. Now, though, Sally was going to Scotland and he'd never see her again.

No, he agonized, it couldn't be true. Sally loved Arthur, he was sure of it, but she was now putting an impossible distance between them.

'Christ, mate,' he said, glancing at Arthur, 'I can't believe it.'

'Neither could I at first, but she's definitely going.'

'I've got a bit of news too, Arthur. As you know, my place is a bit of a dump, so when Patsy moved out of her flat, I arranged with the landlord to take it on.'

'Blimey, that's great. It was good of you to get her out, and I don't know why I didn't think of it.' Arthur then gave a wry laugh. 'Well, at least there's no chance that I'll be accused of having it off with you.'

During the rest of the journey Arthur hardly spoke and sat slumped in his seat. Joe tried to lift his spirits, but his replies were monosyllabic.

When they arrived at the site it was full of activity and once again Joe felt a thrill of excitement. The development was taking shape, and soon he hoped they'd see a large return on their investment. 'It's looking good, Arthur. The show house will be finished in another month or two. We'll need to show it at its best advantage and it could do with a woman's touch to get the décor right.'

'Sally would have been great at that. She's got a good eye for interior design.'

'Talk to her again, Arthur. She may still change her mind.'

'No, it's too late. She's leaving for Scotland in the morning.'

Joe sighed, wishing Arthur would put up more

of a fight. He was about to voice his thoughts, but his friend climbed out of the car, his face etched with pain as he headed for the site office.

They had only one visitor in Candle Lane that evening. Mary called round to say goodbye. She couldn't get time off work in the morning and now clung to them. 'What time is the van coming in the morning?'

'It'll be here at eight, but it won't take long to load. There's only Mum's furniture, a couple of cartons and our cases.'

The telephone rang and Sally went to answer it. It was Arthur's sister, Ann.

'Sally, I can't believe you're doing this,' she said without preamble. 'All right, what Arthur did was terrible, but you can't take Angel away from him.'

'I'm not. I'm only moving to Scotland and he can still see her.'

'Huh, it'll be once in a blue moon.'

'Ann, I'm doing what I think is best.'

'I can't see how taking her away from her father is best for Angel.'

'She'll be living in a better environment, in clean fresh air and, as I said, Arthur will still see her.'

'Oh, Sally, don't do this. My brother made a mistake, a stupid mistake, but he's told me that Patsy meant nothing to him. All right, he was daft to let us think he was going to marry her, but it's over now, finished.'

'So is our marriage, Ann.

'Sally, you're being unreasonable.'

'*I'm* being unreasonable!'

'Yes, I think you are.'

Sally clenched her teeth. 'I wonder if you'd say the same if it was *your* husband who'd been unfaithful.'

'I think I'd be more forgiving.'

'Well, Ann, I hope you never have to put that theory to the test,' Sally said. Oh, she'd had enough and didn't want to talk any more – to think any more. 'Listen, I don't want to argue with you. Suffice to say that it was Arthur who committed adultery – *not* me. Now if you don't mind, I'm busy and have to go.'

'All right, go then, but I still can't believe you're doing this to my brother.'

She felt a surge of anger and slammed the receiver down, only for it to ring again a few seconds later; this time Elsie was on the line. She could hear the pain in her mother-in-law's voice, and when the phone was passed to Bert, his voice was thick with emotion too.

Sally spoke to them for a while, her voice cracking, and when finally replacing the receiver, she felt bruised. When she returned to the kitchen she hardly spoke, the conversation a buzz around her, but thankfully no one passed comment.

At ten, Mary rose to leave, and it was an emotional goodbye. Sally clung to her aunt, and when she finally left, Sally was glad to go to bed, her brain and her emotions numb. Everything was ready, and with all the pictures taken

341

down and ornaments packed, the house looked as desolate as she felt.

She lay in bed, wishing the spiritual presence would come to comfort her, but saw only shadows cast by the moon. How was it possible, when she had just found her father, to feel so lost and alone?

Sally closed her eyes, but couldn't sleep, and behind closed lids she recalled the pain she had seen in Arthur's eyes. Was she being unreasonable? Was she punishing him? Was this her way of getting her own back for the hurt he'd caused?

Her mind turned to all the things that had been said – Aunt Mary's words, Ann's words and those of her in-laws. Yet as she finally drifted off to sleep, it was Nelly Cox's question that remained in her mind: *Do you really want to spend the rest of your life without him?*

Sally felt as if she'd only been asleep for minutes when her mother was waking her up again.

'Come on, Sally, it's six thirty.'

Blearily she opened her eyes and with a small nod, sat up. So this was it, the day had arrived. In just a few hours they'd be leaving Candle Lane. It was going to be a long day for all of them, and as Angel was still asleep, Sally decided to leave her for another half an hour.

Gran was up when she went downstairs, and as her mother made a pot of tea she was smiling happily. 'What do you want for breakfast, Sally?'

'Nothing, Mum. I'm not hungry.'

'You should try to eat something. We've got a long journey ahead of us.'

Sally sat down heavily, Nelly's question still on her mind and as her mother handed her a cup of tea, she stirred it absently. Unbidden, tears welled in her eyes. 'Oh, Mum.'

'Sally, don't start. We've got too much to do this morning and there's no time for tears.'

'I don't know if I'm doing the right thing.'

'Don't be daft, of course you are. We'll be out of this dump, and living in Scotland will be so much better for Angel. She loves her granddad and will thrive there.'

Sally stood up, her shoulders hunched. 'All right, I'll go and get washed and dressed before getting Angel up.'

'Good girl, but don't spend too much time in the bathroom. I'll need to sort Tommy out too.'

Another hour sped by, and now Andrew had joined them. Moments later, Denis called round, looking hung over as he said goodbye to Tommy. 'Be a good boy, and I'll come up to Scotland to see you whenever I get the chance.'

Tommy didn't seem concerned when his father left, the parting surprisingly easy, and now Ruth began to run around like a headless chicken, checking drawers and cupboards for anything she might have failed to pack.

'Calm down, darling,' Andrew said. 'Look, here's the removal van.'

Sally felt as if she was in a dream, her head floating. They were going – they were *really* going.

Whilst the removal men were shown Sadie's furniture, Sally stepped out into Candle Lane, memories flooding back as she looked at it for the last time. In her mind's eye she could see her and Ann as children, skipping and playing hop-scotch. Arthur too, a cheeky boy who often teased her, but he'd grown into a handsome man who'd stolen her heart.

Sally looked along the lane again, but then froze. Arthur! In a dream she watched him walking towards her, her heart feeling as though it had turned a somersault.

He drew closer, but still she didn't move. 'Sally, I had to come – had to see you. Please don't go,' he begged. 'Please give me another chance.'

As she stared up at him, Nelly's question seemed to fill her mind again. Yet could she put it behind her – could she trust him again?

'Sally, I love you, and I swear I'll never be unfaithful again.'

Sally shivered, suddenly remembering her own attraction to Joe Somerton. She hadn't slept with him though. Unlike Arthur, she hadn't been unfaithful, yet in her mind she had wanted the man, and at one time had dreamed of feeling his arms around her. Was she any better? And if Arthur hadn't been so ill in hospital, would it have gone further?

Then, as they gazed at each other, another thought forced itself into her mind and Sally had to face it at last. She could have tried harder when Arthur had first come home from hospital – could have shown him more affection, but instead she'd kept her distance. Her fear of sex had arisen again after the attempted rape, and she'd used his leg wound as an excuse, used it to justify keeping a distance between them. Part of her had wanted to feel his arms around her, yet another part had been repelled by the thought. Was it any wonder that he'd turned to Patsy?

Maybe Arthur saw something in her expression, Sally didn't know, but as he took another step forward, she found herself in his arms. She told him, the words stumbling at first, but at last all her fears came out into the open. 'I ... I should have shown you more affection, but ... but after what that man did, I was scared.'

'Oh, darling, why didn't you tell me before? I knew they'd beaten you, but you never mentioned that one of them had tried to rape you. God, if I could get my hands on him I'd tear the bastard from limb to limb. Christ, Sally, I thought you were keeping a distance between us because you couldn't stand the sight of my leg. I was gutted, and pretended to be asleep every night.'

'The loss of your leg doesn't bother me, but at first I really was worried about hurting your stump. That was another reason why I kept a space between us in bed.'

'If only we had talked – if only we had brought everything out into the open. Sally, please, it isn't too late. I love you, and I know that what I did with Patsy was unforgivable, but please, I beg you, don't go to Scotland. I can't bear to lose you.'

'What if I can't ... well, you know.'

'It doesn't matter. I'll be patient, I promise.'

Sally snuggled close to him again, and somehow knew that it would be all right. She smiled, her mind made up. 'Nelly Cox asked me a question and at last I know the answer.'

'What question?'

'She asked me if I really wanted to spend the rest of my life without you.'

'And?' he asked eagerly.

'I ... I still love you too, and I don't want to be without you.'

He lifted her up, swinging her round in a full circle, his voice loud with joy as he shouted, 'Nelly Cox, I don't know how you did it, but I love you.'

'I don't think she can hear you,' Sally said, smiling at last. 'Nelly left Candle Lane and she's moved into Osborn House.'

'Then I'll go to see her with the biggest box of chocolates I can find.'

Sally's face sobered. 'Arthur, I must tell my parents, and not only that – we had better stop the removal men before they put my cases on board!'

They walked into the kitchen, hands clasped. Ruth became still when she saw them.

'Mum, Dad, I'm sorry, but I've changed my mind. I won't be coming to Scotland.'

'Daddy!' Angel squealed, dashing up to her

346

father. 'I knew you'd come. I knew we wouldn't be going to Scotland with Nanny and Grand-dad.'

Arthur swept her up into his arms. 'How did you know?'

'The lady told me.'

'What lady?' Sally asked, but somehow she already knew the answer.

'The one who comes in the lovely light.'

Andrew spoke, his voice full of wonder. 'My mother sees something similar.'

'Me too,' Sally said. 'And now it seems my daughter will be following in our footsteps.'

Ruth spoke at last, her eyes sad. 'I can't believe you're not coming.'

'I'll visit you in Scotland as often as I can.'

Andrew moved to Ruth's side, taking her hand. 'I know you're upset that our lassie won't be joining us, but take a good look at her. She's happy, and that's what matters.'

'Yes, but for how long? You're out of your mind, Sally. What if he hurts you again?'

'Ruth, I won't,' Arthur said. 'I'll never make the same mistake again.'

'See that you don't, laddie,' Andrew growled.

'We'll be all right, Dad,' Sally said. 'There were faults on both sides, but we're going to put it all behind us and start again.'

Tommy looked bewildered, his little face puckering. 'Ain't you coming wiv us, Angel?'

'No, I'm staying with my daddy.'

'I don't wanna go. I wanna stay here too.'

Ruth crouched down, pulling Tommy into her

arms. 'Listen darling, Angel will be coming to visit us in Scotland, so you'll still see lots of her. If you stay here you'll have to live with your daddy, but if that's what you really want, then ... then of course you don't have to come with us.'

Tommy's lower lip was trembling, his eyes full of confusion. Ruth then said, 'It's up to you, darling, but I ... I love you and would hate to leave you behind.'

Tommy looked at Ruth, his uncle, and then with his head down he plucked his earlobe, obviously deep in thought. The room was hushed, even Angel silent, and then with a grin the boy looked up. 'All right, I'll come wiv you, Aunty Ruth.'

They all heard Ruth's sigh of relief, and, after giving Tommy another hug, she turned to look at Sally, her eyes full of unshed tears. 'Oh, love, I'm so sorry. Everyone's right – I *am* a selfish mother. You're my daughter and I wanted you with me, but I was only thinking of myself. I can see now how happy you are, and ... and I'm pleased for you.'

Sally ran across the room, wrapping her arms around her mother. 'You're not selfish. You're the best mother anyone could have and I love you. I'm going to miss you so much, but you're getting married soon, and no matter what, I'll be there – we all will,' she said, turning to look at Arthur.

He nodded, and now Sally went across to her gran, kneeling by her side. 'I'm going to miss you too.

'And I you, but I think you're doing the right thing.'

'The van's loaded,' a voice said.

'Right, thanks,' Andrew replied brusquely. 'And if I'm not mistaken, that sounds like our taxi.'

Sally's breath caught in her throat and rising to her feet, she found herself in her father's arms. 'Be happy, my bonny lass.'

He let her go abruptly, his eyes moist, and Sally watched with tears now streaming down her cheeks as they all said goodbye to Angel. Her daughter looked bewildered, and as Arthur swept her up again, she clung to his neck.

Arthur crooked her with one arm, whilst he took Sally's hand. 'Come on,' he urged, leading her outside.

Sally watched as her father helped her gran into the taxi, then Tommy climbed in, followed by her mother. She felt torn in two – one part of her heart here with Arthur and Angel, the other half wanting to dive into the cab and go with her family. 'No, no,' she cried, unconsciously moving forward.

Andrew came to her side, hugging her again. 'I know how you're feeling, lassie, but your place is here. We'll all see each other, and often, so hang on to that.'

He then turned swiftly, climbing into the taxi, and as the door closed behind him, the engine started.

They were all waving as it pulled away, Sally

watching and waving back until it turned the corner, her heart cracking with emotion.

Arthur took her hand. 'Don't cry, darling. As your father said, we'll see them all again soon.'

Yes, we will, Sally thought, drawing in juddering breaths. She looked up at Arthur, saw the love reflected in his eyes, and knew that she had made the right decision. Her place was here, with her husband. They loved each other, and just like Nelly and George Cox, many happy years stretched out ahead of them.